WHAT WAS GRIMWOOD'S SECRET?

Dr. Grimwood flipped on the switch in the room in which the beautiful mannequin was stored.

"Now," he said proudly, "in a moment you'll see her start to—"

He stopped and stared. She was nowhere to be seen.

"She—she's been kidnapped!" Dr. Grimwood cried.

"How could she have been?" Pete asked, much too sensibly. "Jeff and the detail have only just now left. Not even Houdini could have managed it."

Abruptly then, deep in the bowels of the house on Kemble Street, they heard a man's wild laughter, suddenly released and just as suddenly cut off.

"There *can't* be anybody in those passages!" Pete shouted. "What's going on?"

"You are right," said Liselotte. "It was not from the rooms. It was not from the passages." She faced them, white as death. "That laughter came from—*somewhere else!*"

Reginald Bretnor

A KILLING

IN SWORDS

A KANGAROO BOOK

PUBLISHED BY POCKET BOOKS NEW YORK

Another *Original* publication of POCKET BOOKS

POCKET BOOKS, a Simon & Schuster division of
GULF & WESTERN CORPORATION
1230 Avenue of the Americas, New York, N.Y. 10020

ISBN: 0-671-81313-7

First Pocket Books printing February, 1978

Trademarks registered in the United States and other countries.

Printed in the U.S.A.

FOR ROSALIE,
who drove me to it.

Contents

I

The Death of Don Juan

The mayor of San Francisco was stabbed to death at approximately ten thirty on the evening of October twelfth, while Alastair Alexandrovitch Timuroff was at the opera. This was fortunate, for on a number of occasions Mr. Timuroff had stated publicly that the city, and indeed the world, would be better off if His Honor came to an untimely end. The people who afterward remembered this and made unkind remarks would have recalled it much more vividly and unpleasantly had there been any doubt as to his whereabouts.

Timuroff always took his closest friends to hear *Don Giovanni:* Liselotte Cantelou, dark and full of fire, who was Viennese and his mistress; his secretary, blonde Olivia Cominazzo, and her husband, Inspector Peter Cominazzo of the homicide detail; and Judge Clayton Faraday, small, elegant, precise, who was as devoted to Liselotte as he was to the opera. Timuroff had first taken them to dinner at the little Russian restaurant on Hayes Street, a block from the opera house, which he said appealed to the Muscovite in him because it was rather like dining with Nabokov's Pnin, and to the Scot because its charges were so moderate. Then they had gone on to a really splendid performance, marred only when their neighbors in the front row of the dress circle recognized Liselotte, began to buzz about it, and had to be quelled by the Cominazzo frown usually reserved for culprits in the morning lineup. They stayed, applauding until after the final curtain, and left their seats only after the crowd had thinned.

"Memorable! Absolutely memorable!" exclaimed Timuroff as they walked down the staircase. "The Don Giovanni was the best I've heard since Ezio Pinza's. As for the Dona Elvira—*ah!*" He blew a kiss in the general direction of the muse of music. "One soprano only, in all the world, could have done it better."

"Thank you, dear," murmured Liselotte.

"But I was remembering Elisabeth Schwarzkopf!" said Timuroff, all innocence.

"*Beast!*" She dropped his arm. "For this, never, *never* will I let you make an honest woman of me. Go away!"

She stamped her foot to punctuate the statement, which had already attracted the attention of three old ladies and a plump young clergyman. They stared, first at her in some astonishment; then at Olivia, bright and tiny; then at the contrast between Pete Cominazzo's football frame and Judge Faraday's small-boned fragility; and finally at Timuroff's five-foot-eleven fencer's figure and the scar that ran from his Tartar cheekbone to the trim corner of his graying moustache. The old ladies drew back, twittering. The clergyman smiled doubtfully, as though unable to decide whether their social standing merited a stern rebuke or an enlightened tolerance. And Liselotte, trilling her famous laugh, daintily slapped Timuroff's behind, repossessed his arm, and told him that she loved him anyhow.

"Oh, I remember Pinza," Olivia said, "though I only saw him once when I was little, in *South Pacific*. He looked just like Pete."

"Now that's *true* love," declared Timuroff. "Most wives would've said Pete looked like Pinza. So you love Pete, and Lise says she loves me—though she loves her alimony even more. And tonight's performance *was* a splendid one. Let's celebrate. Champagne must flow."

"Not for me," said Judge Faraday. "I've a hard day ahead of me tomorrow."

"But tomorrow's *Saturday*," protested Liselotte.

"Yes, dear Lise—but a man's last year on the federal bench is as demanding as any of the others. I have my homework to get done if I'm to be worth my salt on Monday."

Clayton Faraday's parents, both Kentuckians, had endowed him with a patrician nose, a surprisingly deep and well-modulated voice, and a stern courtliness which evoked the law's majesty wherever he presided. People seldom argued with him.

Liselotte made a face, told him that she was *désolée* because only he could keep her Timmy out of mischief, let him kiss her hand, and then suddenly embracing him, kissed him good-night.

They parted with regrets and promises.

"I just can't get used to it," Pete said. "He's a great guy, but somehow I always see him in black robes, under the Great Seal of the United States." He shook his head. "Well, how about coming up to our place? We've a couple of bottles already chilled. I'll make the drink that ex-cavalry character invented at Fort Bliss—jigger of tequila, jigger of brandy, fill it up with champagne. Smooth as a horse's nose, he said it was."

"He didn't invent it at Fort Bliss," said Timuroff, wrinkling his nostrils. "He invented it in Juarez, across the river, where liquor was cheaper."

"You see?" commented Liselotte pleasantly. "My Timmy was also in the cavalry. We wait, and all comes to light. Now at last we learn why he did not remain in the army of the Argentine Republic. Evil companions and this terrible drink made him seduce his colonel's wife, like me. It was a great disgrace. In the army of the Argentine, they are even now forbidden to mention him by name."

"Dear Lise! How much more fun it would've been if it were true. But—" he touched his scar—"I was separated from that service quite honorably after a serious motor accident in Uruguay, which I must tell you all about some day. Think of it, except for that, I might now be dictator of Argentina, or at least a general, instead of humbly selling antique arms in San Francisco."

"Uh-huh," said Cominazzo. *"Humbly."*

"How else?" asked Timuroff.

"Pete, I don't think we ought to go to our apartment. Tonight's been so much fun, and you know what'll happen. Kielty will phone you, or Harrell, that someone's just been shot or something, and everybody's sick, and can't you help out just this once? Just this once! It's happening twice a week. It—it simply isn't *fair!*"

"Sweetheart, tonight the chief himself couldn't roust me out. We'll crack those bottles, and fix some lobster archiduc. Like in Vienna, Liselotte. You know, young hussar officers trying the routine on lovely ballet girls, and ancient field marshals trying it on lovely ballet girls? With Strauss waltzes played by poor Gypsies hopelessly in love with lovely ballet girls."

"I do not understand. In the convent, they did not tell me of such things." She gave him her best mother superior look. "Perhaps this used to happen long ago, when our good Franz Josef ruled. Or maybe you have just been reading naughty books?"

Olivia giggled. "They confiscate them from juvenile delinquents," she said, "but there's not much in them about ballet girls, or field marshals, or even lobsters. Well, okay, I give up. Only I warn you, the lobster and champagne's just a blind. Pete has The Pistol out of safe deposit, and he's all set to show it off, as if we all hadn't seen it fifty or a hundred times."

"Ungrateful wench! Who was it helped me trace my Italian ancestry to the greata Lazarino Cominazzo of Brescia? Who gave us this pistola made by him? Your boss, that'sa who. He gets lobster and champagne. Tim, you'd like to see the great pistola, wouldn't you?"

"Absolutely!" said Timuroff, loyal to his wedding present.

Olivia winked at Liselotte. "A nice little station wagon would've been more practical, and it would've cost less."

"Or a platinum mink coat," suggested Liselotte.

"You have to *buy* those," said Timuroff. "You can't just trade collectors out of them."

They waved good-night to the uniformed sergeant directing traffic out of the opera parking lot, and drove off in Liselotte's apple-green Rover, up Van Ness, then a block east on Greenwich. Timuroff, at the wheel, talked of his ancestor, Alastair Drummond of Skrye, who had escaped from Cromwell to serve under the czar Alexei Mikhailovich, father of Peter the Great, and who had died in Muscovy full of years and honors in 1696, the very year of the great Lazarino's passing—giving Pete a chance to mention the great Lazarino's artistry once or twice. Olivia and Liselotte put in a few pointed remarks about how silly it was for men to waste so much time on outdated firearms and ancestors deader than doornails.

They kept it up in the garage and the elevator, breaking off only when Pete unlocked the door. He headed for the kitchen; and Timuroff, making an unkind remark about people who thought only of their base appetites, took The

Pistol from the mantelpiece. It was a lovely Brescian snaphaunce, its steel mounts carved and intricately pierced, made while Charles II still reigned in England. He regarded it with affection: it was in perfect condition; he had obtained it for a quarter of its value; by giving it he had rewarded one firm friendship and cemented another; it was one more pleasant grace note to the evening.

There was a muffled *pop* from the kitchen, and presently Pete came in again, grinning, carrying a silver tray with chilled glasses and a champagne bottle. "Come on, girls!" he called over his shoulder. "Mr. Lobster can wait while we drink a few toasts."

"To me?" Olivia called back.

"To the pistola," Pete replied.

And then the telephone rang.

The silence was instant and complete. The thing rang again. Olivia and Liselotte appeared at the door.

"It's for you, Mr. Inspector Peter Cominazzo," Olivia said bitterly. "If it's your friend Harrell, with the news that someone's aunt's been murdered, tell him that your little wife hates his guts. If it's Kielty, make that a double."

"*Damn.*" Pete put down the tray. "Darling, I *told* you. Don't worry—"

He picked up the phone. "Cominazzo," he growled. Then, "Oh, for God's sake!" A long pause. *"You've got to be kidding!"* A much longer one. "Well, who *did* it? . . . Yeah, I know you said that, but what kind of pigeon do you take me for? . . . Hell, of course I've heard of him, who hasn't? Nutty as a fruitcake. Oh boy, just wait until the press gets hold of this!"

His tone had changed; its anger suddenly had vanished. All of them, even Olivia, realized that something had occurred that made the spoiling of their party unimportant. Pete said nothing more for two full minutes, while the phone talked at him. Then, "All right," he told it. "I'll be over. Half an hour be okay? . . . Uh-huh. . . . Yeah, sure, I'll bring him with me."

He hung up and turned to face them. He seemed a little dazed. He said, "Don Juan is dead."

Timuroff raised an eyebrow. Liselotte giggled. Olivia said, "Yes, dear. We *know*. They sent the statue clomping after him to pull him down into the flames of Hell. We were right there."

"I don't mean *that* Don Juan. I mean *our* Don Juan.

You know, Lover Boy. His Honor Errol Vasquez Munrooney, all things to all men, one thing to all women, and mayor of San Francisco. He's been murdered."

"Not shot, I hope?" exclaimed Timuroff. "Any man who wanted a police permit for every flintlock musket in the city deserved a baser death."

"Don't worry," Pete replied. "He didn't give his antigun pals any ammunition. He got stabbed."

"I don't suppose the Devil sent a stone Commendatore after him?" said Timuroff, pouring the champagne. "He was much too cheap a wolf to rate VIP treatment." He passed the brimming glasses and raised his own. "Well, here's to the public benefactor who sent our Errol to his just reward."

"Timmy!" Liselotte was genuinely shocked. "You must not speak this way. It is not funny that this man was murdered. He was a human being, with a soul. Are you not ashamed?"

"All right," grumbled Timuroff, "for your sake I'll try to be ashamed. But all my sympathies are for the poor girl who stabbed him." He turned to Cominazzo. "It *was* a woman, wasn't it?"

Pete nodded. Abruptly, he drained his glass and held it out to be refilled.

"Have they arrested her?"

"They haven't, and they aren't likely to. Her name's Lucrece. She wears a flimsy sort of toga thing, and lies on a chaise longue, and recites poetry. It happened at a party, at this Dr. Grimwood's—"

"Not *the* Dr. Grimwood's?" exclaimed Timuroff.

"That's right, the one and only. I guess I've never quite believed he was for real. There was this party going on, about forty of 'em, mostly little big shots, would-be jet-setters, one or two names in the news, and a lot of weirdos. They all say Munrooney was alone with her upstairs in her room. She has one all to herself, just like the other two, only hers has Roman plinths, and statues, and all that sort of jazz."

"Do you mean that this doctor has three *petites amies*," asked Liselotte, "all in the same house together?"

"Girl friends? Well, yes and no. He's a retired brain surgeon, with enough dough so he's eccentric instead of just plain crazy. He's got a hobby." Inspector Cominazzo blushed. "He—well, he makes these mechanical women in his basement. There's Lucrece, and there's Muriel Fawzi—she's a Middle Western belly dancer—"

"Surely you mean a Middle *Eastern* belly dancer?" interrupted Timuroff.

"No, Middle Western. Her father was an Arab, but her mother was a little girl from Cairo, Illinois. She plays some weird kind of instrument and does this belly dance. Then there's a beautiful brunette who—I'm quoting Harrell quoting Dr. Grimwood—won't be born till Tuesday."

"The man's a genius!" laughed Timuroff. "Gears and springs and all sorts of good things—that's what pretty girls are made of. I've always suspected it." He looked Liselotte up and down. "What could Errol have been trying to do to her?"

"Ha! I do not believe she was mechanical. Why would any man make such an automaton when—when—?" Liselotte gestured expressively at Olivia and herself. "It is ridiculous."

"They wouldn't have to buy them drinks or dinners, or clothes or furs or diamonds," Olivia told her. "They could spend all their money on lovely guns and swords."

"That would be nice," said Timuroff. "But let's be serious for a moment. Today's senseless tragedy should be a lesson to us all. To protect our dedicated, self-sacrificing leaders, *mechanical women must be registered!*" He finished his champagne. "And now, if our host and hostess will be so kind as to attack the lobster and the other bottle, let us return to our revels."

"Quit kidding, Tim." Pete put his own glass down regretfully. "You know what the man said. Maybe we've got time for just one more, a quickie. Then let's get on our horse."

"We?"

"*We.* Us. You and me. The chief's there, personally. He's riding Harrell, and Harrell says I'm to be in charge. To make it worse, Judson Hemmet and Mario Baltesar—you know, Munrooney's law partners—they're out there raising hell. So everybody's going to be riding me. Where you come in is this: Lucrece stabbed Lover Boy with an old dagger—a real antique, with gold on it and a stone handle. You've got to look at it and find the murderer."

"What murderer? According to the Constitution, English Common Law, and probably the Code of Hammurabi, mechanical women can't commit a murder. They're not legally responsible."

"Okay, the guy who programmed her, the fiend who took advantage of her clockwork innocence."

"Our public benefactor," said Timuroff. "I cannot do it."

"Come on, let's get rolling."

"By all means!" Olivia glared daggers at them both. "You know you wouldn't miss it for the world. Roll on out of here, you party-poopers! One real pig and one honorary one. I hate you!"

"Madame"—her husband bowed—"after one more glass we shall remove our porcine presence from your sight."

"The police are not allowed to drink on duty," asserted Liselotte. "Judge Faraday would not permit it, and when I tell him he will be greatly shocked. Besides, I hate you too. Olivia and I shall devour the lobster. We need the bottle to get drunk on."

"Then we'll go down to—to the Edinburgh Castle, and dance wild Scottish dances, and pick up two big sailors from a Belfast freighter."

"You'll find it pretty much a waste of time." Timuroff smiled. "They'll make you buy their beer, and fill your lovely little heads with boring anti-Papist propaganda. Take my word for it—I've read their slogans on the men's room walls."

"Already you are jealous!" cried Liselotte, laughing and shooing them toward the door. "Now go away."

II

The Rape of Lucrece

They took Liselotte's Rover, Timuroff remarking that it served her right for threatening to get drunk and eat the lobster, and turned left on Van Ness.

"Corner of Broadway and Kemble," Cominazzo told him. "Way out by the Presidio. He's got some kind of queer old mansion there; Harrell says he got it during the Depression, from the widow of a patient."

"You make him sound a little grisly," said Timuroff. "As I heard it, she left it to him out of gratitude. He did an operation no one else would try, and won her husband a few extra years."

"Could be, Tim. You've been out there?"

"No, but everybody else has. I've had a few of those catch-all invitations—you know, come and bring a friend, where I was supposed to be the friend. Young Coulter asked me several times—the doctor has some pretty decent armor—but always when something else was on."

"Harrell was there right after that nasty butcher business in the Haight. Old Grimwood likes to spice his parties up with somebody sensational; I guess getting Jake was next best to getting Mr. Murderer himself. Anyhow, Jake sat around drinking up his bourbon, which didn't hurt a bit, and answering gruesome questions, which in this racket can get pretty boring, as you know. Also, he had to watch himself, because Hemmet and Baltesar were there that

17

time too. Anyhow, he got to meet the ticktock girls, plus a real live one who's Grimwood's secretary or something."

Timuroff turned west, up Pacific Avenue. "Those two—Hemmet and Baltesar. Did you know that Baltesar is married to Munrooney's sister? And of course he's also on the board of supervisors. You knew that they're both customers of mine?"

"Olivia's mentioned them, and I think you have too. The boys in the Department don't have much use for them. They helped Munrooney with the dirty work when he cut Pat Samson's throat and put his own lad in as chief."

"Chiefy?" asked Timuroff.

"Yeah, *Chiefy*. Can you believe a chief of police whose wife calls him Chiefy, and who calls her Wifey, out before God and everyone? The bastard ought still to be opening limousine doors for the high and mighty down at the opera house, like when he was lieutenant. Believe me, it's really going to be a mess. He's playing he's personally in charge, and he'll keep it up till the publicity fades down."

"It could get pretty complicated, Pete. Do you realize it's only about three weeks to election day—and that Munrooney would've been a sure winner?"

"It's bad enough without that. A murder on the second floor, and forty people, more or less, around the place. How're you ever going to sort them out? Especially with legal sharks like Baltesar and Hemmet on the premises."

"Did Jake mention anybody else?"

"Only one or two by name. Socrates Voukos—remember, with all those millions in rundown real estate, who raised such hell when digit dialing took away his HEmlock phone number? And Wade Kalloch, and Amos Ledenthal. That's all I know about."

"Here we go again," murmured Timuroff.

"How's that?"

"Socrates and Kalloch are also customers of mine—you must've heard Olivia speak of them—and so, of course, is Amos, besides being a friend."

"That last I don't get," Pete said. "Ledenthal collects Japanese swords just like you do. Seems like you'd naturally be rivals."

Timuroff smiled. "He buys almost all of his from me, and naturally he loves me because I give him such good deals. Well"—his smile disappeared—"let's hope it's just one big coincidence. Things could get downright sticky where you're dealing with His Honor and His Honor's crew. You'll have fun enough without my being involved."

Cominazzo groaned. "I'll have problems finding out anything, and problems if I don't find out anything, and worse problems if I find out the wrong things—which chances are I will."

"I will pray for you," said Timuroff sanctimoniously. "Would you prefer Church of England or Russian Orthodox? I am equally well versed in each."

"Look, Expert Witness, either one will help. But first give Jake the lowdown on the dagger—that's what they're going to pay your fee for."

They drove past mansions converted into guest houses, new and insulating high-rise massifs, and still-moneyed mansions bravely pretending that McKinley was not dead and that there was no servant problem. They passed the gray Hotel El Drisco, full of retired naval captains, ancient ladies, and antique Episcopalian clergymen. They turned down Baker Street to Broadway, turned left for half a block, and slowed where Kemble starts its short, steep plunge down the hillside. A cold wind from the Golden Gate, bringing with it a breath of colder rain, had blown the smog away; one could smell the sea and, like the mansions, pretend that San Francisco had not changed since Ambrose Bierce's day.

In that day, the residence of Dr. Hector Grimwood would have been thought a rather modest mansion. Its architect had labored to minimize its size, and behind iron gates and a small formal garden, its Georgian façade displayed two perfectly proportioned stories. Timuroff recalled that a tycoon of the later nineties had built it for the bride whom he had seduced away from two careers, one as the wife of a Parisian postman, the other as the pampered darling of a successful wine merchant. She had developed into a grande dame of unusual splendor, whose romantic story was still slobbered over regularly by the city's columnists; and it was she who had made the doctor the beneficiary of her gratitude. He sketched this background briefly for Pete's benefit; then, finding no parking available on Broadway, turned downhill on Kemble.

He parked at right angles to the curb, the car at that San Francisco angle which forces passengers to climb out against the full weight of the door while the driver is literally decanted.

"I'll bet the old lady still haunts the place," Pete said. "Can't you just see her spooking around the doctor and his automated girl friends, chasing off socially inferior ectoplasms?"

"If she does, Mr. Munrooney must have had a very rude reception when he popped out on her astral plane."

From Kemble Street the house was more imposing. A driveway led through another pair of frilled iron gates into a paved courtyard containing a converted stable—an area now crammed with silent police cars—above which the house soared, all alight. Now it was possible to see another story below the ground floor, and under that a stone retaining wall with a blank door and two high, barred windows hinting at mysterious chambers half underground.

"Shall we use the service entrance," asked Timuroff, "or go around to the front door pretending we're gentry?"

"The front door," Pete declared. "We must be impressive. Our mere appearance must plunge the unknown malefactor into a state of helpless terror."

"I'll make my Ivan the Terrible face," promised Timuroff.

The door was opened instantly by a big, bald plainclothesman who started to tell them that he was sorry but Dr. Grimwood was not available, and then, recognizing Cominazzo, smiled sheepishly and stepped aside. "Come in, Inspector. Hi, Mr. Timuroff. I guess I make a pretty good butler, huh?"

The hall was high-ceilinged, Persian-carpeted, paneled in a light warm golden wood. A staircase, strong and delicate, flowed to the second floor; and beyond it Timuroff saw a gilded birdcage elevator, obviously dating to a time when such devices were new and wonderful. In the corner next to him, by a narrow Sheraton side table, a suit of Maximilian tilting armor stood silent guard.

"Where is everybody, Jeff?" Pete asked.

The plainclothesman gestured at a closed door to the right. "The chief's in there, in the library. Lieutenant Kielty's with him, and his secretary, and he's questioning everybody. I guess it's pretty much for looks, and we'll get down to doing the real work later on. Anyhow, the lab guys are upstairs, with the medics. Captain Harrell said for both of you to go on up."

"What about all the guests?"

"The chief corraled 'em in the living room—all except

Mr. Hemmet and what's-his-name Baltesar. They're helping him."

"They're *what?*"

"Helping him ask questions, I guess. He's got a guy named Ledenthal in there right now, mad as a hornet."

"*That* should be interesting," Timuroff remarked. Amos Ledenthal was known for his terrible temper, and he had nothing but contempt for Judson Hemmet.

"What about the doctor?" Pete asked.

"Grimwood? See that door opposite the stairs? It's sort of a My Lady's Sitting Room, fixed up way back when. He's in there holding his girl friend's hand—his live girl, not the windup kind. She was with them when they found the corpse—him and Baltesar and Sergeant Wallton. Wallton was doing the body-guarding bit; he got anxious when the mayor said he was going to the john and told him to stay put, and then was still gone after a half hour."

"Well, I guess we'd better get along upstairs, Jeff. Thanks for the rundown. Come on, Tim."

In the little lift, snail-slow but surprisingly quiet for its age, Timuroff said, "You look worried, Pete."

"I *am* worried. Munrooney was a clown, but he *was* the mayor, and a lot of people thought he was the man with the brass balls politically. I sure wouldn't want to be in Denny Wallton's shoes. He's black, and tomorrow the militants and half the press are going to crucify him as a Tom for letting Lover Boy get stabbed. And Godalmighty—Hemmet and Baltesar helping at a police interrogation! I'd hoped Jake could talk you-know-who into leaving the job to us working artists, but it looks like he's dead set on hanging on to it. Meaning he'll take the credit if I solve the case, and I'll be the fall guy if I fail."

The elevator jerked and halted. As Pete slid the door open, the sound of voices down the hall told them where murder had been done; then a solemn uniformed policeman took them in tow and, quite unnecessarily, escorted them twenty feet to the open door.

The floor of Lucrece's room was tiled; so was the miniature pool, displaying Neptune and his nereids, that graced its center. The walls were frescoed with classic temples set in pastoral scenes where prancing nymphs and satyrs pursued each other. Members of the San Francisco Police Department were everywhere; their equipment cluttered the three stiff Roman chairs, the one low table, and the lion skin, which some returning conqueror had tossed down carelessly. In an alcove behind all this, on a couch of silver, silk, and ivory, Lucrece reclined. A blonde with the features of Pallas Athena, her glorious hair heaped high to fall again in cascading ringlets, she regarded them with serene gray eyes, quite undisturbed by murder or its noisy aftermath. Her exquisite left hand hung down, utterly relaxed; her right was out of sight behind her back. One knee was drawn up. One graceful foot in a gold sandal peeped from beneath a white-and-golden toga so diaphanous that it revealed not just the beauty of her body but its astonishing completeness. On the floor in front of her, on a plastic sheet, lay the late mayor of San Francisco; and even the thread of blood from the corner of his mouth could not conceal the fact that his expression, instead of betraying pain or horror, was one of pleased surprise, as though someone at a political convention had just mistaken him for Teddy Kennedy.

Once, Errol Vasquez Munrooney had been a very handsome man. More recently, showmanship and charisma had combined with what was left to charm not only a succession of impressionable women but much of the general electorate as well. Now the flamboyant personality was gone; the vulgar magic had run out.

"Well," said Timuroff, considering the remains, "he may have rated a few imps, perhaps even one or two noncommissioned demons—but a stone Commendatore? Never! Still, don't underrate the dead. His Honor can make more trouble for you now than when he was alive and kicking."

"You know," Pete remarked thoughtfully, "he looks sort of like an overblown Richard Burton run to mod. Look at that outfit—right out of *Esquire*'s fashion section, shaggy curls and all. He must really have been sucking for the teenage vote."

Abruptly, before Timuroff could suggest that the mayor had probably had more carnal reasons for trying to bridge the generation gap, Jake Harrell bulled his way out of a busy knot of criminalists. "Pete!" he boomed. "Boy, am I glad you're here! We're almost through. After Tim tells us all about the dagger, I'll fill you in. Then—thank God!—the detective bureau can go hit the sack. You want to look around awhile before we wrap things up?"

"No need. Your boys know their job."

"Okay, they'll bring you everything they have tomorrow."

He gestured at the body. "How about him? Any fond fare-wells?"

Pete shook his head. "Just tell me, did he die there at her feet, or what?"

"He was half on, half off. Looked like he'd grabbed her, then she'd stabbed him, then he'd reared up and fallen back again. See how her nightie's torn around her breasts? When he was found, his head and shoulders were hanging over on the floor, her right hand was above his wound, and the dagger was still sticking in him."

"Did you turn her on again? Maybe she'd want to make a statement."

"Funny man! Sure we turned her on, but not until we'd questioned Grimwood to find out how she works, and then we videotaped the whole procedure to make sure we'd fouled nothing up. All she did was start her recitation over again right from the start."

"Well, that's it, I guess," Pete said. "At least for now."

"Fine. The *Chronicle* just phoned, and they're on their way. The *Trib* and everybody'll be right on their tail. I want all this cleaned up before they get here." He turned aside. "All right, Doc, you can have him now. Jimmy, bring the dagger over here for Mr. Timuroff. Bring both of 'em."

"*Both* of them?" asked Timuroff.

"Yeah. She's programmed for a fake one, a stage dagger. When you turn her on she starts reciting this long piece about some Roman rape case way back in B.C. Then, if anybody makes a pass at her, *whammo!* She screams and lets him have it in the back. All nice, clean fun—only this time the dagger was for real, and the fake one was stashed in that vase up there. Thanks, Jimmy—" He took the daggers, wrapped in Pliofilm and neatly ticketed, and held them out to Timuroff. "You want me to undo them, Tim?"

"It won't be necessary," Timuroff said slowly, stroking his moustache. "I had a feeling the weapon would be some-thing special when you asked for me." He handed back the rubber dummy dagger. "And it is special. I can tell you when it last was sold, and where, and for how much, and to whom." He turned the weapon over. The blade was about ten inches long, slightly curved, double edged. "It is a khanjar, Indo-Persian, and there are lots of them around —but not like this. It's said to have belonged to Nadir Shah, and it was sold at Sotheby's in London roughly six or seven weeks ago for seventeen thousand, seven hundred pounds."

"You mean," exclaimed Harrell, "that some nut paid that kind of money for a sticker just so he—so he could—?"

"Kill our Heroic Leader?" Timuroff smiled. "I doubt it very much. But the man who bought it was an agent named Strickland, acting for our friend Socrates Voukos."

Grimly, police glances were exchanged.

Timuroff shook his head. "Somehow, I can't believe Socrates is involved. He'd have too much respect for it. He actually threw a party for it when it arrived; I was invited, but I was down south. See how delicately the hilt is carved from spinach jade, inlaid and overlaid with gold and precious stones. Look at that splendid fretwork! And even though the blade is bloodied, you can still see that its damask and carving and inlay are unmatched. Master craftsmen created it." He handed the dagger back regretfully. "I hope you'll wipe that blood off before too long— just in case Socrates decides to sell it to some honest local dealer when this is over. You didn't find the scabbard, by the way?"

"No," Harrell answered. "Ought there to be one?"

"There was. It matched the rest, gold and more jewels, with velvet carefully chosen to complement the jade, though that of course had faded quite a bit over the years."

Harrell signaled, and the man who had been taping Timuroff's remarks hustled his gear away and disappeared. Suddenly the room was empty; everything—cameras, extension cords, hand vacuum cleaners, chemicals—had been removed. Moments before, everyone had been packing frantically; now the only sign of activity was the slow march to the door of the ambulance crew carrying the discreetly packaged mayor.

"What about Exhibit A?" Pete pointed at Lucrece.

"Leave her here," said Harrell. "You can't subpoena her, and trying to pry her out could wreck the evidence. I've ordered a lockup on the room until the picture clears. You just explain it to the chief in case he starts to throw his weight around, ha-ha!" He slapped Pete reassuringly on the back. "And now I'll brief you on what we've learned so far, which won't take more than about two minutes. Tim, do you want to sit in on this?"

"I'd rather prowl around a little, Jake. This is a fine old place; I'd like to look it over. Pete, is that okay with you?"

"Sure. Just don't let Kielty give you a bad time. And leave word with someone if you go anywhere you'd be hard to find."

Timuroff shut the door silently behind him, and strolled toward the staircase. Here the walls were paneled in a glowing hardwood much darker than those downstairs. The high ceiling was of modeled plaster, the sort of work once done for the great houses of Horace Walpole's England. The only pictures, incongruously, were half a dozen modern Japanese prints, all of them wonderfully dramatic cats by Tomoo Inagaki. Timuroff regarded them approvingly, recognizing that they had been chosen by someone who didn't give a damn for the opinions of interior decorators, and his estimate of Dr. Grimwood went up accordingly. At the head of the stairs, in an alcove, he spied what appeared to be a first-rate suit of Renaissance half armor, possibly from Nuremburg, but he remembered that the press was on its way and hastened on. Downstairs, he walked politely around a livid Amos Ledenthal, who, just released from questioning, was furiously shaking his grizzled mane and enormous fists, and telling the imperturbable plainclothesman at the door how he was going to bring about the downfall of Judson Hemmet, Mario Baltesar, and the chief of police, in that order. Ledenthal didn't even notice him, but his partner in the heavy-construction business, Reese Guthrie, was waiting for him in the background, so Timuroff said hello to him instead. "Amos seems upset," he said. "I can't say I really blame him."

A much younger man—young enough to have been a captain in Vietnam—Guthrie had impressed him favorably on the few occasions when they'd met. He was a southerner, from one of the Carolinas, strong and courteous and soft-spoken—and under all of it, taut and battle-hardened. Now he returned the greeting, and glanced over his shoulder at the altercation. "I just got here," he answered. "They tell me Munrooney's been killed. Too bad it had to happen here at Grimwood's. Otherwise, I don't think the country's suffered a great loss. I hope they don't think Amos had anything to do with it."

Timuroff said he didn't think so, then told him about Lucrece, the locked door, the strong suggestion that the mayor's intentions had not been of the noblest, and the khanjar.

Guthrie laughed aloud. "Well, that dagger puts Amos in the clear. He would've used a big katana or—what's the other one?—a tachi."

"Like any sensible man." Timuroff smiled. "Though it'd be a shame to risk a blade in perfect polish on someone like our Tarquin." Seeing that Ledenthal wasn't even beginning to run down, he decided to resume his tour. He said good-night to Guthrie, asked him to say hello to Amos for him, and wandered down the hall until it merged, through two stately doors standing open, into the living room. There he stopped to chat with Pascoe, another of Harrell's men, and to survey the guests.

The room extended more than forty feet across the rear of the house. Its paneling was of Circassian walnut, framing the windows and the mirrored mantels, one at either end, and setting in relief the precious First Empire paper on the walls. Fires in both fireplaces blazed cheerfully; and on the right, another door through which a caterer's waitress was carrying a tray of empty glasses betrayed the existence of a bar and butler's pantry.

Most of the guests looked apprehensive. Like livestock in a blizzard, they had huddled into more or less homogeneous knots. Before one fireplace, rebelliously sitting on the floor, were six or seven male and female hippies, probably chosen for relative cleanliness from the fringes of the English Department at U.C. They were paying court to an epicene but hairy person in a once-white swami suit, whom Timuroff recognized as a poet who had achieved public notoriety by publishing amatory verse involving a large section of the animal kingdom.

To counterbalance these, before the other fireplace were gathered those with pretensions to prestige, position, money, and high fashion: pretty people, vain people, inheritors of new money and onetime possessors of old fortunes—people who kept the gossip columnists alive.

Between them and the hippies, scattered by twos and threes, were the most valid people in the room. Socrates Voukos, squat and bristle-bearded, was talking seriously and softly with Wade Kalloch, a speculator and subdivider whose smooth, plump face and rimless glasses concealed the social conscience of a wolverine. Miranda Morphy Gardner, gaunt and diamonded and sheathed in silver, a power in the shadow world of ruthless moneylending, sat with one hand on the thigh of her effete male secretary, watching a well-known architect swiftly sketch imaginary designs on a burnished tabletop. Rear Admiral Houston Melmoth, retired, towered above them silently, grim-faced, turning his highball glass slowly in his hand.

Timuroff knew them all. They were all customers of his. But now he realized that he had never really looked at them before. From the beginning, the murder of the mayor, like the man himself, had had something so far-out about it that he had thought about it only as good theater: a farce, a travesty of the believable. Suddenly this had changed. Indefinably, on the edge of consciousness, a breath of cold and deadly purpose had reached out and touched him. It came and it was gone, leaving the world transmuted.

Timuroff had experienced it before in more than one of his several strange careers, and he had learned that it was not to be ignored. He surveyed the room again. There were a dozen others there whom he recognized, but they were unimportant, uninteresting. He looked again at Voukos and Kalloch and the looming admiral. He looked again at Miranda Gardner. He smiled at Pascoe. "Quite a party, isn't it?" he said.

"Weird, real weird." Pascoe shook his head. "Can't see why the chief keeps 'em here. Hell, we can haul 'em back for questioning anytime." He broke off, cocked an ear to listen. "Doorbell," he said. "That'll be the media. Boy, is this place going to be a nuthouse for a while!"

"It's certainly going to be confused," Timuroff agreed. "I think I'll wander down and get a drink."

"I wish I could," sighed Pascoe.

III

The Fearful Guest

Long ago, Alastair Alexandrovitch Timuroff had learned
how to move unobtrusively, so that strangers did not notice
him and acquaintances immediately forgot that he was
there. Now, on his way toward the bar, he was recognized
only by a moulting actress, who blew him a moist, crimson
kiss, and by young Coulter, who nodded vaguely and instantly turned back to the young lady he had his lustful
eye on.

He made friends with the middle-aged Filipino barman,
received a double brandy and soda instead of the single he
had asked for, then shifted into Spanish for a chat. The
barman was disturbed. The people here, he said emphatically, were very strange, more so than any group he'd ever
served. It was no wonder the poor mayor had been slain!
He gestured, dismissing the hippies and the real and aspir-
ing idle rich contemptuously. He dropped his voice. "But
there are others here, señor, who frighten me—and I,
Florencio Pambid, who was a sergeant in the constabulary
at nineteen and fought the Japanese as a guerrilla, I do not
frighten easily."

Timuroff, familiar with their combat record, was impressed. "I would value your opinion highly," he replied.

"Señor, I know you were not here before, that you came
with the police. Listen!" He pointed at Miranda Gardner.
"That woman looked into my eyes, and she is dead inside.
But worse—" Almost surreptitiously, he crossed himself.

29

"There was a man here who is gone. A big man, very cold, with a loose skin and pale eyes. But it was what he was, not how he looked. When the Japanese held my country, such men came. They came from here, from there, but they were all the same. They lived only to kill, to give others pain. You understand?"

"I understand," said Timuroff. "I have met such men. My friend the police inspector, who will be in charge, will speak with you."

"I will tell him everything I know—that the man went away before they found the mayor had been killed, that he stayed by himself and, I think, spoke to no one."

"*Mil gracias.* I will write the inspector's name on my card. If you think of more that you can tell, speak to him only or telephone me. The police know where to reach you? . . . Good."

There was a hubbub at the door; the gabble of the guests died suddenly; a strobe or two went off. Timuroff, realizing that the newsmen had arrived, paused only long enough to have his glass refilled. Then, as waitresses came up with trays of orders, probably for the press, he faded back into the butler's pantry, and out of it into a service hall. Rather to his surprise, the policeman there was the one who had opened the front door to them on their arrival. He was staring disconsolately into a cup of coffee.

"Hello, Kerry," Timuroff greeted him.

"Glad to see you, Mr. T. The chief booted me back here when the newsmen came. Where's Pete?"

"Still upstairs, I think. Your captain was briefing him when I came down."

"I sure don't envy him. All those characters. And would you look at this joint—twenty different ways in and out."

Timuroff saw that in addition to the service stairs there was a service lift, another little hall with a mysterious door at its end, a door announcing the probability of a john, a door to the main hallway, a great many closets and cupboards, and finally, at the dead end, a taller and more ornate door obviously opening into the library.

"Anybody in the library now?" Timuroff asked.

"Uh-uh. It's empty. Nobody's been there since the media came. Why?"

"Maybe I'll hole up there and kill my drink while I wait for Pete. Think anybody'd mind?"

"Can't see why." Kerry, who had hoped for company

and conversation, sounded disappointed. "You want me to tell him where you are if he shows up?"

"Tell him to come in and wake me." Timuroff turned the handle of the door. "It's been a long, hard day."

Some of the lights had been left on, and being fond of libraries, he was pleased to see that this was more than one in name only. Between the windows, and on either side of the high fireplace, bookshelves rose from floor to ceiling. Morocco, calf, and vellum spoke of centuries spanned; specially made slipcovers and shelves high enough for folios and tall quartos hinted at fine printing and probable rarity.

Everything was mahogany: the paneling, the great desk in the center of the room, where presumably Chiefy had been putting people to the question, the dictionary stand that flanked it, the wheeled library ladder, the heavy chairs, the huge Victorian couch before the fire. Two lovely Ting Yao bowls, almost a pair and obviously Sung, were on the mantel, next to a French clock extravagantly gilded and enameled, with at one end a dying gladiator and at the other his mourning wife and minor children, all in bronze. Timuroff was enraptured; he stood and stared, and presently the clock went *bong!* sepulchrally, as though announcing the sad end of the Franco-Prussian War.

He drank a toast to it, then let his gaze continue round the room. Beside the door to the main hall stood yet another suit of armor, dark and nobly Gothic, almost unornamented, made for an unusually tall man, its steel hands crossed over the hilt of an enormous broadsword. Idly, he raised the visor.

His reflexes were extremely quick, so he did not quite drop his drink. From within the helm, a human skull glared at him. It had ferocious teeth, bright blue glass eyes, and a lank yellow wig. Its jaws opened. In hollow tones and with a distinct Scandinavian accent, it cried out, " '*Speak! speak! thou fearful guest!*' "

Timuroff let the visor drop, and the skull was silent. Almost at his elbow, though, he heard a chuckle, and, turning to his right, found himself face to face with an elderly gentleman wearing a glen plaid suit, who seemingly had appeared out of nowhere. He was a vast crag of an old man, still mighty though falling into ruin, with stooped shoulders broad as a caber thrower's, a once-broken nose, a slightly cauliflowered ear, great grizzled eyebrows, sideburns, and moustache, and eyes which seemed at once quite mad, immensely shrewd, and wholly innocent.

"How do you do?" He beamed at Timuroff. "I'm Dr. Hector Grimwood. I see that you've met Eric here. What do you think of him?"

"Well," Timuroff replied judiciously, "he certainly isn't 'in rude armor drest.' "

"He isn't, is he? I tried to put him into Viking armor, but he just wouldn't hold together—there's so little to it, just thongs and bearskins and perhaps a byrnie—so we compromised. I bought him this suit at Fischer's in Lucerne. It was just his size."

"At the Mannheim-Esterhazy sale?" asked Timuroff.

"How—? *But of course!*" The doctor slapped his knee. "You're that arms expert the police brought in. They think my poor Lucrece used that peculiar dagger to stab our wretched mayor to death. Don't you believe it, sir. She is as gentle as a kitten. I know—I made her, after all. Or if she did, believe me it was justified. The man had a disgraceful reputation; I'd never have invited him if Mario Baltesar hadn't pressed me to. But all that's unimportant. Your nice police friend told me about you. It's lucky I ran into you. Wasn't your ancestor a Drummond?" He pointed to the couch. "Come, come. Do sit down. I've read about him. He married the daughter of some sort of princeling, didn't he?"

Timuroff thanked him and sat down. "Yes, he escaped out of the Tower with Drummond of Cromlix and Old Tom Dalyell of the Binns, and all three became generals and fought the Polonian and the Turk. When Charles the Second was restored, they were permitted to go home— a rare thing in Russia in those days—but by that time he'd married the daughter of Prince Dmitri Timuroff, who claimed descent from Tamerlane the Great, Timur the Conqueror. She was prettier than good King Charles, I dare say, so he stayed where he was. Our name is really Drummond-Timuroff, but it's simpler just to shorten it."

Under the circumstances, Timuroff did not think it strange that he should be sitting at the quiet center of a homicide investigation discussing his own forebears with an aged eccentric who, having contrived the apparent means and setting of the murder, was quite clearly a prime suspect. He had forgotten neither the premonitory chill he had experienced in the living room nor the doctor's silent, still unexplained appearance in the library. But he had taken to the old man instantly; a bond of sympathy had passed between them, and he suspected that the foundations for a friendship had been formed. For the next ten minutes, he told about the various Timuroffs: how through the centuries they had always kept in close touch with their Drummond relatives, sending at least their eldest sons to British schools and sometimes on to Edinburgh or Oxford, and quite frequently bringing back English or Scottish brides. He told the doctor how, in 1926, when he was nine, he himself had been shipped from Istanbul, where his family had fled after the revolution, to an ancient school at Inverness, still noted for its Stuart sympathies, where he had spent six years before his father sent for him, this time from Buenos Aires, where he had become a fencing master to the army.

"There, of course," he said, "I had to learn my Spanish, and do my military service, and finally my father pulled some strings and they commissioned me, probably because by that time I was as good as he was with the sabre."

"Your background makes my own seem rather humdrum, Mr. Timuroff," replied the doctor. "My ancestors were all New England Yankees, except a single scapegrace southerner who disappeared to everyone's relief. But still my life has had its more exciting moments." His eyes twinkled, and Timuroff observed that they had curious dark green flecks. "At Johns Hopkins, I had to wrestle my way through, quite literally—a bout here and there during the term, and taking on all comers with a carnival in summertime. I kept it up until I started my internship. That was how I acquired these mementos." He touched his damaged ear and nose. "And I learned how to make the most horrendous faces, to say nothing of marrow-chilling grunts and groans. Yes, my career started out eccentrically, and it's really not surprising that now most people think I'm crazier than a bedbug."

Politely, Timuroff started to demur.

"No, no. They do, you know. If, like so many of my colleagues, I spent my money flying a hundred-thousand-dollar aircraft at speeds much lower than a commercial airliner's and a risk many times as high, everyone would consider me enviably normal. If I maintained a mothballed harem of divorced wives, they'd undoubtedly admire me for marrying a cute office nurse a third my age. As it is,

I live here happily with Penny Anne—that's Mrs. Short, my secretary—and spend my time contriving little ladies like Lucrece, and give my parties for the floating world. So of course I'm mad. And it amuses me. What I do resent are the nasty stories that have been going around lately."

"What sort of stories?" asked Timuroff.

Dr. Grimwood frowned. "About my girls. One or two of the columnists have been printing loathsome hints, especially that professional Irishman, the one with the bad temper and the porous nose. I love perfection and completeness, and naturally I know anatomy. Therefore, because Lucrece's garment is transparent, they've heard that she has everything a woman ought to have. Of course, it's all nonfunctional; the poor little thing's equipment, like beauty, is no more than skin-deep—but apparently they don't know that. If they'd been joking, I wouldn't mind at all, but they've been serious. We've even had some filthy phone calls, and Penny has been dreadfully upset."

Timuroff agreed that this was understandable.

"That's why I'm avoiding newsmen at the moment. You can imagine the sort of questions they'd be asking me! Besides"—the doctor lowered his voice—"I am convinced that my Lucrece *was* used to lure Munrooney to his death, and that these stories somehow played a part in it."

For a few minutes, Timuroff had been hearing the sounds of busyness outside, a rise and fall of voices, occasionally a few that were peremptory, and stampings up and down. Now someone tried the door, waited a moment, tried harder. There was a knock.

"It sounds as though they've come downstairs and are out looking for you," he told the doctor. "What do we do now?"

The knock was repeated, and a hoarse voice shouted, "Dr. Grimwood? Are you in there, sir? I'm Rop Millweed of the *Chronicle*. I'd sure appreciate a moment of your time."

"I'll be the sacrificial lamb," offered Timuroff. "I can run out, tell them you aren't here, and bring Pete to the rescue."

The doctor's mood changed instantly. He leaped up, a sudden pixyish smile on his lips. "Don't worry—they'll never find us in this house if we don't want them to!"

Raising a cautionary finger, he moved toward the paneled corner of the chimneypiece.

As Timuroff joined him, he halted, chuckling delightedly. He reached into the bookcase next to him, turned something—and in utter silence the entire case swung out toward them. Behind it was a lighted passageway. "Come with me!" he whispered, entering it.

Timuroff followed him, pleased that the mystery of his abrupt appearance in the library had been solved, and they waited as the case closed behind them. The passage, no more than twelve feet long, connected with two narrow staircases, one going up, one down. "I love these secret passages," remarked Dr. Grimwood, heading for the lower stair. "The house is full of them, and I've wondered why old Mrs. Albright's husband built them in. I've heard he was involved in shady business dealings, smuggling and all that sort of thing. At any rate, I'm very grateful for them. They *are* convenient."

Timuroff wondered how these convenient passages would further complicate Pete's already tangled task, but he said nothing.

At the bottom, Dr. Grimwood unlocked another door, opening into an even narrower passageway. "This one," he said, "connects the wine cellar and my workshop. We're all the way back on this floor; it's shorter than the upper ones—the hillside cuts it off. My shop used to be some sort of storage room in the old days, but I refitted it and cut more windows through. I want to show you how I work, and all my tools. The art of making automata is as exacting as the finest gunsmith's. I'm sure you'll find it interesting—"

He turned a key, snapped a silent switch—and Timuroff found himself regarding a long and narrow room which, at first glance, might have been either a workshop or a surgery. Everything looked too white and sterile: the shelves and cabinets along the inner wall, the cluttered workbench on the window side. The bright white lights were clearly surgical. Some of the tools appeared to be dental; others to have been borrowed from the aerospace industries. In the exact center of the floor, under fluorescent tubes of an especial brilliance, stood an operating table. And on it lay a human figure discreetly covered with a sheet.

"We doctors!" chuckled Hector Grimwood happily.

"We're all alike. We enjoy playing God. Some of us terrorize our patients by dramatizing our power of life and death. Others, a little more humanely, just make them wait forever in our waiting rooms. But I prefer to do it by making my own people, who cannot feel, who're always in the best of health, who cannot hate me for my failures. Now, let me introduce you to my masterpiece—"

For a moment, when the first passage swallowed them, Timuroff had wondered whether, despite his liking for the doctor, he might indeed not be on his way to a demise even more extraordinary than Mayor Munrooney's. Then the enthusiasm in Dr. Grimwood's voice had reassured him; it was so clearly that of the dedicated craftsman, the monomanic hobbyist. Now, as the hobbyist strode to his operating table and seized a corner of the sheet, Timuroff experienced a new twinge of apprehension.

"There!" the doctor cried. "Isn't she beautiful?"

Timuroff's eyebrows shot up. She was beautiful indeed—every astounding bit of her. She lay there naked, with her legs very slightly spread and a sweet smile on her countenance. For an instant, he entertained the fantasy that Dr. Grimwood, under contract to Hugh Hefner, had gone into the business of manufacturing Playmates. Then he saw that between her breasts a little door was open, revealing an extremely complex mechanism.

"This is Evangeline," declared the doctor. "Eventually, of course, she will be dressed as Longfellow envisioned her, but under all that cloth and frippery she will be perfectly complete." He turned toward the workbench; seized forceps, little jars and canisters, and a small, needle-pointed electric instrument. "Now watch! I want to show you how I affix these pubic hairs—"

Timuroff watched, fascinated, while Hector Grimwood, working swiftly and with precision, discussed his problems and techniques: how he had developed a synthetic skin that not only looked but felt extremely natural, and the difficulties involved in coordinating changes of expression with voice recordings and movements of the body.

A good listener, he interrupted only at appropriate intervals with genuinely interested questions. After twenty minutes, he and the doctor were "Alastair" and "Hector." The fact that there had been a murder in the house had been comfortably sidetracked, and he himself had half forgotten the reason for his being there. Then, just as Dr.

Grimwood finished implanting a final slightly curly hair, the phone rang. It rang softly but insistently from the workbench, and the doctor, with a sigh of exasperation, put his forceps down and went to answer it.

"Hello, hello! . . . Yes, Penny dear, I'm down here. Yes, working on Evangeline. . . . Mr. Timuroff? He's with me. Why don't you join us? I'm sure you'll like him too. . . . Well, tell Inspector Cominazzo where we are, and bring him with you. . . . You will, after the newsmen leave? Good, good. Yes, in the poker parlor. I'll see you there in a little while."

He hung up. "Penny Anne has been wondering what became of us. But now Chief Otterson has gone, and she says the reporters are finally giving up." He looked down at Evangeline, and patted the locus of his latest creative effort with affection. "That *is* a pretty little pussy," he declared. "Really, I'm quite proud of it." He pulled the sheet back up again. "Alastair, I do hope you'll come again. Goodness knows there's going to be enough for me to do. I suppose I'll have to make some changes in Lucrece, now that all this has happened. And I've been wondering about Eric. Penny Anne thinks I ought to give him some of the horrible noises I learned to make when I was wrestling. But it seems to me that Longfellow's *The Skeleton in Armor* in its entirety is quite adequate. Don't you agree?"

"I do indeed," Timuroff assured him. "Most people would never get past 'Speak! speak! thou fearful guest!' "

The doctor's answering chuckle cut off abruptly. His troubled countenance, as he turned from his workbench, announced another sudden, total change of mood. "This evening at the party," he said, speaking very slowly, "we *really* had a fearful guest. I had forgotten it; I suppose the murder drove it from my mind." He began pacing up and down. "Have you ever met a man you absolutely loathed and feared *on sight*? I never had before, but that was how this man affected me. How can I say this? I felt at once that I could kill him without conscience or compunction. The thought shocked and frightened me, and it still does."

Timuroff felt his hackles rise. "Was he a big man, with rather pale eyes, and a skin that seemed too large for him?"

His host stopped short. "How did you know? Why, you weren't even here!"

"No," said Timuroff, "but others were." And he told the story Florencio Pambid had told him. "There are people who radiate such undiluted evil that sometimes normal men—at least men with any sensitivity—feel the immediate impulse to lash out at them. They don't, of course, and usually they end up more scared of themselves than of the other fellow. I believe it because I have experienced it myself. Your own reaction needn't worry you. Having him in your house, especially with a murder following, would cause me more concern. Why did you invite him?"

"Invite him? I didn't. I wouldn't have. Somebody must have brought him—I let people whom I know do that at my parties—but I've no idea who. Penny Anne may know."

"Do you recall his name?"

"Yes, I believe I do. It was van Zaam. He had some sort of accent, and I suppose he could have been a Hollander. I exchanged a few words with him, and I believe he came up and introduced himself. Someone told me later that he'd left early."

Timuroff tensed; again the cold wind had blown. "Well, it'll be interesting to see if the police can find out anything about him. With his name, and your description and the bartender's, I'm sure Pete'll be able to run him down."

"I hope so! For a while I really thought I'd lost my mind. But I still wish I'd never seen the man." Like a bear trying to shake the frost of winter from its shoulders, the doctor shuddered. "Well, let's go to the poker parlor, where we can have a drink. Lord knows I need one."

He double-locked the workshop door behind him, and they followed a corridor into another hall almost as formal as the one above, where there was a smaller staircase and an elevator entrance. "This used to be the billiard room," he said, opening a door far over to the left, "but now I use it for my porcelains and general loot and clutter."

They walked between a small army of glass cases, between unctuous celadons and fragile Sung whites, quiet teadusts, glowing peach blooms, rich Imperial yellows. The door to the poker parlor was standing open. They went in. Paneled in another unknown hardwood, the room contained much more than the Diamond Jim Brady poker table—a table at which one could see fortunes being won or lost—under a pendant Tiffany lamp at its very center. It had a scattering of large leather chairs, a bar and mirrored backbar, a brass ship's clock fastened to the bulkhead, a fireplace in which a fire was magically roaring, and, in its inner corner, a vast armoire of age-blackened walnut. The bar was L-shaped, with one door which Timuroff guessed must lead into a service hall. An ardent poker player, he recognized a poker player's paradise, and said as much. "This place is wonderful! You do play here, I hope?"

Hector Grimwood brightened perceptibly. "At least twice a month, when I can get a group together. Usually on Saturdays." He went behind the bar. "Would you like to join us? That is, if you don't mind a lot of wild games? I could let you know."

Timuroff indicated that he enjoyed all poker, straight, wild, or in-between.

"Now what can I offer you? I'm going to have a shot of Bushmill's. . . . No? . . . Brandy and soda? Of course, but it may have to be domestic."

They drank a silent toast.

"Hector, I envy your house. I can't imagine anyone who lived here ever leaving it."

"Well, it costs me a pretty penny to maintain, but it's worth it—and after all, I *have* a pretty penny. Brain surgery is not unprofitable, and my investments have happily been shrewd ones." The doctor chuckled. "You'd have liked old Albright, Alastair. He was a bandit, I suppose, but he was good company. If he hadn't been—well, I just might not have risked my reputation to give him those few extra years."

"Did he put this room in, or did you?"

"Oh, it was his, of course. They were great gamblers in those days. His games started right after lunch, and he'd have dinner served in here; then they'd keep on playing far into the night, interrupting only for a midnight snack. Often they were still going at breakfast time. We seldom push it quite that hard these days—we almost always break up by two A.M."

"And the only way in is the way we came?" asked Timuroff.

"He didn't like unexpected interruptions, so he made the place a little hard to reach. It has its private washroom— that door by the fireplace opens into it. But"—Dr. Grimwood winked—"Albright did love his exits and his entrances, so he installed one other. I'll show you." Putting down his drink, he went to the huge armoire. "Come and take a look. There's a sliding panel in the back, another in the wall behind it, and of course a secret passage with a flight of stairs going back upstairs. The cabinet's from the Low Countries, and it's an ancient one. It weighs at least a ton, with those enormous wrought-iron hinges and that lock—" He broke off suddenly. For a long moment he was completely still. "That's strange!" he said. "I could've sworn I closed those doors myself this afternoon. And what is *that?*"

The doors stood a tiny fraction of an inch ajar; and Timuroff saw that *that* was a white piece of pasteboard showing its corner under one of them.

Frowning, the doctor picked it up. *"Look,"* he said, and handed it to Timuroff, and when he said the word the half-forgotten chill swept through the room again.

The card was crushed and torn. Timuroff took it, and on its face he read: *Hendrik J. van Zaam,* and under that *Industrial Liaison,* with an address in Los Angeles.

The doctor's face was gray. "Wh-what was he doing in this room?" he asked. He asked it of the air, a question to which there could be no answer. Then, without thinking, he pulled the armoire doors open—and recoiled instantly.

High on its left side, Timuroff saw a great black iron hook.

Van Zaam, his loose skin pallid as a shroud, was hanging there.

IV

Their Exits and
Their Entrances

Metallically, the ship's clock struck six bells into the silence—and Timuroff realized that it was three o'clock and marveled fleetingly that so short a time could have encompassed all that had occurred since the curtain fell on *Don Giovanni*.

Van Zaam hung suspended by a cord wound twice around his weight-stretched neck, a cord so hard and thin that it had cut and bruised the flesh it violated. His almost colorless blue eyes bulged sightlessly. His cruel mouth hung open, showing a sagging, swollen tongue. He was only too clearly dead. But the terror and revulsion he had inspired in others had not died with him. His life was gone, but evil clung to him like a miasma—to be dissipated, thought Timuroff, only with his body's ultimate decay. Florencio Pambid had been quite right about the man, but certain people must have found him useful—a thought quite as disquieting as he himself had been, or as his murdered body, hanging there.

Forcibly, Timuroff turned his mind into more pragmatic channels. He saw that Dr. Grimwood, hands trembling violently, was staring blankly at the terrible corpse; and very quietly he closed the doors of the armoire. He urged the doctor down into a chair. He fetched his glass.

41

"Hector," he said, "you'd better drink this down. Do you think you'll be all right?"

"Th-thank you. I'll be . . . better in a moment." He downed his drink; held out his glass. "Till now," he said, as Timuroff refilled it, "Munrooney's murder didn't seem quite real. But this one—this is different. Everything's been changed." For a moment, he closed his eyes. "This sort of thing—till now I've kept it out."

"Well, when it forces its way in," said Timuroff, "the best thing one can do is act. I'll call Pete Cominazzo."

"Good Lord! Penny'll be here any minute now. She—she mustn't see *that!*" He struggled to his feet. "My God, I hope she isn't bringing him down through the passageway!"

"Is there a phone here?"

"B-behind the bar. Push the white button down. Then dial nine—that rings them all."

Timuroff pushed and dialed, and almost instantly three voices answered. "Inspector Cominazzo?" he snapped, and two phones clicked down as Pete replied. "That you, Pete? Can you get hold of Dr. Grimwood's secretary? . . . She's right there? Good. Tell her she's *not* to come down here. But *you'd* better get here on the double. . . . Yes, there's something new—another murder. . . . What?" He heard a woman's voice, anxious, in the background. "No, he's all right. . . . Yes, I'll put him on."

He gave the phone to the doctor, and waited till Mrs. Short had been informed and reassured. Then, "Pete'll be here directly," he said. "Hector, this all keeps getting curiouser and curiouser. First there's a rare old khanjar, and now we find *him*"—they both glanced round at the armoire—"strangled with a bowstring. The Turks were always fond of that—back in the seventeen hundreds, they did it to a relative of mine. This string looks very much like one of theirs. I'm not just making tasteless jokes, but if anyone wanted me involved, this would be just the way to manage it."

"But *why,* Alastair?"

"Perhaps because my low opinion of His Honor is well known. Perhaps to make confusion even worse confounded. Perhaps because somebody thinks I can be exploited or manipulated—"

He was about to add that the last possibility was one he found distinctly irritating, but at that point quick steps and voices came from the billiard room, and a moment later Pete Cominazzo entered with a wiry, gray-haired detective named Stevens. They looked harrassed and tired.

Pete took the room in at a glance. "So we've got another one," he said bitterly. "We would—at three A.M. Who is it this time—the governor? Jimmy Hoffa? Joan Baez? Don't anybody tell me. Just let me guess."

"You aren't even warm," Timuroff answered, pointing at the armoire. "But then neither is he."

Pete reached the doors in three strides; jerked them open. He stepped back abruptly. For a moment, he made no sound at all. Then a low, unsteady whistle escaped his lips. *"Whee-e-ew!* Thanks for the shudders!" He turned. "Tim, who *is* this guy?"

Stevens said nothing. He held his breath for a few seconds, then released it with a gasp.

"He—he was not a guest," Hector Grimwood told them unhappily. "That is, he was not—invited."

"I should hope not! Christ, I wouldn't invite that creep to his own funeral!"

"Somebody did," Timuroff pointed out, handing Pete the business card. Then, briefly, he filled him in on the bartender's story and the doctor's reaction.

There was a long, long silence while Pete stood there frowning, as though the act of waiting could force that hanging corpse to tell whatever secrets lay behind its presence there.

"In case you're wondering," Timuroff remarked presently, "that is a Turkish bowstring round his neck."

"I don't like it," Pete muttered, not really answering him. "I don't like *any* of it. I was hoping we'd be up only against local talent. If this buzzard's what he seems to be—and that *'Industrial Liaison'* can cover up a lot of nastiness these days—the media are really going to go ape." Firmly, he closed the armoire doors again. "Well, all we can do about it is get to work."

"How did he get down here?" Stevens asked.

"There are several ways," the doctor answered. "We have two elevators and two sets of stairs, as you know. He could've used the main ones or gone down through the service areas. Or of course somebody could've led him through the secret passages."

"The *what?*" Pete exclaimed. "What was that you said?"

"The secret passages," repeated Dr. Grimwood, almost cheerfully. "The house is honeycombed with them. I always try to show them to my guests. Alastair—that is, er, Tim—will tell you. I brought him through one from the library to this floor, behind my workshop. But all are more or less connected. This one from the armoire leads, one way and another, to the formal sitting room, to Lucrece's room, to Penny Anne's, and to a closet off the main hall."

"You mean one of them comes out *here,* out of the wall, right behind that body? And that it goes straight up to where the mayor was killed?"

"Well, not *straight* up, Inspector. But it does get there."

"My God!" sighed Pete. *"Now* they tell me."

"Oh, dear!" said Dr. Grimwood. "I suppose I should have mentioned it. But we've always taken these passages so much for granted—" He broke off helplessly.

"Well, we'll just have to do the best we can in the barndoor-locking department. Jeff's been on the horn to headquarters, and some of the boys are coming back to do the spade work on this van Zaam character. When he's been carted off, I'm going to leave Inspector Stevens here in charge and try to catch up on a little sleep. Tomorrow's going to be a big and nasty day. Before I go, though, I want to make absolutely sure those passages are clear. Why don't we take a tour of them right now?"

"Surely you—you don't want to start *here?*"

"Behind van Zaam? God, no! We can start someplace else and work back. By the time we've made the circuit, they'll have him taken down. Till then, Steve can stay and hold his hand so he won't be stolen."

The bowels of Dr. Grimwood's residence turned out to be even more ramified than Timuroff had suspected; and the guided tour convinced him that unless one belonged to some dedicated special interest group—the Borgias, for example—secret passages could very soon become a bore. No clues turned up; no carelessly dropped handkerchiefs, no subtle cigar ashes, not so much as a torn clipping from the morning paper. Timuroff politely stifled yawns, and Pete Cominazzo patiently insisted that every door and sliding panel be secured and sealed. By the time they reached the poker room again, van Zaam was gone; and when they finally went upstairs once more the lab men had done their job and taken off.

Penelope Anne Short was waiting for them in the library. She rose to greet them, and Timuroff, caught off guard, barely suppressed his instant impulse to exclaim, "Hello, Evangeline!" Instead, he acknowledged Dr. Grimwood's introduction as gracefully as possible, considering that Mrs. Short was very lush indeed and that his mind insisted on undressing her with a quite indecent intimacy. Indeed, it took him several seconds to realize that Penny Anne—red lips, dark eyes, black hair, and all—was much older than her mechanized twin sister, or even to notice the stocky middle-aged woman to whom she had been talking, whom the doctor presented as his housekeeper.

"Mrs. Hanson and her husband have been with me almost since I got the house," he said. "When was it exactly, Mrs. Hanson?"

"September eighteenth, 1944, it was, sir." Mrs. Hanson blushed a shocking pink. "How could I forget it? Hanson just discharged from the navy on his disability—and me, a little virgin fresh from Lassen County." She sniffled sentimentally. "Or almost one, at least—we'd only just got married. Imagine! Coming to this house, with the doctor, and his mechanical lady—there was but the one in those days—and, well, everything!"

She subsided, and Dr. Grimwood completed the introductions ceremoniously, announcing that Timuroff was the world's foremost authority in his field, that Inspector Cominazzo was a splendid fellow even if his name did sound like the forced marriage of two extremist parties, and that the murders would speedily be solved.

"They'd better be!" declared Penny Anne. "It was quite bad enough when the mayor was killed, but this one —*ugh!*" She shivered. "Do—do you think it's safe for us to even stay here, Heck?"

The nickname came as a surprise. Her voice was deep and musical; and the way she spoke it, together with her whole manner to the doctor, at once defined their relationship as firm and normal and affectionate. Timuroff decided that he approved of her.

"Now, Penny Anne," said the doctor soothingly. "The Inspector here has everything in hand."

"I'm leaving three men here, Mrs. Short," Pete told her. "We've searched the secret passages, and they're clean. Now they've been locked and sealed; so have the poker room and . . . er . . . Lucrece's room upstairs. I don't think you have to worry." He turned to Dr. Grimwood. "Doctor, are all your phones on the switching system?"

"Why, yes—though Penny has a direct outside line."

"Good. Why don't you show us how to work it? The press is going to start bugging you the minute they catch on there's been a second murder, and if you want your rest you'd better let the PD run interference for you."

"That would be good of you. Calls from friends can be turned over to the Hansons—their apartment's over the garage. They'll know who to put through to us." The doctor patted his secretary's well-rounded arm. "Penny Ante here has had a very trying day, so I'm going to prescribe a sleeping pill for her."

Relaxing visibly, Mrs. Short smiled back at him. "Heck always calls me Penny Ante when he's quieting me," she told them. "It's a put-down, sort of, coming from an old poker player, but I don't really mind."

Pete surveyed the room, as though uncertain whether yet another murder might not still turn up. "I guess that's all for now," he said.

"If you gentlemen could stay a little longer," offered Mrs. Hanson, "I'd fix you ham and eggs."

"Inspector Stevens and the boys just might take you up on that," Pete answered, "but it's four thirty—Mr. Timuroff and I are going to head on home."

"I'll bet you have a pretty little wife just waiting up for you." Mrs. Hanson, regarding Inspector Cominazzo's manly frame, turned pink again. "Well, we enjoyed your being here anyhow. That is, we would of excepting for those awful murders. That is—"

Gently, Hector Grimwood shushed her. He thanked Pete Cominazzo for his kindness. He thanked Timuroff for making a bad time much easier to bear. He walked them to the door, and ushered them courteously out into the chill of early morning.

The door clicked to behind them, and they walked in silence to the car. Timuroff backed it out and, in low gear, sent it down the dark declivity of Kemble Street.

"You're strangely quiet," he said to Pete after a block or two.

"I'm sulking," replied Pete morosely. "I tell you, Tim, I wish Chiefy had put his boy Kielty in instead of me. Then when the roof falls in it'd be him under it."

"Calm yourself," said Timuroff. "I'll not abandon you."

"You mean you'll stand at my right hand and keep the bridge with me? Well, at least that's appropriate. Do you know why our friend Dr. Grimwood made Lucrece? No? Well, as a boy they sent him to a Christian Brothers school. There was a Brother Padraic there, who had a thing on Ancient Rome. So little Hector had to memorize 'Horatius,' with gestures, and give it every time they had the parents in—and in a toga. Anyhow, when he'd made his pile and could do anything he wanted, he got to thinking: if Lucrece had just put up a fight instead of lying back and then committing suicide, Lars Porsena wouldn't have marched on Rome, Horatius would never have had to keep the bridge, Macaulay's poem wouldn't have been written, and he himself would have been spared his ordeal. So he programmed his little lady so that if anybody tried to spread her legs apart, even the least bit, she'd stop reciting, scream, and stab him. Okay, no Tarquin, no rape, no Etruscan army, no bridge, no poem, no performance for young Hector. It sure put Brother Paddy in his place, even if he was forty years dead."

"And our mayor in *his*."

"Tim, you don't know the half of it. The PD doesn't often suppress evidence, especially in this kind of murder, but this time we did, for the time being at least. We even swore Doc Grimwood and his Penny Anne to secrecy. Maybe we can keep it quiet until the trial—if there ever is a trial."

"It must be something really interesting," said Timuroff.

"Oh, it is, it is! When they found His Honor, His Honor was exactly where they said. Only he hadn't any pants on. And his shorts were lying there next to him. And he had the door all locked from the inside."

Timuroff was surprised but not astounded. He said as much. "And you retrousered him before the photographs were taken?"

"No, Harrell has better sense than that. He took the first shots himself with Wallton and a couple others looking on, and didn't touch a thing until Chiefy got there. That was only a few minutes, because Wallton phoned him at home right after calling headquarters. Chiefy gave the order to reshort, retrouser, and reshoe his Leader—Munrooney did have socks on, by the way—and of course the damn fool brought Baltesar and Hemmet in on it, so now they know about it too."

"There!" said Timuroff. "That is why young men become photographers. Can't you imagine Harrell's shots in *Playboy*, probably with a profound interpretation by some expert, say Eldridge Cleaver?"

"I'm glad somebody has a sense of humor," grumbled Pete. "Just don't forget—the van Zaam bit isn't half as funny, and they both happened in the doctor's house. By the way, what do you think of *him?*"

Timuroff was serious instantly. "He is a dirty old man," he answered. "But he's a very rare and superior sort of D.O.M. Most of them are just dirty young men or dirty middle-aged men grown senile. He isn't. Pete, I like him. Of course, he's mad—but then he's a gentleman, and you have to be insane to be one nowadays." For a long moment, he was silent. "But I also realize," he added slowly, "that it was *his* house, *his* mechanical woman, and *his* party. Besides, even at his age, he is probably still strong enough to have strangled van Zaam and hung him up there single-handed. So there we are."

"Not quite," said Pete. "That's *one* alibi we have established—that and Socrates'. From the time Munrooney went upstairs—and it seems like he took off before van Zaam—until they started up to look for him, neither one was out of Denny Wallton's sight. Neither was Penny Anne. And your Filipino friend—Pambid?—he swears to it too. Of course, Grimwood could still be an accessory, or even the murderer if he really did put that dagger in Lucréce's hand."

"That, Pete, is just about impossible. Has it occurred to you that our little friend Lucrece almost certainly did *not* stab Lover Boy?"

"Come again?"

"Whether she has the strength or not, I just don't know. But that khanjar is all wrong. It's a heavy dagger for its type, broad and slightly curved—and the human back is full of bones, the spine and all the ribs, not at all easy for a programmed blow. If anyone were trying even to make the thing look plausible, they'd choose a different type of blade, narrow and straight. No, it just doesn't wash."

"All right, if Lucrece didn't do the job, who did? I hope you're right—Grimwood's much too picturesque to put in jail."

"Well, some of his friends aren't exactly colorless," said Timuroff. "Hemmet, Baltesar, Voukos, Ledenthal"—he ticked them off—"Kalloch, and Admiral Melmoth, and don't forget Miranda Gardner. Even Tommy Coulter, though he hardly counts. Remember what I said? They're all arms collectors, every one of them, and customers of mine. They all know Grimwood, and I understand that most of them have been mixed up in business deals together. But that's not what's so odd. The really odd thing is the choice of weapons. Have you questioned Socrates about the khanjar?"

"Yeah. He really blew his stack. He swore he'd locked it in his safe after his party, before he flew to Greece. He got back only yesterday, he said, and you were a damn liar—it couldn't be his dagger—and you were jealous because he was so rich he could outbid you on it. Well, then we showed it to him, and he got off his horse but started right in weeping—why hadn't we cleaned the blood off right away? and how he'd sue us if we got it rusty. Anyhow, he checks out, and Jake and I both think he's okay. He didn't even know about Grimwood's gettogether till Penny Anne phoned him this afternoon."

"Someone must've stolen the khanjar at his party. Did he say who was there?"

"Several times. Some characters out of the de Young Museum, and a few rich Greeks like him, and every collector you just mentioned, plus what's-his-name—Guthrie—who came with Ledenthal. Even Grimwood and his Penny Anne were there."

"Hemmet collects edged weapons, mostly late Renaissance," said Timuroff. "Baltesar buys whatever strikes his eye, and doesn't bother to learn anything about it. The admiral is an armor man, and Kalloch goes in for high-art firearms, like your pistola, though he never keeps anything he can make a buck on. Miranda Gardner is a serious and well-informed collector of kidney daggers, stilettos, and other pretty little things' people stick into people. Coulter buys crud mostly—brand-new commemorative Colts and Winchesters, and rusty sawed-off shotguns wicked antique dealers have stamped W.F. and Company. Even Heck owns a few suits of armor, though he really isn't a collector. The only one who isn't in on it is Guthrie."

"He wasn't really in on it tonight, either," said Pete.

"Jake said he showed up late. Who is he, anyway? Seems like a nice guy—who might be rough to tangle with."

"Amos's partner. Ledenthal started in business with his father years ago, and took the son in when he came back from 'Nam after the old man died."

In his mind's eye, Timuroff reviewed the faces. Hemmet and Baltesar, Voukos, Kalloch, Melmoth, Miranda Gardner. They were the faces of acquaintances, of customers, of people talked to, smiled at. "Most arms collectors," he said, speaking almost to himself, "tend to be a bit less hostile than the average, perhaps because they take out their aggressions by playing with swords, or duelling pistols, or whatever. But these are different. I had to see them all together to realize it. Except for Amos and young Coulter, and maybe Baltesar, they're wolves."

"I noticed," Pete replied. "Jake had a lot to say, and there's plenty of gossip about some of them."

For a block or two, nothing more was said. Timuroff suddenly was tired and tense, and he could sense that Pete was too. Finally, as they turned into Van Ness, he said, "I wonder. I wonder if any of them did engineer it?"

"Well, your sword-collecting friend Ledenthal isn't wondering. He *knows*."

"What the devil do you mean?"

"You haven't heard? He yelled at Chiefy that by God it must've been Hemmet and the Gardner woman—that with friends like them Munrooney had no room for honest enemies."

"Amos must've been hysterical. Hemmet and Munrooney were like Siamese twins."

Pete laughed a little wildly. "Don't you envy me?" he cried. "Maybe I should've been a Jesuit, like my cousin Austin. By God, I don't know what keeps me from joining them right now."

"I can think of at least two things," declared Timuroff. "The first, as Mrs. Hanson wisely pointed out, is probably waiting up for you. The second is too little Latin and less Greek."

He turned the car into the garage, and Pete stepped out into its concrete stillness. "Tim," he said, "sometime today could you sit down and tape what you remember about tonight? Everything—people, things, gossip, hunches. I'd appreciate it. I'll be in touch, probably around Olivia's quitting time."

Timuroff agreed, saying he'd do his best. Then, trying to shake off the remembered grisliness of the night's events, he drove the Rover home through the still almost empty streets.

V

A History of the Eighteenth Century

Timuroff's shop occupies the third floor of a very old, very narrow stone business building on Battery Street, one which has survived simply because, in today's economy, it could not be replaced profitably. Huddled against an insurance company's structural display of wealth in glass and steel, it never is really noticed by the weighty businessmen and hurrying young executives and attractive secretaries who pass its door.

That, of course, is how its tenants like it, for none of them is anxious to attract casual passers-by. The ground floor consists, at least visibly, of nothing but a tiled hall containing a wall directory, an elevator, and the locked door to a staircase; the rest—warehouse space, boiler room, and a garage opening on Magruder Alley—is out of sight. The first floor has for decades accommodated a changing congeries of petty steamship companies, busily engaged in moving cargoes of dubious origin and smelliness between unlikely ports. The second floor houses a discreetly prosperous firm of Dutch exporters and importers. The third, according to the wall directory, belongs to *A. A. Timuroff—by appointment only,* which is adequately uninformative.

Olivia Cominazzo came down at her usual hour, 9:30— for Timuroff almost always opens on Saturdays. She was not quite her usual bright and cheerful self. Pete had not wakened her when he came in, and she had carefully not disturbed him when she left. However, she had turned the news on very softly during breakfast, and had heard enough to understand that he was having problems. Very promptly, she had forgiven him, and a little later, feeling magnanimous, had forgiven her employer for contributing, even if involuntarily, to his delinquency. Now she was worried, as she always was when the media cascaded news of death and danger into her life.

She walked into the elevator hard on the heels of two large Levantines who were conversing emotionally in a tongue she did not understand. "Good morning, Mr. Karazoglu," she said to one of them, glad for the little touch of normalcy. "How is everything?"

Mr. Karazoglu, who had been deploring the effect of cheap air transport on the once-rich trade of carrying Moslem pilgrims through the Red Sea to Mecca, broke into an olive-oil smile, bristled his moustache, and said that, yes, yes, everything was wonderful, such a nice day! and such a *pretty* lady, yes. He thought of how profitable a little property she would have been, installed in an establishment his brother had once operated—though only for a most exclusive clientele—in Marrakech.

"And how is Mrs. Karazoglu?" inquired the pretty lady. "And the kids?"

Mr. Karazoglu sighed a little wistfully, and replied in a deflated voice that they were, thank you, thank you, very well. He then introduced his friend, who spoke no English, and whose name sounded like Mr. Asterisk. They escorted her to her floor, exchanging several private comments on the way. As they said good-bye, Mr. Karazoglu informed her that Mr. Asterisk had asked what business Mr. Timuroff was in. "I have told him, because he is a very fierce man from Anatolia, who has fought in Korea. Now I speak to you what he says." Laughing heartily, Mr. Karazoglu made a swift and graphic gesture of throat-cutting. "He says that with all these guns and swords this fine city could kill one mayor every day. He is pleased. That is sometimes what they do in Anatolia."

"You've just made *my* day," remarked Olivia through set teeth.

"Thank you," said Mr. Karazoglu, as the elevator parted them.

Olivia paused for a moment, breathing heavily. Then she took out her keys, deactivated one burglar alarm, unlocked the door, deactivated another, picked up the mail, and went in. The shop consisted of one large salesroom, with armor and long arms arranged along its walls, and horizontal cases filled with smaller weapons in between. Surprisingly, it also had a dozen tall and glittering mirrors, three crystal chandeliers, and, in Timuroff's own office at its end, a vast and antique safe—all inherited from a previous occupant, an expensive and fashionable, but unfortunately dishonest, furrier.

Olivia subconsciously inventoried everything, and was happy to find everything as it should be, including Timuroff's martial painting and engravings and his bronze bust of Prince Kutuzov chuckling over the dismal fate of *la Grande Armée*. She went on into the office, where again all was well—the two First Empire cabinets, two desks, filing cases, bookshelves, the little bar with its refrigerator, all under still another chandelier.

There were newly arrived sales catalogues to be sorted, from Christie's, from the Hôtel Drouot in Paris, from auction houses great and small. She leafed quickly through them, looking for special goodies to which Timuroff's attention should be called. Then she turned to the first-class correspondence. A letter from Major Hugh Drummond-Mowbrey, a Hallamshire cousin, she set aside unopened; the rest went into her *Action* tray. She called the answering service and learned that there had been no calls. Finally she got up, made sure that the shop door was locked and bolted, returned, opened her desk drawer, checked out the 9 mm Colt Commander that lived there, and settled down to her typewriter. The fact of murder frightened Olivia, but it did not dismay her.

Timuroff showed up at eleven thirty, having walked from the Golden Gateway tower where he and Liselotte lived together decorously in adjoining apartments. She had not forgiven him as quickly as Olivia had forgiven Pete, but eventually she allowed him a late Australian breakfast of eggs and bacon and a small filet, garnished with biting comments on faithless lovers bemused by gadgetry to the point of preferring it to the real McCoy; and he had given her a blow-by-blow account of the events at Dr. Grimwood's, only toning down the gruesome details of the discovery of the hanged van Zaam. Afterward she had kissed him ten-derly, cautioned him against unnecessary risks, and promised to let him take her out to dinner. Then he had gone forth into one of those rare San Francisco autumn days when the sun shines brightly on all men and all women are beautiful.

It was the sort of day when it is hard even to believe in the existence of people like van Zaam, let alone that one may find them murdered; and Timuroff, enjoying it, greeted Olivia with his usual cheerfulness.

She glared at him. "Isn't it bad enough having my husband messing around with murders all the time, without my boss having to get in on the act? Why can't you be satisfied with 'humbly selling antique arms in San Francisco,' unquote?"

"I'm being an involved citizen," he answered.

"That's what I'm scared of. Believe me, I have enough of it at home without its following me to work. Now, how about telling the hired help what happened? I left Pete snoring like a hibernating bear, so all I've heard was what the radio told me."

Timuroff frowned. He sat down, turning his chair to face her. "I'm afraid someone *is* involving me, whether I want to be or not. I promised Pete I'd tape everything I could remember about last night. Why don't you listen in and ask me questions? That'll keep me from forgetting anything important."

She checked the tape deck in her desk's upper-left-hand drawer. "Your secret microphone is ready, Oh-Oh-Seven."

His account was militarily concise, precisely factual, and extremely vivid. It took about twenty minutes, and he was only interrupted four times: when the phone rang to ask whether he cared to discuss business with the M.C. of a midnight quiz show called *What's Your Murder?*, again when Lieutenant Kielty tried vainly to get through to him, once more as Olivia cried out involuntarily at the finding of van Zaam, and finally when, having heard of the bowstring by which the body hung suspended, she felt compelled to tell him nervously of her encounter with Mr. Karazoglu in the elevator.

Timuroff soothed her. "I don't know about his fierce friend, but if Karazoglu ever had a bowstring he'd have sold it long ago, probably to buy rock-'n'-roll records for his offspring. He is a distressingly bourgeois Turk, not at all like those my family used to run into in the good old days."

"I hope so," said Olivia fervently. "My blood can stand just so much curdling."

Timuroff ended the recording at Pete's arrival in the poker parlor. Then, out of courtesy, he filled her in on how Pete had checked the secret passages, on Mrs. Short and her relation to Evangeline, and on the matters he and Pete had discussed on the way home.

"So you see," he told her cheerfully, "it looks as though someone's been weaving a very tangled web indeed—perhaps more so than he originally intended. We'll take whatever precautions we can think of, and play the thing by ear."

For a few seconds, Olivia simply stared at him. "I do admire you, Tim," she finally said. "I-I'm awfully fond of you. And you know how I love Pete. I just wish—I just *wish* you two stupid bastards weren't en-enjoying all of this so much! Please pass the Kleenex."

For half an hour or so, the answering service kept them busy. There were a couple of legitimate long-distance calls, and one or two that smelled as though someone were trying to run interference for some columnist. Judge Faraday phoned to tell Timuroff how much he had enjoyed *Don Giovanni,* and remarked that, according to the morning news, it was just as well he hadn't come with them after the show; he sounded definitely concerned, and made a luncheon date for Tuesday, the first time he'd be free.

Then Pete called. "You want the latest on van Zaam?" he asked. "We've got the autopsy report."

"He now can be officially considered dead?" said Timuroff.

Pete snorted. "They found out how he died. He wasn't strangled."

"What do you mean? He looked about as strangled as anyone can get."

"Well, the examiner thinks that was just an added touch. Technically, he may still have been alive, sort of, when it happened, but what really killed him—or would have anyhow—was getting stabbed, at the back of the skull, right up into the brain."

Timuroff was astonished. "My God, what did the murderer use this time—a skene dhu, a nice sharp golok, an aikuchi?"

"Guess again, Expert Witness. As near as anyone can tell, he used an ice pick."

"Well, that lets me out. I don't know any ice-pick collectors."

"Any day now," Pete said dismally. "It'll probably start a trend—like Avon bottles. Anyhow, we also got some poop out of the federal boys about the guy. It goes back when he was only about twenty, the last year the Nazis were in Holland. The gossip was they had him working for them, but nobody proved anything. After that, he drifted here and there: first Italy and somewhere in the Near East, then South America till a few years ago, when he came over here. Suspicions, questionings, even an arrest or two, but no convictions. He keeps just enough contacts with foreign companies for his 'industrial liaison' to look plausible, but everybody's sure it's a cover—only for what? Here in the Bay Area, they say he's been working with the Hanno Agency, and they're as crooked as they come. Their specialty is what they call industrial intelligence—which means they snoop and steal. Now, are you all set for the rest of the bad news?"

Timuroff replied that he had braced himself.

"All right, Kielty's making trouble. He's been getting under foot all day. This morning he was over to the Hansons' quarters, and she let him paw over everything—because he's a policeman, she said. I hear he came out looking like he'd made the jackpot. Has he been pestering you?"

Timuroff told him of Kielty's calls, and assured him that, if by some miracle the lieutenant did get through, nothing would be discussed except khanjars and Turkish bowstrings. "And while we're on that subject," he inquired, "have you learned any more about what happened to the khanjar?"

"Yeah," grunted Pete disgustedly. "Socrates opened up his safe, and it wasn't in the leather case he keeps it in. All there was was a big, cheap hunting knife. It weighed about the same. I guess somebody swapped it at his party, but nobody saw anything. All everybody says is what a swell host Socrates was, and what terrific drinks he poured —which could explain how the knife-swapper got away with it."

Pete hung up, and instantly Liselotte was on the phone, demanding whether Timmy had given poor Olivia a chance to go to lunch, calling him a heartless brute when she found out he hadn't, and announcing her imminent arrival to repair the damage.

"Go and get prettied up," he told his secretary. "Lise has taken pity on you. How that woman eats four or five meals a day without putting on weight I'll never know."

"Partly it's being Viennese," Olivia told him, tidying her desk, "but mostly it's just worrying about you."

She disappeared into the powder room, and he spent the next few minutes with his mail, whistling as he worked. By the time Liselotte got there, he had finished his reminders for the day, and Olivia was regarding him disapprovingly.

"Has he been behaving nicely?" asked Liselotte, entering like a flame.

"He's just been sitting there whistling 'Lilliburlero,' as if this was a nice sunny day in the eighteenth century."

"Only to you will I tell my secret—to my Timmy, *le dixhuitième siècle* has never ended. You would think he was Maurice de Saxe and I, Adrienne Lecouvreur—though I admit that perhaps he has more finesse in some things than Maurice." She kissed the top of his head condescendingly, and handed him a newspaper. "While we are gone, he can perhaps find out if Catherine the Great is dead."

He walked them to the elevator, and heard his phone screaming at him to be picked up again. It was the answering service girl: Was Mr. Timuroff available? Mrs. Miranda Gardner's office was on the line.

Frowning, Timuroff told her to put them on.

"Mr. Timuroff?"

He recognized the too-smooth voice of Mrs. Gardner's current male secretary.

"Mr. Timuroff, Mrs. Gardner wishes to know whether you will be open there this afternoon? She will be in your vicinity at about one thirty, and would like to drop by if it's convenient. I know that she is looking forward to seeing your latest acquisitions. May I inform her that you will be expecting her?"

"You may."

"Thank you, Mr. Timuroff. She will be very pleased when I tell her. Good-bye."

"Good-bye," Timuroff said. He sat back slowly and stared at the telephone. *What next?* he asked himself. Miranda Morphy Gardner, ice cold and hard, was not a woman who did things by coincidence. The feeling he had

had the night before, of hidden forces, of dark designs and unguessed relationships, was reinforced.

"Telephone," he addressed the instrument, "how dare you intrude into my century with women like Miranda Gardner? My forebears managed very well without you. Tyrants used often to execute the bearers of bad news, but I'm forbidden by your owners to do anything no matter how obnoxious you become. Beware, telephone! One of these days I'll—"

The telephone shrilled at him offensively.

"For God's sake!" muttered Timuroff. "The thing's alive." He lifted it gingerly by the nape of its neck. "Yes?" he said.

The answering service informed him that Dr. Hector Grimwood wished to speak to him, that it was urgent. A moment later, he heard the urgency quite unmistakably in the doctor's voice. Hector Grimwood was a frightened man.

"Tim? Tim, something's happened. I didn't want to phone from home, so I'm calling from the pharmacy on Union Street. I've tried to reach Inspector Cominazzo, but they keep telling me he isn't there—"

"Whoa there, Heck! Slow down a minute. What's happened?"

"Somebody's been tampering with my Muriel!"

"Muriel? You mean your belly dancer?"

"It's uncanny, Tim! The house has been alive with police and with reporters—you can imagine how it's been. That miserable Lieutenant Kielty spent half the morning here too, nagging me about Munrooney and van Zaam, and hinting broadly that somehow I and Penny Anne are mixed up in the murders. And yet it must've happened while they were here. I went into her room just half an hour ago, and she had changed position! She does her dance kneeling or sitting down, and she just wasn't as I left her. It was as though someone had turned her on for just a minute. But it's *impossible*—that is a room to which I have the only key!"

"You're *sure?*"

"I'm absolutely sure."

"Have you told the police?"

"Tim, how do I know that some of them aren't mixed up somehow with the people who're behind all this? I tell you, the room was locked all morning, and the secret passages are sealed—just as you and Inspector Cominazzo left them."

"Heck," Timuroff said, "you're a precisionist; you'd certainly not imagine nonexistent mysteries where your own creations are concerned. You're right to take this seriously. But don't let it frighten you. I'll get in touch with Pete, and he'll look into it. In the meantime, stay out of Muriel's room, keep the door locked, and don't tell another soul. . . . No, I can't come out there right now, but if you and Penny Anne have nothing planned, maybe we can get together this evening for an hour or two, perhaps at my place?"

Sounding slightly reassured, the doctor made a few more comments about what a pest the police and newsmen were making of themselves, and accepted the invitation eagerly.

Once again, the weapons shop was silent, and Timuroff shook his head philosophically. "Well, I may be living in the eighteenth century," he told himself, "but no one can deny that my small section of it is a lively one!"

VI

And of the Twentieth

Miranda Morphy Gardner arrived at one forty-five. She did not come alone; nor was she, as usual, attended by a secretary. Judson Hemmet entered with her.

Timuroff concealed his surprise when he met them at the door. He knew, of course, that the firm of Munrooney, Hemmet, John H. Braidstone, and Baltesar were her attorneys; and both she and Hemmet had bought a good part of their collections from him. But he could not recall ever seeing the two together, and certainly never in his shop. He said that it was nice of them to come, that Mrs. Gardner hadn't been around for quite a while, that seeing Hemmet was an unexpected pleasure. "So perhaps I can kill two birds with one stone——" He laughed. "Or are my clients ganging up on me?"

The effect was instant. Miranda Gardner, grimly female and unfeminine in the light of day, beauty-shopped into a strangely unconvincing simulacrum of youth and beauty, said not a word. Judson Hemmet smiled coldly with his lips alone, and answered in his cold and cultured voice, "Well, Tim, in a world of dead birds and thrown stones, sometimes ganging up is called for." Then he too laughed, as though a joke that was not there could somehow be evoked.

Timuroff changed the subject, telling him about a small group of rapiers he had just purchased out of Portugal. Casually, he led the way toward the case that held them.

Judson Hemmet was in his early forties. At first glance, his face seemed almost frighteningly austere, that of a Puritan, a hanging judge; one had to look more closely to see the marks and lines of unrestrained rapacity and arrogance. His New England ancestors had been among Hawaii's first missionaries, turning false piety into outrageous profit; and Timuroff had once remarked that he himself looked like a reformed missionary out of a Maugham story. Now, measuring Hemmet, he felt simultaneously that his own measure was being taken, not as the potential buyer weighs the seller but much more intimately, as the experienced duelist weighs a possible opponent.

In the background, the office radio had been tuned softly to an FM good-music station, and a harpsichord was playing a dark and gay and lovely piece by Jacques Champion de Chambonnières, written largely for the bass in a century when gentlemen wore swords and perhaps slew each other a little carelessly, and sometimes paid more than lip service to art and beauty. Timuroff, showing the rapiers, wondered what sort of person Hemmet might have been had he lived then—Hemmet and, for that matter, Miranda Gardner.

In college, and for some years after, Hemmet had been a fencer, never a champion but still quite a good one; and Timuroff wondered why, for fencing has no practical and natural place in today's world, and Judson Hemmet, whatever else he was, was a twentieth-century man, with the materialism of the industrial and computer revolutions in his blood and bones.

Yet in his hands, suddenly, the swords became weapons once again. Three were Spanish, two Italian, two from Germany, one each from Austria and England, all of fine quality. Hemmet weighed them, put them aside, returned to them; finally he settled on a seven-ringed Spanish sword with a blade more than four feet long—scarcely, Timuroff thought, a modern fencer's choice, and obscurely the idea troubled him.

"I'll be taking this one," Hemmet said, setting it apart. "But that's not why we came up here today."

Miranda Gardner, uninterested, had wandered over to the cases in the center of the room. She was standing over one full of poniards, misericords, hunting daggers, savage bowie knives. She had opened it herself, and was examining a leaf-shaped push-dagger with transverse ivory hilt, made in the Gold Rush days by Will & Finck, in San Francisco. She brought it with her as she returned to them, a sudden feral satisfaction on her face.

"Miranda," Hemmet said, "I've just been telling Timuroff that we aren't really here as customers."

Timuroff smiled. "I didn't think you were, but it's always nice to do a bit of business by the way." He glanced toward the office. "Why don't we sit down? How about a drink?"

They exchanged glances. They followed him. They took their chairs.

"What'll it be?" he asked.

"Nothing," Hemmet said, his voice expressionless.

"Canadian?" Fondling the small dagger, Miranda Gardner looked up with her expensive, fleshless smile. "On the rocks."

Suddenly, as he poured—one for her and a long, wet one for himself—Timuroff saw her as another of Hector Grimwood's contrivances, conceived perhaps in a moment of depression after awakening from a nightmare. His fancy showed him a complex mechanism behind that smile, gears and springs and motors giving life to her long hands and incongruously long and lovely legs. He shook the idea off, and, as he had before with Judson Hemmet, began to wonder what really animated her. He raised his glass. "Cheers!" he said. They drank.

"We want to talk to you about last night," Hemmet began. "I understand that you were called in by the police to check that dagger, that you arrived while everybody was still there, and that you were actually with Grimwood when he found the second body—what was his name? Van Zaam?"

"Hendrik J. van Zaam," said Timuroff. " 'Industrial liaison.' So his card said, at least. And a most unpleasant sight he was, too."

"That's what the papers said." Hemmet leaned forward. His voice dropped confidentially. "Tim, this is a nasty situation. You didn't like Errol. Even I didn't see eye to eye with him on everything. But he'd become a major national figure. He'd pretty well bridged the racial gap, and the generation gap, and Lord knows how many others. Can you imagine how many political applecarts have been knocked over by his death? Especially considering the crazy circumstances? How do you think I feel about it, as his law partner? Or Miranda here, whom we represent? She's been associated in almost all his business enterprises."

Timuroff sat on the corner of his desk and sipped his drink.

"But even with all that," Hemmet went on, "until this second murder it seemed like—well, something we could understand. People like Errol gather all sorts of enemies as they go along—organized crime, right-wing extremists, just plain nuts. That's the risk they take. But this van Zaam thing is different. There are too many overtones and undertones. He had some sort of record overseas, they say."

"And?" said Timuroff.

"Tim, there's something here that's unpredictable. It makes you ask yourself *Who's next?* Baltesar and I are working very closely with the chief of police. We want this business cleared up as soon as possible, for the country's sake, and for the city's, and for our own. You seem to have a special relationship with homicide—I know you've worked with them before—and there's no real reason why we can't help each other, is there? Maybe we can smooth out some of the police department's rivalries and jealousies?"

Timuroff could think of no good reason why they couldn't, but a voice inside him kept crying *False! False! False!* insistently.

Miranda Gardner held her glass out, and he did the honors. "Jud, I appreciate your confidence," he answered. "But I'm determined to be just an expert witness. I identified the khanjar and told the police where Socrates bought it. But they'll have to take it on from there. My secretary's married to a homicide inspector, as you know, and they're both close friends of mine. I'm going to keep my distance."

"I'm sorry you feel that way." Hemmet's voice chilled. "When a man like Errol's murdered, all sorts of things get stirred up, and some of them aren't nice at all, and sometimes they actually get dangerous. Wouldn't we be better off to stand together?"

Miranda Gardner put down her glass. Carefully, she placed the ivory-handled dagger in her handbag, and Timuroff scribbled himself a mental note to bill her for it. She leaned toward him, still wearing her edged smile. "Mr. Timuroff, it must have been tremendously exciting, helping the police to solve those other cases. Lieutenant Kielty told me all about them, how you worked practically alone, not telling anybody anything." She licked her lips. "Weren't you afraid somebody might try to kill you?"

Abruptly, Timuroff's perch on his desk changed its character: it had been a relaxed and easy seat; now it became a point of balance, a center for poised forces held in close control. Judson Hemmet felt it instantly. Miranda Gardner stirred uneasily in her chair.

"To kill me?" repeated Timuroff. Both iron and irony were in his voice. "Of course I thought of it. Some people get these silly impulses."

There was a silence. Then, "I envy you your confidence," Judson Hemmet said.

I wonder, thought Timuroff, *whether I ought to envy yours?* But he said nothing. He sat balanced there, smiling at both of them.

Then it was over. Abruptly, Hemmet turned the conversation back to swords. He promised to send somebody to get the rapier, and Miranda Gardner asked him not to sell one or two other items she had her eye on.

Over the radio, Wanda Landowska, long since dead, played a bright, sunlit something by Rameau, a background of cut-crystal sound to the ritual politenesses with which hostility is so conveniently concealed; and Timuroff began to wonder how long they'd take to go, when—for once opportunely—the doorbell announced a visitor.

"Business is thriving," he commented. He rose; and they rose with him. He escorted them under the cut-crystal chandeliers to the door, and opened it.

Framed in it, great and gray, stood Amos Ledenthal.

All movement ceased. It was as though, without a sound, all the cut crystal had shattered in the air, leaving the threat of an explosion still unfulfilled.

Timuroff saw Ledenthal's fists clench, his knuckles whiten, his gray eyes smoulder suddenly under the shaggy mantel of his brows. Then he looked at Miranda Gardner, and saw the same expression she had worn when, a few minutes previously, she had suggested that perhaps someone might have tried to kill him—the same expression, but vastly more intense, as though something had stripped her face of its humanity, down to the bare, bleached bones of hatred. They stood frozen there, a set piece.

What goes on here? thought Timuroff.

And Judson Hemmet, his expression utterly unchanged, said in his flat voice, "Don't worry, Amos. We're leaving."

Ledenthal said nothing. He moved aside, and it was an act not of courtesy, but of aversion.

Then Hemmet and Miranda Gardner walked past him to the elevator door.

"Go on in, Amos," Timuroff said. "Be with you in a moment."

He saw them on their way, and neither of them made any comment on the incident. He turned back into the shop, locking the door behind him.

"Well, Amos," he called out, "you aren't trying to buy my Yasumitsu away from me, are you? Not *again?*"

Ledenthal turned to face him. Sideburned and moustached, booted and silver-buckled, he looked like a Frederick Remington frontier marshal expensively redecorated in Scottsdale, Arizona; and both his temper and his ancestry reflected in minuscule the stormy history of the West. His great-grandfather, a German-Jewish merchant, had let the Gold Rush sweep him to Salt Lake, where—to his own surprise—he was converted first to Mormonism, then to a pleasantly prospering polygamy. The blood of Scandinavian immigrants flowed in Amos's veins, mixing with that of Scotch-Irish mountain men and women, of Plains Indians, and of long-forgotten *voyageurs*. Timuroff attributed his chronic irritation to the fact that there no longer was a frontier to contend with.

The unbuyable Yasumitsu blade was a standing joke between them, but Ledenthal ignored it completely.

"Timuroff!" he shouted. "You goddamned fool! What the hell d'you think you're doing, getting yourself messed up in this Munrooney business? It's going to get a damn sight uglier! You wait and see!"

He came forward as he spoke, and they shook hands.

"I'm just an expert witness, Amos," Timuroff said placatingly. "I'll speak my little piece and leave the stage to the important people. Believe me, I won't get involved."

"Dammit, you *are* involved! Some militant on KPFA just go through asking why the pigs called you in at all, when it's well known you're a White Russian reactionary, and that you threatened the late St. Errol publicly. Then he demanded that they investigate your whereabouts last night. You better have a damn good alibi."

"I didn't threaten him," Timuroff answered reasonably. "I merely said the world would be a cleaner, sweeter place without him—which it is. As for last night, I *was* in at the death of a rather despicable wolf, but it was quite legal. I was with Liselotte and the Cominazzos, and we had a federal judge there besides."

"Bah!" shouted Ledenthal; and Timuroff reflected that he had never met another man who could say the word and make it sound like an enraged gravel truck grinding broken gears. "Bah! So thanks to Mozart they can't pin *that* on you! You listen to me, Timuroff——" Abruptly his voice dropped, losing none of its intensity. "Tim," he growled, "I came down here to *warn* you. Have you any idea at all what kind of people you're playing with? What kind of people that stinking Hemmet and his she-vulture really are?"

"Let's sit down," suggested Timuroff. "I still have most of a drink left. I'll make you one."

"Make mine light—I'm driving. Going out to Pleasanton to see my Arabs. Nice, clean horse turds are going to smell pretty good after the characters you just said good-bye to."

He sat down while Timuroff put the drink together. He leaned forward intently. "You listen, Timuroff. I'm going to tell you what I told that fat-assed chief of police last night. You want to find out who killed Munrooney or had him killed? Okay, you don't have to look any further than his friends. I'll lay you ten to one that Hemmet and that Gardner woman are back of it. *That's* what I told him—and Baltesar and Hemmet too."

Quietly, Timuroff put the drink down at his guest's elbow. He said, "Doesn't that sound a little bit unlikely, Amos? They'd have had nothing to gain and a lot to lose by killing him."

"Damn it, I know, I *know!* That's the way it looks. And naturally that's what Hemmet and the chief both said, besides Hemmet threatening that he'd sue me. But you don't know the way that crew does business. I *do*—I've been in business with them. Tim, I feel it in my bones. Did you see the look that harpy gave me?"

Timuroff nodded.

"She hates my guts because she knows I know—even if I can't prove anything. But watch what happens—they're going to do everything they can to pin it onto someone else, and in a hurry. It could be you or me; it could be old man Grimwood, which is a lot more likely." His forefinger stabbed the air. "Timuroff, does Caldwell, Jolly and Company, Incorporated, mean anything to you, or the San Francisco Parks Recreation and Ecology Master Plan?"

"Not much," Timuroff answered. "Caldwell, Jolly are big developers, and I'm pretty sure some of my customers are mixed up with them—Socrates, I think, and Melmoth? As for the Master Plan, all I know is that it's been touted as a Munrooney stroke of genius, so I'm against it."

"You're damn right customers of yours have been mixed up in Caldwell, Jolly—and not just those two, either. I was, and Kalloch too, and Hemmet and Miranda Gardner and Baltesar, besides a few who weren't your customers— old Braidstone, Hemmet's senior partner before he died, and of course Munrooney, and Heck Grimwood—"

Timuroff looked surprised.

"Yeah, him too. He bought in for damn near nothing at the start, when all they owned was a brickyard and a few acres of pineapples in Hawaii. The old bastard always manages to do that. Maybe he gets his inside information digging into brains. There were a few others too, people you don't know. Anyhow, up till a year or so ago the more or less good guys had control—then Hemmet and Munrooney and that bitch-wolf pulled a fast one on us. They pried all Braidstone's shares out of his estate—*she* bought them up. That put them in the saddle. Then they made it plain who was doing the handwriting on the wall, and most of us who didn't see eye to eye with them sold out. By that time, we knew what we were up against, especially after what Hemmet did to Reese, though that's neither here nor there—"

Timuroff looked at him inquiringly.

"It was a personal thing—something Reese wouldn't want talked about. There was a girl involved. Anyway, the only ones who stayed were Melmoth, because he thinks he's big and tough enough, and Grimwood, because he's too far-out to know what kind of company he's in. Then, after we were out, they sprang this Master Plan, complete with a City Parks Foundation that calls itself 'a non-profit group of concerned citizens.' It's got a lot of tame Ph.Ds and hired city planners pooping for it, behind a false front of prominent old farts with more dough than horse sense. But the real power is Caldwell, Jolly—and Caldwell, Jolly *is* Miranda Gardner."

"What do they plan to do?" asked Timuroff.

"They plan to cut Golden Gate Park into three parts!" roared Ledenthal. "Like Gaul, goddamnit! They say—I quote—'to make more efficient use of the environment,

with lower taxes and maintenance, and better policing'—
that's so our underprivileged citizens can have more fresh
air fun and commit fewer fresh air crimes! And the three
hunks of park are going to be separated by big 'developed
areas'—and guess who's going to slice the millions in *that*
pie! I tell you, Timuroff, it's *big*. And it's damn dangerous.
That Gardner woman's like a swarm of army ants. No
matter who's the loser, she's going to win. *Don't* get mixed
up in it."

He stood and killed his drink. "Well, that's enough for
now," he growled. Suddenly and surprisingly, he smiled.
He told Timuroff to kiss la Cantelou's hand for him. "That
is a lovely lady, Tim. You're a lucky man."

"So are you, Amos," Timuroff replied. "Give Jessica our
love."

At the mention of his wife's name, the gruffness ebbed
away. "Good-bye, Tim," Ledenthal said softly, courteously.
"I guess you aren't convinced, but I'm glad we had our
talk. You'll learn. I'll see you in a day or two."

After he had gone, Timuroff tried to go back to work,
but his visitors had really hung an albatross around his
neck. It annoyed and worried him, and it just wouldn't go
away. Partly, it was what Hemmet and Miranda Gardner
had said and how they'd said it, but even more it was
Ledenthal's accusation which, despite its logical absurdity,
insisted on assuming a strange dramatic rightness in his
mind.

He tried to read his cousin's letter, all about foxes and
people who spent their time hunting them, but finally he
swore softly in English and in Russian and gave it up.
"Damn you, Munrooney!" he proclaimed aloud. "You now
have my full attention."

He phoned Pete at headquarters and, saving the story of
the visitors for later, told him about Hector Grimwood's
phone call and the mystery of Muriel Fawzi's getting herself turned on; and Pete, though he obviously didn't take
it very seriously, promised to head out to Kemble Street as
soon as possible.

Timuroff then resorted to the news. The paper Liselotte
had left for him was, as he expected, completely dedicated
to the sensational display of Munrooney, Munrooney's murder, Munrooney's wife and children, Dr. Hector Grimwood
and his eccentricities, Lucrece with and without dagger,
and photos of various luminaries at the party. Most of the

material was from the paper's morgue, but enough hasty
writing and rewriting had been squeezed in to assure not
only its entertainment value but its immediacy. Mention
was prominently made of several ladies with whom the
mayor's name, if not the mayor himself, had been en-
twined. Much was made of his romantic origins and picturesque career; and Timuroff, long a collector of Mun-
rooneyana, amused himself by filling in omitted data with
which he was familiar.

Thus, where the paper simply stated that the Mun-
rooneys had originated in the same part of Ireland as the
Kennedys, he was reminded that this was not discovered
until the Kennedy star had risen in the East. When the
reporters went into minor ecstasies over the aristocratic
Old Californian forebears of Trudie Vasquez, the mayor's
sainted mother, he recalled that they had been a secret
long after her family returned from Puerto Rico (where, it
seemed, they had fled to escape the Yanqui imperialism of
the Gold Rush) and had been resurrected only after the
Third World began to show its head, when mere hidalgo
ancestry quickly evolved into a direct connection, first with
Tiburcio Vasquez, a folk hero known to the law officers
of his day as Three-Fingered Jack, and then with a Span-
ish-Californian governor whose progenitor had, by a happy
coincidence, been a mulatto.

On the editorial page, Timuroff found a moving eulogy
that wept over the untimely quenching of so bright a flame,
over the loss suffered by the nation and especially by the
poor and oppressed, and over their now shattered hopes
for any peaceful, prosperous, and enlightened future. The
writer hinted broadly that the dark influence of the firearms industry was behind the murder, and cited as evidence the significant fact that it had *not* been committed
with a gun. Finally, he called upon the poor and oppressed
to make their voices heard in protest.

The initials with which this piece was signed were those
of the editor in chief, a person who, in Timuroff's opinion,
had missed out on a career in the underground press only
because of superannuation and inherited wealth. Therefore
he was not surprised to find no mention of Munrooney's
tortuous business dealings—dealings so dubious and so immensely profitable that they had aroused the enquiring interest of bar associations, congressional committees, humor-
less federal agencies, and once even the Sierra Club.

His equanimity more or less restored, he put *Lieutenant Kijé*—which always made him feel very nostalgic and Russian—on the record player. He called his answering service and was not perturbed to hear that there had been two more calls from Lieutenant Kielty—about whom, he told himself, Prokofiev would never have written as much as one sour note. Then he made an unenthusiastic effort to get back to business, and succeeded only in shuffling papers back and forth. Finally, when the last notes of Lieutenant Kijé's death and burial had died away, he turned on a newscast reporting the discovery of van Zaam's horrible corpse and telling of an apparent attempt by a radical group claiming to represent the poor and oppressed to memorialize Munrooney by bombing a Berkeley branch of the Bank of America.

The clock informed him that it was now nearly four; and he reached again for his cousin's letter, thinking that there still might be time to answer it before Liselotte and Olivia returned. He began once more to read it—

There was a peremptory knock on the door.

"Damn!" said Timuroff, no longer feeling Russian or nostalgic. "Who the devil's that?"

Then, as the knock was twice repeated, he strode to the door and threw it open.

Lieutenant Kielty and a plainclothesman were standing there, Kielty small, pinch-mouthed, red-faced, and hostile, the plainclothesman heavy-jowled and not much interested.

"Yes?" said Timuroff.

Kielty was trying to keep his antagonism veiled, and not succeeding. "You're going to answer a few questions, Timuroff," he said, entering uninvited. "I tried the phone, but you weren't answering. Now we can get it over with."

"I think not," said Timuroff.

"What d'you mean, you think not?" The veil was slipping; Kielty's voice was shrill. "I can damn well hold you as a material witness, Timuroff. How the hell do we know *you* didn't kill that van Zaam character—you and Grimwood? We've only got your word you found him hanging there."

Timuroff turned his back, and walked back to his office, Kielty at his heels. The plainclothesman lagged behind, fascinated by the weapons in their cases.

"You've been doing your smart-ass detective act just long enough." Kielty was crowing now. "Maybe Pete goes for it, but a lot of us at headquarters, we're fed up to the gills. This once, you'd better find some real sharp answers!"

Timuroff sat down. He smiled with all the warmth of a Siberian winter. "Mr. Kielty, if you had consulted your medical examiner, you'd have realized that neither I nor Dr. Grimwood could possibly have killed van Zaam, because we were elsewhere when he died. It would have saved you from attempting so absurd a bluff. As for holding me as a material witness—try it." His voice hardened. "Pete Cominazzo is a friend of mine. You aren't. I trust him absolutely. I don't trust you at all. He is, as you are probably aware, in charge of this investigation. Therefore I will not answer any of your questions, now or in the future. Do I make myself clear?"

"Mister, you'll damn well answer if you know what's good for you. I've got all the authority I need, and from the chief himself." Kielty's voice had risen almost to a shout; now suddenly he lowered it. "Look," he hissed, "there's two of us and only one of you. I've got a witness. If anything should happen, like maybe you attacking me, it'd be *our* word against yours. Get me?"

"Is that a threat?" asked Timuroff.

"It's a promise!"

"It would be more effective if you didn't flap your wings. Let us be realistic, Lieutenant Kielty. The chief was very much the mayor's boy, and I'm sure that you're very much the chief's, but I doubt very much that Officer Pickering there—it is Pickering, isn't it?—is *your* man. If he had been, you'd not have dropped your voice to make sure he wouldn't hear you threaten me." Timuroff's own voice rang out loud and clear. He saw the plainclothesman look his way. "Now, with the mayor gone, you and the chief are skating on thin ice, and anyhow I'm certain that Mr. Pickering would never testify to anything except exactly what he'd seen and heard."

As Kielty started sputtering, Pickering grinned at Timuroff embarrassedly. "Who the hell wants him to?" yelped Kielty. "Don't try to smear me, Timuroff! What the hell d'you think you're hinting at?"

"Just that there's really nothing more to hold you here." Timuroff smiled. "Unless, of course, you'd like to start collecting swords and guns and things?"

Kielty snarled incoherently. He whirled. "Let's get out of here!" he snapped at the plainclothesman.

"Good-bye, Mr. Timuroff," called the plainclothesman from the door; and, "Good-bye, Pickering," called Timuroff cheerfully as it banged shut behind them.

He leaned back, his good temper returning. For a few minutes, he busied himself composing a limerick for Liselotte:

> I prefer the seventeenth century
> With its wars and wining and wenchery
> To the one we are in
> Where sinners and sin
> Are sordid instead of adventury.

Pleased with his effort, he told himself that she'd been wrong, that he was really a seventeenth-century man, not an eighteenth-century one. He decided to tell Hugh Drummond-Mowbrey all about it, and picked the letter up again.

The doorbell rang.

Timuroff lifted his eyes to heaven, decided that no heavenly help would be forthcoming, and marched to the door prepared to demolish whoever might be there.

He was pleasantly surprised to find Florencio Pambid, the perceptive bartender of the night before, accompanied by a dainty Filipina.

"Señor, something has occurred," began Pambid in Spanish. "It is, I think, important—especially since the cruel one has been killed. I have told my wife about it, and about you, and she also thinks we should inform you of it."

Timuroff smiled at the girl, said that it was only fair that so brave a soldier should be rewarded with so beautiful a wife, and asked them in. "Come," he said, "we shall sit and talk, and this time I shall be the bartender."

Mrs. Pambid smiled; her husband courteously demurred; each finally accepted a Tom Collins and waited while Timuroff refreshed his highball.

"To your bride," proposed Timuroff.

"Of three years already," added the bridegroom proudly. "With one child, a boy."

They drank.

Then, suddenly grave, Florencio said, "Now I shall tell you what—"

"*Un momentito!*" interrupted Timuroff, remembering that he had a tape recorder, and kicking himself simultaneously at the realization that he could have taped Kielty's entire attempt to bulldoze him. "My friend, may I turn on the recorder so that Inspector Cominazzo can hear what you have to tell me?"

The Pambids nodded.

"Twice we called the police," Florencio said, "and each time they said we could not speak to him. Then one man, a detective . . . well, I did not like the way he spoke. So I told him nothing, not even who I was."

"You have acted wisely," Timuroff assured them. "What you tell me shall be heard only by Inspector Cominazzo."

"Muy bien." Florencio leaned forward. "It was necessary for me to stay very late last night. We were not able to clean up everything until the police had finished. Even after the waitresses had been sent home, I stayed and helped the ones who work for Dr. Grimwood—"

"The Hansons," put in Timuroff.

"Pues. They are nice, except that he is a little crazy in the head. I helped them bring glasses, bottles, other things downstairs to put away. You will remember the place where they play cards. Behind the bar, a door goes out into a little hall where the service elevator comes, like upstairs. I had just put down my tray to unload. Then I thought perhaps I had not closed the elevator door, which does not close itself. I started out into the hall—and then I stopped! Luckily, I made no sound. Quickly, I drew back, leaving only a crack to look through. There was a policeman, a small man not in uniform. Near the elevator there is a—how do you say?—an alcove. He was just bending to pick something up. He looked at it. Very quickly, he put it in his pocket. Then his glance darted every way, to make sure nobody had seen."

"What was it?" asked Timuroff.

"It was a key. An ordinary key on a small chain, perhaps with something else attached."

They regarded each other silently.

"That he should pick it up and put it in his pocket was not strange," said Florencio Pambid. "But that he should be frightened of being seen—that, I think, was very strange indeed."

"Very," Timuroff said softly. "Tell me, my friend, can you describe this small policeman?"

"His face was very red, with a thin nose, and a mouth like this—" Suddenly, Kielty's expression was mirrored on

Florencio's countenance. "I had seen him upstairs, giving many orders."

"So that's how the land lies!" murmured Timuroff. "Listen, if anyone asks why you came here to see me—and they may—it was at my request, about a party to be given by my friend Madame Cantelou and myself, a party where the food must be the finest, like that served at the Presidential Palace in Manila."

Florencio grinned. "I understand. I hope you speak of a real party, señor. There is no cook, even in Manila, like my Carmencita."

Timuroff smiled back. "We will celebrate as in the days after the liberation."

"*Bueno!* The truth is always easier to tell." Florencio rose. He drained his glass to Timuroff. "Let us hope that Inspector Cominazzo will catch the murderers."

"He will thank you," answered Timuroff. "Now we can only wait and see if Mr. Kielty reports the finding of the key—which will prove most instructive."

He sent them off after one more exchange of compliments, and actually managed to get his letter to the major well under way before Liselotte and Olivia arrived parcel-laden.

"I didn't mean to be so late," Olivia said. "That is, I hope things didn't get too rough for you . . . or, or anything."

"Nonsense!" declared Liselotte. "He has been drinking with his customers. Here in the cool shop, while we were trudging the hot streets."

"One of the great advantages of the seventeenth century —not the eighteenth, my dear—is that old-fashioned courtesy compels one to drink with all one's visitors, except perhaps the more hostile members of the police department. I have had an interesting and quite profitable afternoon. I sold a Spanish rapier to Judson Hemmet and an expensive push-dagger to Miranda Gardner."

"That woman gives me the creeps." Olivia shuddered.

"If Timmy were a gentleman," said Liselotte, "he would go immediately and mix for each of us a small restorative."

Timuroff growled something about women who boozed in bars all afternoon and then demanded more alcoholic stimulants. "Hogarth would have been interested," he told them. "It would have given him another horrible picture for his Gin Alley sequence."

"He was in the eighteenth century, not the seventeenth," pointed out Liselotte. "So you must make the drinks for us at once. We have time for at least one or two before Pete arrives."

Olivia, reminded of three dry Manhattans and of work left undone, blushed guiltily and began to stammer that, really, she didn't need anoth—

The phone rang shrilly. Mechanically, she answered it. "A. A. Timuroff. . . . A message for him? Yes, of course." For a few seconds, the phone made subdued noises. "I . . . see." Suddenly her voice was practically inaudible. "Th-thank you. I . . . I'll tell him."

She hung up. She turned around. Her blush had drained away. "That . . . was the . . . answering service, Tim. There was a call for you. He . . . he wouldn't state his business, but—" Her voice broke. "He said he'd . . . call again. He . . . left his name."

"What was it?" asked Timuroff.

Carefully she leaned against the desk. "Van Zaam," she said.

Instantly, Timuroff was at her side. "Take it easy. Somebody's doing his level best to scare us, but it's not van Zaam. Believe me, van Zaam's not phoning anyone. Anyhow, I don't think whoever made that call is dangerous. Dangerous people don't waste their time on fun and games. They strike and vanish. This fellow sounds to me as if he may be running scared himself."

"It sounds to me," Olivia answered, a shadow of her smile returning, "as if my boss is whistling in the dark."

Turning toward the bar, Timuroff winked at her.

VII

Deaf Heaven

Twenty minutes later—when Olivia, despite Timuroff's reassurances, was beginning to get anxious—Pete phoned to say he was delayed, as usual, and where were they going to have dinner?

"How much longer will he be?" asked Liselotte. "Perhaps it would be better to call the Jade Pavilion, for a good Chinese dinner to be sent up to the apartment. You will be my guests."

Timuroff nodded. "Good, then he won't have to waste time waiting around a restaurant."

Olivia passed the word along, and told her husband—but without conviction—that there'd be no going back to work for him that night if she could help it. She sighed. "He says if you don't mind waiting he'll have a squad car drop him here. Then you and he can come on over. He means he wants to talk without us girls."

"Yes," said Liselotte, picking up purse and parcels, "we know when we are not wanted. Olivia and I will go away and prepare the dinner. Come, Olivia."

"Don't think it's not appreciated," replied Timuroff. "The thought of you two slaving over a hot martini is downright inspiring."

They left, and he settled down to scan the paper Olivia had brought with her and to wait for Pete. The front page glared at him gruesomely with the news of van Zaam's death, and offered a last-minute boxed editorial suggesting that, in view of van Zaam's reputation, the Federal Bureau of Investigation drop all other activities to expose the sinister political and economic forces which—doubtless with the connivance of the political party the paper was not supporting at the moment—had driven the great and good Errol Vasquez Munrooney to his martyrdom.

Timuroff read it and clapped his hands politely; and at that point Pete arrived, so far ahead of time that, for a moment, he suspected him of having waited out of sight just long enough to make sure the girls had gone. However, his friend looked too preoccupied to have authored even this small duplicity.

"You look very down in the mouth," said Timuroff sympathetically, pouring cognac for him.

"I *am* down in the mouth," Pete answered.

" 'When, in disgrace with fortune and men's eyes,
    I all alone beweep my outcast state,
    And trouble deaf heaven with my bootless cries.
    And look upon myself, and curse my fate . . .'

"And don't look at me like I was your first talking horse. Haven't you ever heard a homicide inspector quote Shakespeare before?"

"Usually," said Timuroff, "you quote *Hamlet* or *Julius Caesar* or one of the *Henrys*. It must be something really distressing to make you quote the sonnets. However, don't forget that you are still 'with friends possessed.' "

"I haven't. That's why I'm here unloading on you." Pete put his untouched glass down on the desk. "Look, I get almost no men assigned to me, when—hell!—I ought to have the whole detective bureau. And Chiefy not only puts the pressure on—the dumb bastard's phoned me twenty times today—but he gives Tom Kielty some kind of hunting license to run his own investigation. Everybody from Doc Grimwood and that phony admiral—Melmoth, isn't it?—to that creep who buggers beasties and calls himself a poet has been calling in to howl about his pushing them around. Honest to God, if that son of a bitch ever takes his hat off he'll get run in for indecent exposure!"

"He called on me," said Timuroff, "and went away without buying anything." He gave Pete a blow-by-blow account of Kielty's invasion and retreat. "If I'd had the sense

God gave a gray goose, I'd have turned the tape on and got it all."

"It's a damn shame you didn't. We'd have had a piece of first-class evidence." Pete picked his glass up, drained half of it, remembered it was cognac, looked ashamed of himself. "Tim, this case looked wild enough last night, but it's a lot worse than that. Chiefy isn't acting as if he wants it solved—he acts like he wants the whole mess pushed out of sight before anyone can get a good close look at it. Kielty's leaning hard on Hanson, Grimwood's man. He's trying to pin the murder of van Zaam on him, I think, and maybe he'll succeed. Hanson's naval disability was a Section Eight job, and he has a couple of arrests on the record way back when for beating up on characters—drunk and disorderly, unprovoked assault, that sort of thing. And one time he skipped bail, which makes it worse."

"Do you think they'll actually arrest him?" Timuroff asked, thinking of what Amos Ledenthal had said.

Pete's face was gloomier than ever. "They'll do whatever the people who pull Chiefy's strings decide they want. You know, Tim, lately the Department's been pretty clean, at least until the sovereign people elected Lover Boy. If this gang gets in solidly, we'll really hit the skids." He groaned. "I wish you could've gotten Kielty's performance down on tape—that threat especially."

Timuroff smiled ruefully. "I'm afraid I'm learning rather slowly, Pete. I didn't even tape the Tim, Judson, and Miranda Show, or Fifteen Minutes with Amos Ledenthal. But I did get A Candid Interview with Mr. and Mrs. Florencio Pambid. Solid entertainment. No commercials— not even my own. You can check it when you get a chance."

"How about filling me in right now? Just the high spots."

"Well, I guess the ladies will give us a few minutes."

Pete was a good listener. He interjected comments a few times, and asked two or three questions: when Timuroff reported Kielty's finding of the key, and when he repeated what Ledenthal had told him.

Finally, when Timuroff had finished, he said, "That's *very* interesting; Kielty especially. We'll talk about him later. As for Ledenthal's notion about Hemmet and Miranda, forget it. Okay, they acted pretty strangely when they came to see you, and I agree with him about the kind of slugs they are, but otherwise he's flipped."

"I wonder," Timuroff said slowly. "Amos seems to have been right about their trying to sweep the whole thing out of sight, and he does know them pretty well."

"*No way,*" Pete said emphatically. "With Munrooney they stood to make I can't even guess how many millions out of that Master Plan."

"And without Munrooney?"

"Without Munrooney, even if they clear the case before election day and get their own man in—Baltesar probably —they won't have half the chance. Could that be why we're now without Munrooney?"

Timuroff stroked the scar under his cheekbone. "Well, when the press gets around to it, I suppose they'll scream that whoever dunnit, dunnit to keep the poor from getting better parks. But that won't wash. Anybody against that sort of looting would be too sane to go around murdering. That's certainly not it. Now, how about you? Did you pick up any leads?"

"Maybe, maybe no. That weirdo poet—his name's Elia Stitchgrove, by the way—said one thing when he called that stuck with me in spite of what he is. After he'd sung his song about Kielty and his rights and police brutality, he hinted maybe he'd picked up something so important it scared him. I told him to come in and we'd be good as gold, but he said no, he didn't trust us enough to come into our lair, but if *I* was polite, I could go up there to his ashram or whatever. He's got a place this side of St. Helena, where he's started up some kind of cult. He calls it Kaula —K-a-u-l-a—and he'd be happy to instruct me. I didn't argue with the guy. I didn't even say that we could pull him in for questioning; he sounded scared enough already. Maybe I'll take a run up there, just in case. Unless, of course, they get the whole case buried before I get a chance."

Timuroff frowned. "The Kaulas are a real sect in India, about as nasty as they come. Well, nowadays the worse you are, the easier it seems to be to attract followers. You mix it in with drugs and peace talk and communal living, and kids fall for it."

Pete shook his head. "It's almost enough to drive a poor simple cop to drink. What would Will Shakespeare have thought of a so-called poet none of whose stuff scans or rhymes, and most of which sounds like the chorus lines from 'Old McDonald Had a Farm'? He got kicked out of the Audubon Society for molesting a young turkey—I'm not kidding! And would you believe his cult's getting to be real big around U.C.?"

"A few years ago, I wouldn't have believed it—but then I wouldn't have believed there'd be wide-open pony shows in North Beach either."

The telephone summoned him peremptorily. Liselotte was offended; she was shocked to find her Timmy full of anti-Chinese prejudice; if he could be so bigoted about his food, how would he feel about his Liselotte, who was mostly Austrian, but also part Hungarian, part Italian, and part Gypsy, with perhaps some French from the Napoleonic wars?

Timuroff made soft, cooing sounds, and promised that he and Pete would come without delay.

Pete was already standing when he hung up. "The dinner bell?" he said.

Timuroff was pleased to see that he was grinning. "I'm glad it cheered you up," he answered. "Or did you just enjoy seeing a seventeenth-century man put down by an every-century woman?"

"Believe me, Tim, I know what you mean. But it wasn't that. It's just that all day nothing's clicked, and now all of a sudden a few bits of information—like Kielty tampering with the evidence—look as if they might fit together somewhere."

Timuroff started on his routine of locking up. "I hope you're right, Pete. At least, I'm beginning to see some glimmerings of a picture. Do you remember what I said this morning about our little friend Lucrece almost certainly not stabbing Lover Boy? Well, has it struck you that, except for one small thing—the khanjar—it wasn't a bad plan at all. If the weapon had been an ice pick like the one that killed van Zaam—or better yet a sharp and narrow knife from Mrs. Hanson's kitchen—the whole thing might've held together and they could have charged Heck directly with the murder, though I think Jake would have seen through the Lucrece bit—in which case they'd have been after Hanson, just as Kielty is now. Anyhow, I think we can assume that their plan was sound—the setting, the confusion, everything was for them. Then the khanjar queered it. Ergo, we can assume that someone brought the khanjar in expressly for that purpose. Therefore we ought to see some more fireworks before too long."

"Just what we need," said Pete.

"Have your lab men come up with anything?"

"They hadn't when I left, but Jake's working overtime. He said to call him; I guess I'd better, just in case."

While Pete made the call, Timuroff went about his business, putting a few precious pieces into the safe, locking the cases, setting his alarms. Pete's end of the conversation was monosyllabic and uninformative, and he had almost resigned himself to more bootless cries when its tenor changed. "Hey, no kidding?" Pete exclaimed. "Well, I'll be——!" There was another extended silence. "So that's the way it was! Okay. . . . And you say Kielty knows about it? . . . Yeah, let me know. I'll be at Tim's for dinner— you have the number. Thanks, Jake. Thanks a lot."

He hung up and turned around. "Well, you were right," he said. "Lucrece is cleared. Jake says they found a little piece of skin tissue, like perhaps a hangnail, and just a touch of fingerprint. The skin was on the dagger's handle, where a sharp little piece of gold has been bent out. The print, almost wiped away, was on the door into the secret passage. Neither, Jake says, would've been any use to chase anybody down with, but they fit what we've got. Munrooney was murdered by van Zaam."

Timuroff showed no astonishment. "That's very interesting, but when you say van Zaam you're saying *what,* not *whom.* He was a useful tool, just like the khanjar; somebody wielded him just as he wielded it. To that extent, we're still where we started."

"Kielty doesn't think so. Jake couldn't say much on the phone, but from what he hinted things are going to start happening almost anytime. That's right in line with what I told you about Chiefy's great big hurry."

Timuroff made sure the door was locked. "We'd best get on to dinner before Lise decides to poison me. Besides, I've invited Hector Grimwood and his Penny Anne to drop in afterwards."

"I'm afraid you're going to have to cancel that one, Tim. I couldn't get out there this afternoon, and I promised him for sure I'd try and find out who turned on Muriel Fawzi. Anyhow, I really should be there just in case Kielty tries to pull a fast one."

Timuroff pushed the button for the elevator. "Grimwood won't mind a raincheck, but Lise will be disappointed.

And suppose Kielty does pull a fast one, with Chiefy's backing—where would that put you?"

"Right back in the deaf heaven–bootless-cries department," Pete answered.

VIII

Up in Muriel's Room

Long ago, Liselotte Cantelou had learned how to dominate an audience; and what she had accomplished at the Met and Covent Garden and the Staatsoper, she of course managed easily enough at her own table. Murder was not allowed to show its ugly head; and Timuroff and Pete, after a few ineffectual sallies, let her have her way. Liselotte, the cuisine of Szechuan Province, wine and the opera, and the possible love lives of Lucrece, Muriel Fawzi, and Evangeline dominated the conversation; and Timuroff admitted to himself that probably, because of it, a better time was had by all. However, he could see that Pete wasn't really with it, and when dessert was interrupted by an agitated phone call from Dr. Grimwood, to his own surprise he was glad the play was over. He listened to the doctor's disjointed recital, asked one or two pointed questions, and promised that he and the inspector would be there immediately.

"Now what's happened?" Pete asked.

"Judson Hemmet just turned up at his front door to tell him that Kielty's on his way out there to make a pinch. He, Lawyer Hemmet, wants to do all he can to help his old friend Dr. Grimwood. He feels that Hector's bound to be dragged into it."

"Grimwood isn't buying that garbage, for God's sake?"

"Not he. He smells a rat. He has a hunch that Kielty's

after Hanson, and—though he didn't come right out and say so—I feel that he mistrusts Hemmet's motives."

"He'd better." Pete was on his feet. "Come on, let's go."

"I am coming with you," proclaimed Liselotte. "You promised you would introduce me to your doctor and his Penny Anne. No, do not argue. He will fall in love with me at once. Perhaps he will even use me for a model for one of his creations, and she will sing lovely arias to amaze the world."

Timuroff, who could deny her nothing, looked at Pete.

Pete shrugged. "Well, he invited you, Tim, so it's unofficial. There's no real reason why Lise can't come too. It's not as if Olivia came along—we'll have to drop her off at home on the way out."

"I *never* get to go anywhere interesting," complained Olivia. "Lise, don't say I didn't warn you—when old Grimwood makes your Doppelgänger, he'll probably cram her full of tapes of Joan Sutherland and Anna Moffo, and then you'll wish you'd stayed at home with me."

"Heck's such a *completist*," chuckled Timuroff. "You'd find your sittings with him rather disconcerting."

But Liselotte already had her purse, her hat, her coat, and was heading for the door. She chattered gaily all the way to the house on Kemble Street, *oohed!* and *aahed!* at her first glimpse of its jewel-box façade, and exclaimed with delight when she was introduced to the doctor and his Penny Anne.

Mrs. Short won her over instantly by crying out how simply wonderful she'd been as the Queen of the Night at the Sydney Opera House ten years before. The doctor, though obviously distraught, expressed his pride and pleasure, and his wild gray-green eyes looked her up and down, taking her measurements with a connoisseur's eagerness.

"See, I told you!" she whispered to Timuroff as they were escorted to the library. "I shall be the most beautiful of all his dolls!"

"And at midnight," Timuroff whispered back, "you'll turn into a clockwork pumpkin."

In the library, like a cold dark shadow, Judson Hemmet was awaiting them. He was standing next to Eric's suit of armor, and as they entered, he smiled mirthlessly at Timuroff and raised the visor to show the grinning skull.

" '*Speak! speak! thou fearful guest!*' " cried Eric, moving his lower jaw gruesomely.

Liselotte squealed and clung to Penny Anne. Timuroff glared. Pete grunted contemptuously. And Timuroff, again, felt the sudden, absolute conviction that, against all logic, Amos Ledenthal had been right.

Still smiling, Hemmet dropped the visor. "Well," he remarked, "our little party grows."

"Inspector Cominazzo's here to examine Muriel," explained Hector Grimwood, "and I invited Mr. Timuroff. Have you met Madame Cantelou?"

With an impatient inclination of his head, Hemmet indicated that he had. "Hector, I don't think you understand how serious this thing is. Lieutenant Kielty has a warrant, and judges do not issue them without impressive evidence. Hadn't you better concentrate on how we're going to handle it?"

"No, Hemmet." Dr. Grimwood was visibly annoyed. "I do not think I should. You tell me you don't know whom the lieutenant is going to arrest. If even you don't know, what can we accomplish before he gets here?"

"Somebody," replied Hemmet coldly and politely, "is going to need legal representation, and need it badly. That's partly why I'm here—after all, I've been a guest in your house more than once. But, frankly, I've another reason. Whatever happens now, even if it's a police mistake, eventually may lead us to Errol's murderer."

Hector Grimwood stood silent for a moment, appraising his uninvited guest. "Let's hope it does," he said, his voice just as controlled as Hemmet's. "However, I have full confidence in the inspector here. If anybody's going to catch that murderer, he will. But your assistance certainly is welcome. I'm afraid we're facing a rather painful scene, whichever way the wind blows—a scene our ladies should not be forced to undergo." He turned. "Penny dear, why don't you take Madame Cantelou and introduce her to Evangeline? There's a policeman just outside the poker parlor, so you won't feel too lonely there. Later on, when this is over, we can all visit Muriel Fawzi."

There was a swift exchange of glances between Timuroff and Liselotte, between Timuroff and Pete. Obviously, at least for the moment, the doctor was once again on top of things. Timuroff nodded imperceptibly.

Liselotte did not argue with him; and when Mrs. Short showed signs of apprehension and reluctance, she took her arm and whispered that the doctor and her Timmy and

Inspector Cominazzo could handle *anything*. Penny Anne was persuaded, and Liselotte waved gaily as they took their leave. A moment later, the doorbell pealed through the house.

"Well, here's the boarding party," said Dr. Grimwood. He sat down at his desk and pushed a button. "I have a feeling we'd best get Hanson up here."

There was an uproar in the hall, and Mrs. Hanson burst into the room. "Oh, Doctor, Doctor!" she cried out. "They're simply *pouring* in—the police and other people—and . . . and, oh, everybody!"

Hard on her heels strode Kielty, and he was not alone. Two patrolmen flanked him, a pair of sergeants followed him, and behind them, resplendent in his full-dress uniform, came the chief of police of San Francisco. Behind him there surged an eager, motley crowd of newsmen.

"Tim, would you look at *that!*" Pete whispered. "Chiefy must figure it's St. Patrick's Day."

Seen from any distance, Chief Otterson appeared a splendid figure of a man, well over six feet tall. His tailor had made him massive in the shoulders, drawing attention from his more massive midriff; his barber had cut his thick iron-gray hair so that one saw his noble forehead rather than the irresolution of his mouth and jaw. The press admired him, stating repeatedly that he had a warm human touch uncommon among policemen.

Dr. Grimwood, less impressionable, ignored him completely. He fixed Kielty with an angry eye, and demanded bluntly the reason for this intrusion.

Woodenly, Kielty started to reply that he held a warrant for the arrest of one Warren Gamaliel Hanson, charged with the murder of—

But the chief of police was not to be so easily set aside. Assuming his celebrated warm human smile, he ploughed between sergeants and patrolmen, quelled Kielty with a glance, and addressed the doctor.

"I am Chief of Police Otterson," he announced in a deep, rather fruity voice. "My business with you, Dr. Grimwood, may not make me welcome, but it's important to us all. We have come primarily to arrest Mr. Hanson, charged with the murder of the man van Zaam—"

There was an anguished gasp from Mrs. Hanson.

"—but I have other news which should—I repeat, *should* —please us all." He beamed. "I'm glad that you are here,

Mr. Hemmet, for I know that no one was as deeply shocked by Mayor Munrooney's death as you. And you too, Mr. Timuroff, who have been so helpful to the police from time to time. And I'm not surprised to see you, Inspector Cominazzo, right on the job as usual. Well, well! Our news is this: The case is solved! We have identified the murderer beyond the shadow of a doubt."

There was a tumult of conflicting questions from the press.

Otterson held up a hand. "The murderer of the mayor was van Zaam, an evil man out of a dubious past. Physical evidence has proved his guilt. What dark forces were behind this terrible act we do not know. Nor do we know why he himself was killed. But, thanks to Lieutenant Kielty's brilliant work, we now believe we know who killed him, and we are here to take the culprit into custody. Who knows, perhaps protective custody?" He paused portentously. "I shall be available for an in-depth conference as soon as we have carried out our mission here."

He stopped. The room was still. Dr. Grimwood, elbows on his desk, was staring at him fixedly over steepled fingers. "I have made several mechanical women," he remarked conversationally. "But I have never thought of making a mechanical police officer. Perhaps"—he smiled— "I should."

Pete Cominazzo snorted; the two sergeants struggled to keep their faces straight; there was a surge of laughter from the press. From a dramatic standpoint, the chief had had the rug pulled out from under him.

"Watch this," Pete said, *sotto voce*. "He'll not just land on all four feet—he'll make a profit out of it."

And suddenly, as he was speaking, the chief reacted. His eyes crinkled. He grinned. He threw his head back, laughing with a deep, Santa Clausish *ho! ho! ho!* "You do that, Doctor. Believe me, I'll be grateful. He can hold my chair down while I go fishing. My cops won't even know the difference."

"And that's God's truth!" Pete grunted. But now the room was laughing with the chief; the rug was firmly under him again.

At once, the grin dissolved; Santa Claus disappeared. Chiefy's voice rang with regained authority. "It's too bad, Dr. Grimwood, but we just can't play that little game for a while. We have our serious business first."

And abruptly Hector Grimwood was once again only an old eccentric at whom the forces of the law looked askance.

He had no chance to offer a riposte. The back door of the library opened, and Hanson entered. He stopped, blinking at the crowded room—a man as broad as his employer, but much shorter and many years younger. He looked immensely solid and ominously powerful, the sort of squarehead who, in the days of sail, served perilously before the mast so that occasionally he could come ashore to indulge the simple pleasure of tearing apart a waterfront saloon or whorehouse. His hairy tattooed hands echoed his Seabee background, and made his white waiter's jacket and black bow tie seem even more incongruous.

"Yessir?" He looked inquiringly at Dr. Grimwood.

Instantly, Mrs. Hanson was upon him, arms around his neck, sobbing, "Tell them you didn't do it, Gammy! You, named after a President and all! And we've been so h-h-happy since you stopped your drinking, and—"

Hanson shook her, gently but decisively. "Hey, honeybunch, what *is* all this? Tell 'em I didn't do *what?*"

"T-t-tell them you didn't *murder* anybody! Th-they're going to arrest you, and t-take you off to j-j-jail, and I'll—I'll never, never, *never* see you anymore!"

A freshet of tears quenched her momentarily. "Easy does it, chickie," Hanson soothed her. "Quit blubberin'. Now, who's going to arrest me?" He jerked a thumb at Kielty. *"That?"*

Kielty gestured apprehensively to his sergeants and patrolmen.

"Look," said Hanson to the room, "if this funny monkey thinks I killed the goddamn mayor, he's out of his effing head! I ain't killed nobody—not since the war, that is."

"That's right!" his wife put in. "Mr. Hanson w-wouldn't even k-k-kill a mouse!"

Kielty, protected by his squad, stepped forward. "Warren Gamaliel Hanson—" he began formally.

"Get lost, squirt!" growled Hanson, beetling his brows. He advanced a step. Kielty retreated half a step, remembered he was not alone, and came back bristling.

Hector Grimwood broke up the confrontation. "Hanson!" he called out, rising to his feet.

Hanson turned his head. "Yessir?"

"I'm afraid there's nothing we can do to prevent your

being arrested, Hanson. They've charged you with the murder of the man van Zaam, and a proper warrant has been issued."

"Anybody killed that creep deserves a medal," snorted Hanson, "but it wasn't me."

"I'm sure of that, and you're going to have the best legal assistance I can get. Mr. Hemmet's going to help us." The doctor walked around and put his arm around Hanson's shoulders. "And don't you worry, Mrs. Hanson —they won't be able to hold him very long."

Hanson looked dubiously at Kielty. He looked back at Dr. Grimwood. "Well, if you say so, sir," he said reluctantly.

Then, while Mrs. Hanson moaned softly in the background, Kielty completed his arrest. He did it with a politeness that was itself offensive, observing every legal nicety, but even his handcuffs, when they clicked, seemed to click gloatingly. Press strobes flashed. Mrs. Hanson kissed her husband a wet good-bye, and the door closed behind him and his escort. Silently, without a word, Judson Hemmet followed them.

The chief of police stepped into the center of the room. "Well, that's that," he announced. "Now if you people have your questions ready, I'll be glad to answer them."

"Just a minute, Mr. Otterson!" Hector Grimwood strode up to him, fire in his eye. "You have completed your legitimate business here, and my house has no room for anything so deep as your proposed in-depth interview. Leave and conduct it elsewhere!"

The newsmen glanced at Otterson, who shrugged and made the sort of gesture a sane man makes when he is being patient with a lunatic. They started filing out.

"My business here isn't completely finished," the chief declared. "I have a feeling that it won't be for some time. However, as the murder of our mayor has been solved, there's no real reason to keep men on duty here." He addressed the sole remaining officer. "Sergeant, we'll pull off everyone. I want you to seal up the actual room where the mayor was killed, but all the other seals can be removed. You can go now and give the orders."

"Yes sir, right away," the sergeant said, and left the room.

Timuroff had been aware of Pete's gathering anger, and now Pete spoke up suddenly. "Hey, wait a minute! Chief, this case hasn't been solved by a long shot. Van Zaam's whole history shows someone must've hired him. How can I tie up that end of it when you're lifting all security? Any new evidence we find is going to be worthless unless we keep things buttoned up a few more days!"

Chief Otterson did his best to stare Pete down. "There won't be any new evidence," he stated, for the first time letting ill temper sour his voice. "The lab men have already picked up everything. As for van Zaam, the federal people have confirmed his long involvement with reactionary forces. As the papers have suggested, he may have hated Mayor Munrooney for his fearless stand against these elements. In any case"—he shifted his stare from Pete to Dr. Grimwood—"if he was hired, we'll learn who hired him when we find out why he was killed."

He waited an instant for this to take effect. Then, abruptly, his voice and manner became unctuously paternal. "Cominazzo," he declared, "believe me, I'm aware of the great work you've been doing. It's not your fault Lieutenant Kielty cracked the case before you had a chance to. But the fact that he *has* cracked it changes things. From here on, it's just a matter of routine. So you're relieved of your assignment as of now."

Pete took a deep breath—and Timuroff's hand gripped his elbow. It was a fencer's hand and, like a pianist's or violinist's, could be felt. Pete exhaled.

"Cominazzo," the chief continued heartily, "a couple of months back you asked for three weeks' leave. Why don't you take it now? Kielty tells me we can find people to fill in for you. Take your wife down to Disneyland. You've earned it, son. When you come back, you'll be a different man. Mr. Timuroff, don't you agree?"

Timuroff's hand clamped vise-tight. "Absolutely, Chief Otterson," he answered. "Pete's long overdue."

He ignored the deadly looks Pete was giving him; and the chief apparently didn't notice them. Otterson's expression now was that of one who, by a single master stroke, has settled everything. "That's right," he said. "Work hard, but never overdo—that's how to be efficient and stay efficient." He regarded them benevolently. "Well, I'll make sure my men get rounded up. Good night, Doctor. And good night, Mr. Timuroff. Have a nice trip, Cominazzo, and don't forget to have your wife send a postcard from down south to Wifey. She sure loves getting pretty ones. *Good* night."

The library door closed mercifully, and he was gone.

Pete Cominazzo let his breath out with a *whoof*. He disengaged Timuroff's fingers, and confronted him. "Okay, Tim," he demanded. "I was all set to give that silly bastard an earful! I was all ready to resign! Instead, I took the hint. Okay, what gives?"

"It's very simple, Pete," said Timuroff. "If you'd blown up and been suspended, or resigned, you wouldn't have a chance to solve this case. But with a three-week leave, you can still have a crack at it. You have more friends in the Department than Kielty and the chief put together, and a lot fewer enemies. If anything interesting occurs, somebody's going to pass the word along to you."

Pete relaxed a little. "You may be right at that," he answered grudgingly. "Anything I can't find out here, Joe Thieme up in Sacramento will get for me. I only hope you've got a real live line on the murders. *I* haven't."

"As I said before," replied Timuroff. "I think I have a glimmering."

Dr. Grimwood had gone to comfort Mrs. Hanson, who was still whiffling quietly in a corner. Now he returned to them.

"The man's incredible!" he said. "He turns himself on and off so readily that I caught myself wondering whether I might not have made him after all. But then I realized that of course I never could've programmed him with Wifey!" He became serious. "But what do we do now?"

"Who is your lawyer?" asked Timuroff.

"My lawyer? Why, usually nowadays it's young Tommy Coulter. Their firm has always represented me—Primrose, Eisenstein, and Coulter. I started years ago with Tommy's father."

"Well, you'd better get Tommy down to Hanson right away. They do handle criminal cases, don't they?"

"I'm sure they will, under the circumstances. I'm not happy about Hemmet, but I was too upset to think of how to turn him down without offending Mario Baltesar."

"I gather Hemmet isn't a close friend?"

"Hardly. He's been here a few times over the years, and lately he's been playing poker with us pretty regularly. But Mario has played once a month ever since we started, and he has always helped to organize my parties.

He's not at all like Hemmet or Munrooney, and I know
that sometimes he hasn't been too happy with the way they
do things, but he's married to Munrooney's sister, and if
he pulled out she'd bring the house down around his ears.
Anyway, he's a follower, not a leader. Munrooney swayed
the mob the way he himself sways a jury, and while he's
always been dominated by one woman, Munrooney
dominated lots of them. Whenever Munrooney said to
jump, he jumped. But he's an old friend and I don't want
to hurt his feelings."

"Naturally not," said Timuroff. "But Hemmet can't
complain if you have your own attorneys working with
him. You wouldn't want to hurt their feelings either."

"Isn't having Hemmet in on this sort of like getting the
coyote to guard the chicken house?" Pete suggested.

"Perhaps," replied Timuroff, "but sometimes it's a good
idea to know what the coyote's doing, especially when
you have a watchdog watching him. That'll be part of
Tommy's job."

It took several minutes for the doctor to run Tommy
Coulter down, at the apartment of the young lady at whom
he had been looking lustfully the night before, and a few
more to persuade him to hurry to the city jail. By then,
Mrs. Short and Liselotte had returned, accompanied by
Pascoe from the poker parlor, who had paused to say
hello, and to make clear that he and most of his companions neither liked Kielty nor agreed with him.

"See," said Timuroff. "I told you so."

Pete was cheered. He grinned. "Who's up there sitting
with Lucrece until they get her room sealed up?" he
asked.

"Jeff Kerry, the most married man in the Department.
She's safe like in a convent. He should be there fifteen
minutes yet."

"Good, a little later we'll go on up and say hello to
him."

"You staying for a while, Pete?"

"For a while. You've heard I'm taking three weeks'
leave, courtesy of Chiefy? I'll be in tomorrow early and
tidy up."

"I'm going in now," Pascoe said. "You want me to
check out your office? Some busy character might get real
careless and lose something out of it before you get there."

"There's a notebook in my desk drawer which ought

to be good reading on vacation. If Kielty sees you there, tell him I asked you to make sure my files were locked."

"The hell with him!" said Pascoe, and patted Mrs. Hanson on the shoulder as he left.

Pete made sure the front door was locked and bolted. When he came back, Penny Anne and Liselotte were doing their best to comfort Mrs. Hanson, and Dr. Grimwood, his spirits much restored, was telling Timuroff that soon Hanson would be freed, utterly confounding his accusers.

Pete sat down on a corner of the doctor's mighty desk. He listened quietly until his host had finished. Then, "I don't think you'd better count on it," he said, pitching his voice so it could not be heard across the room. He raised a hand to forestall Timuroff, who was about to interrupt. "Let's be frank. We've taken sides. The chief and Kielty are trying to stick Hanson with the van Zaam killing—and if they get away with it, where will that leave you? I'll tell you. Their next step will be to say he did it because *you* told him to—who else?—probably to keep van Zaam from blabbing that you hired him. That's what Chiefy has been hinting at."

Hector Grimwood lowered himself slowly to his chair. "But—but that's ridiculous! I despised Munrooney, and I said so. If Mario hadn't asked me to, I never would have had him in my house. But there was no reason in the world for me to have him killed!"

"Doctor, Kielty and his pals are going to take the line that they don't need to prove a motive. They're going to scream *eccentric* at you so loudly the jury won't even hear any logic."

"They'll mean that I'm insane."

"Yes," said Pete.

"Then what is there to do?"

"Plenty. Tim and I don't believe either you or Hanson had anything to do with this—Tim made up our minds about it yesterday." Pete looked a little wryly at his friend. "And it's not just because we like you. We know for sure there's been dirty business going on, but there's nothing we can do with the evidence we have—not yet. We'll be racing against time, so that the people who're trying to torpedo you won't get the chance."

His voice had risen, and its urgency brought Penny Anne and Liselotte back across the room, Mrs. Hanson following.

"But who would ever want to—to torpedo Heck?" asked Penny Anne, full of anxiety. "He's never done anybody any harm."

"It may be quite impersonal," said Timuroff. "Probably it was the setup—Heck's house, his almost wide-open parties, the passages. Again, somebody may have wanted not just to kill Munrooney but to put Heck on the spot for another purpose. Maybe he owns something someone wants, or is standing in their way. Most criminals, Penny Anne, are pragmatists."

Penny Anne shuddered and drew closer to the doctor, and Liselotte looked accusingly at Timuroff. "Why do you always think of such unpleasant things?" she said to him.

"Because it's better to think of them than to pretend they don't exist. It keeps one from being scared."

"You maybe, Tim—not me," said Pete. "The best way for me to keep from being scared is to get after them." He stood. "Come on, let's finish what I came here for. I want a peek at Muriel Fawzi."

"That's the spirit!" cried Timuroff. "Lise has been nagging for a chance to meet the girls. We can drop in on Kerry on the way, and Penny Anne can introduce her to Lucrece."

"Penny has already introduced me to Evangeline." Liselotte blushed prettily. "She is so lovely! And so delicately made! But"—she smiled at Penny Anne—"I do not think that I would trust myself alone with her creator. You must not believe the stories about rich seducers—it is these artists one must beware of."

Penny Anne looked proud, and Dr. Grimwood shook off some of the depression into which Pete's estimate of the situation had plunged him. "Madame Cantelou"—he rose and bowed—"at my age, you have paid me a great compliment indeed! All is by no means lost." He offered her an arm; Penny Anne took the other. "Inspector, will you lead the way?"

"Huzzah!" exclaimed Timuroff, gallantly letting Mrs. Hanson cling to him. As they set off, he wondered to himself at Liselotte. He knew that she was frightened; yet it had been she who, with a word or two, had brought the doctor back into the fray. She was more than a famous singer, an accomplished actress, he told himself admiringly—she was a great trouper.

Suddenly, as they turned toward the hall, she cried out,

"Wait! I first must see your secret passages! Timmy has told me that they are like those in *The Castle of Otranto,* but I do not believe him. Please let me see them!"

Pete, intent on his investigation, frowned professionally, but Hector Grimwood at once took her part. "Come, come, Inspector—it'll take just a minute. Poor Muriel can wait for us that long. We can start here." He went to the bookcase by the fireplace. "Bother! Here's another one of your silly seals!"

"Okay," Pete said, giving up and removing it, "but let's not take too long. I'll phone Jeff so if he hears noises he'll know it's us."

With a flourish, the doctor took out his little key. The door slid open. They waited for Pete to make his call; then the tour began. Only Mrs. Hanson refused to go along, not when her Gammy was accused of doing such a dreadful thing down there; she'd wait and have some coffee ready for them when they got back.

Timuroff, reserving his opinion of secret passages, listened to Liselotte's cries of scared delight at each new twist and turn and hidden staircase. First, they descended to the cul-de-sac where van Zaam had been found, but did not enter it. Then they returned upstairs, and finally, after Liselotte had been allowed to knock sepulchrally, they walked in on Jeff Kerry in Lucrece's room. He was just starting to seal up.

"I know you have to leave," said Dr. Grimwood, "and that nothing must be touched, but would you mind turning Lucrece on for just a minute for Madame Cantelou?"

Kerry grinned and pushed the button, and Lucrece obligingly turned her head, raised one hand for attention, and began:

> *"From the besieged Ardea all in post,*
> *Borne by the trustless wings of false desire,*
> *Lust-breathed Tarquin leaves the Roman host,*
> *And to Collatium bears the liquid fire,*
> *Which, in pale embers hid, lurks to aspire,*
>   *And girdle with embracing flames the waist*
>   *Of Collatine's fair love, Lucrece the chaste.*
> *Haply the name of 'chaste' unhappily set*
> *This bateless edge on his keen appetite;*
> *When—"*

Kerry turned her off again, while Liselotte clasped her hands and exclaimed at the excellence of her delivery.

"I don't suppose we'd better demonstrate how she defends herself," Dr. Grimwood said regretfully, "under the circumstances."

Kerry walked out with them, sealed the door behind him, said good-night, and left.

"And now we'll visit Muriel Fawzi," announced Muriel's maker, crossing the hall again and opening the door of the room beyond Lucrece's. "She doesn't have a secret passage of her own, and I'm afraid she has to share a bathroom with Lucrece, but we've really gone to endless trouble to give her the right atmosphere."

They filed through into a vision of Araby the Blest, as it might have been conjured up by a little girl from Cairo, Illinois, yearning for a long-lost Arabian father. The color scheme was lush with rose and scarlet, gold, green, and brilliant blue. Rich Oriental carpets adorned the floors and walls. The window frames and fireplace were intricately tiled and inlaid with quotations from the Koran. There were no chairs, and only one low table, but luxurious cushions and silver bowls of Muslim sweetmeats were everywhere.

The doctor flipped a switch, and at once the room was filled with a vast male voice, ululating melodiously.

"That was the muezzin calling her to prayer," declared Dr. Grimwood proudly, turning the muezzin off. "In a moment you'll see her start to——"

He stopped. He stared. They stood there motionless.

From the center of Miss Fawzi's cushions protruded two badly twisted, complex sets of rods, which at the muezzin's call had started to turn and jerk and quiver.

But Muriel Fawzi was nowhere to be seen.

Nor was she in the room. It was, Timuroff thought, as though she had just stepped out daintily to reprove a eunuch, or to order rosewater or hashish from the bazaar.

"She——*she's been kidnapped!*" Dr. Grimwood cried.

There was a long and terrible silence, while the shadows they had half dispelled closed in on them again.

Then Pete said, much too sensibly, "How could she have? The seals haven't been off ten minutes. Jeff and the detail have only just now left. And we've been through the passages. Not even Houdini could've managed it!"

Hector Grimwood's eyes darted from side to side, as

though he hoped to catch her hiding coyly behind a pile of cushions. Nobody said a word.

Abruptly then, deep in the bowels of the house on Kemble Street, they heard a laugh—a man's wild laughter, suddenly released and just as suddenly cut off.

"There *can't* be anybody in those passages!" Pete almost shouted, as though to challenge the impossible. "What's going *on?*"

Again silence fell . . . and Liselotte whispered, in a very small and frightened voice, "Listen! That laugh was not from Hector's secret passages, through which we came. I have known many, many stages, theaters, opera houses. I have been through them, behind them, under them. And I have much experience with the human voice. It did not come from there!"

"It c-couldn't have been from the house—I mean the rooms and hallways," Penny Anne put in apprehensively. "I know this place so well that if it had I—I wouldn't feel this way."

"You are right," said Liselotte, "it was not from the rooms. It was not from the passages." She faced them, white as death. "That laughter came from—*from somewhere else.*"

IX

The Phantom of the Opera

Nobody said it, but the same image came to all their minds, the old familiar one—remembered from how many reruns? —of that terrible, fleshless face, deep underground beneath the Paris Opéra, suddenly turning from the keyboard to confront the audience—and all the old familiar shock and horror returned with it. Who could be lurking in whatever unknown spaces had been hollowed out under that house? *What* could it be that might be moving there beneath their feet?

There are ideas which should not be allowed to grow; and Timuroff came in swiftly. "Heck," he said, in a voice as unruffled as a croupier's, "could anyone have planted a tape player somewhere down below?"

The death mask did not vanish instantly, but he could feel it getting frayed around the edges.

Hector Grimwood considered for a moment. "Tim, I can't imagine how or where. I don't have Madame Cantelou's sense for sound, but I do know every nook and cranny of this house—and I too feel the laughter came from none of them."

"A closet or an air shaft, something like that?"

"I suppose so, but we can't possibly start a search tonight."

"No, we can't!" Penny Anne's voice trembled on the thin edge of hysteria. "Maybe there isn't anyone down there, but *I'm* not going to spend another night here till we find out. Oh, Hector, let's get *out* of here! Let's go to a hotel!"

The phantom evidently had not dissolved enough for her; and Timuroff, with a quick glance at Pete, agreed that leaving might not be a bad idea. "You're right—even if there's nothing there, this house is too much with you. You need to get away from it."

"But not to a hotel!" cried Liselotte, full of sympathy. "They must come to me! Timmy, together we have plenty of room." She hugged Penny Anne. "Listen, I shall make an omelette, and we shall have some wine. Please, say that you will come!"

"Heck, why don't we? Can't we, Heck?"

"I don't know, Penny. After what has happened, I can't have Mrs. Hanson staying here alone, even in her apartment."

"You don't have to leave the place alone," Pete said, "not if you don't mind spending a few bucks."

Timuroff looked at him inquiringly.

"Bill Traeger's between jobs—at least between big jobs. Remember Bill? His agency can get all the men we'd need to guard this place down here in half an hour."

A weight seemed to lift from Hector Grimwood's vast, stooped shoulders. "Is he reliable?" he asked.

"Like a gold certificate in Teddy Roosevelt's day. His line's protecting property and people—he leaves divorce stuff to the private-eye voyeurs. He won't even let Chiefy in without a warrant unless you say so." Pete grinned as though the Phantom never had been there. "Besides, he thinks Kielty pollutes our sweet environment, and that it ought to be de-Kieltyfied."

Timuroff, watching Dr. Grimwood, was amazed at his resilience. His eyes sparkled once again. He returned Pete's grin. "I'm convinced," he said. "Your Mr. Traeger has the best of references. Would you mind phoning him, and making whatever arrangements you think best? When I was practicing, Penny Anne and I could pack our bags and be ready in five minutes, and we still can be out of here just as fast—and I admit it'll be good to get away." He turned to Liselotte. "If you're really sure we won't get under foot—?"

"Of course you will," she answered, "but I will wear soft, small slippers, and you will not be hurt. And if perhaps you are"—she smiled at them—"then I will sing to you."

"She means she'll play you some of her own records," said Timuroff.

"That would be simply *lovely*," said Penny Anne.

"See?" said Liselotte, sticking her tongue out at him.

"There's no point in all of us waiting here for Traeger," Timuroff said. "Heck, why don't you and Penny Anne and Liselotte go on in your car? You do drive, don't you?"

"He drives a Phantom III," Penny Anne answered proudly.

Timuroff ignored the famous Rolls' coincidental name. "Well, it'll be quite safe in our garage. If you can trust Pete and me to brief Traeger's people, I'll join you after they get here."

"Tim, I'm tired enough to take you up on that. Of course, I want to meet Mr. Traeger, but that can wait. What special instructions should I leave for him?"

"Tell him that *no* one is to be admitted, and that all official calls must go through your attorneys. That means the press too. Otherwise, you're simply not available. Incidentally, we ought to have a set of keys to all your passages so that Traeger can have access to them."

"That's simple, Tim. You won't need a *set*." Hector Grimwood fished out a leather key container. "Here is the master key. The others are selective—they open only certain doors. But this key gives access to every secret passage in the house. That's how old Albright planned it." He chuckled. "I suppose for his own dark and devious purposes."

Timuroff took the key. Dr. Grimwood and Penny Anne took off upstairs with Liselotte to get their bags. Pete Cominazzo took up the telephone.

"Tim," he said, "your expression tells me you've just caught the canary." He began to dial. "Maybe you'll tell me what it tastes like?"

"A fine, plump bird," answered Timuroff. "You can have the beak if you're nice to me."

Pete snorted as the phone was answered, apologized to it, then spent a few minutes explaining matters, first to Traeger's answering service, then to the man himself.

"He's on his way," he reported finally. "He's calling three of his best boys, but we won't have to wait for them. All right, how about that canary?"

"First," Timuroff informed him, "I am delighted. Heck didn't hesitate before he turned the whole thing over to us, the key included. That cleared up my last small doubt where he's concerned. Next, though I didn't want to say so near the ladies, I think this house does have its Phantom of the Opera, though I doubt whether he's actually in residence. We ought to have at least a quarter hour to scout around after Heck takes off, oughtn't we?"

"Scout around? You mean looking for your phantom?"

"For him, or at least for the way he'd been getting in and out." Timuroff dropped his voice. "He has to be the man who kidnapped Muriel Fawzi, and it probably was he who killed van Zaam. Pete, there *must* be at least one more passage, leading to a doorway to and from the house. We would've had to figure that out even if there hadn't been a phantom laughing underground."

"Do you reckon van Zaam knew about it?"

"No. If he had, they'd not have brought him in and let him introduce himself. That was insurance in case someone spotted him. Whoever hired him probably had a pat explanation ready for his being there—that and a solid alibi. The act he put on, saying good-bye before Munrooney left to go upstairs, would've been part of it, and I suppose they planned to sneak him out through the side door or out the back after the stabbing. The extra passage would've been a secret they couldn't trust him with."

"Tim, do you really think that sharp old coot upstairs has lived here all these years and doesn't know it's even there? Boy, some canary!"

"Pete, Heck got the house from Mrs. Albright *after* Albright's death. Now, just suppose there'd been some really shady business going on? What better way to cover up than to have passages all through the house? You'd tell your wife and a few friends about all but one or two of them; then every accidental noise would be explained. Does that make sense? Anyhow, can you imagine Heck keeping something like that all to himself?"

"Okay," Pete said grudgingly, "we go down into the catacombs, and hold a phantom hunt. You beat the wash pan, and I'll hold the sack. And if we catch the character, then what?"

Timuroff smiled grimly. "Then probably we'll find we've known him for years."

Hector Grimwood called to them from the hall. He had

his own suitcase and Penny Anne's. "Can Mr. Traeger come?" he asked.

"You're all set up," Pete told him. "Have you left word with Mrs. Hanson about phone calls and all?"

"I've told her just what Tim suggested."

"Good. We'll help you carry your stuff down to the car." Penny Anne and Liselotte came down the stairs, and somehow everybody managed to squeeze into the little elevator.

"Floor?" asked Pete.

"The bargain basement, please," laughed Penny Anne.

Down they went, and the elevator door opened into a hall neither Timuroff nor Pete had seen before. It too was paneled, but very plainly, and a stout door led from it directly to the courtyard, now empty of patrol cars and with its iron gates standing open.

They crossed to the converted stable, and Timuroff made appropriate admiring noises while the doctor brought the gleaming twelve-cylinder Rolls-Royce to life and Pete opened the garage doors. "Remember!" called Liselotte, as the car glided majestically away. "You must come right home!"

The Rolls turned right and vanished down the hill, and Timuroff and Pete closed the iron gates and bolted them. Then they walked slowly back across the cold stone pavement into the house. In the elevator, Pete was tempted to suggest that they might be embarrassed if they found what they were looking for, a real phantom, armed and grisly, waiting for them. Then he recalled his training, his own .38 Chief's Special, and the .45 automatic which, in times of stress, Timuroff carried discreetly in his waistband.

They made their way between the cases containing Dr. Grimwood's porcelains into the poker parlor. Timuroff opened the doors of the armoire, and unlocked the sliding panel at its rear. They turned the light on, and stood inside the cubicle.

"You think we'll find a secret door in *that?*" Pete said dubiously, pointing at the plain panels separated by narrow verticals.

"Perhaps," Timuroff replied. "Usually the keyholes are covered by ornamental detail. You grasp the detail very firmly, pull it out and turn it. And there the keyhole is, quite safe from being found by accident. However, here we're going to have to look for something else."

He was moving from one panel to another, frowning, pressing his ear to each and knocking softly. Finally, at the second from the end, he stopped.

"I think you've got yourself a wild-goose chase," Pete told him.

It took him two more minutes to find what he was searching for. He pointed to it—a mere nothing, a tiny hole almost at the top of a divider, as though the wood-stained putty hiding a finishing nail had fallen out. It had been there a long time. Its edges were very slightly beaten down. "What do we have I could push into that?" he asked.

Pete fumbled in his pockets. "What about a paper clip?"

Timuroff took it, straightened it out carefully. Reaching up, he inserted it and pushed. It met resistance, but the resistance was not hard. The wire went in an inch, a good inch and a quarter. There was a massive, muted *click*.

Timuroff pushed the panel gently. It began to open, against a weight or spring. He moved swiftly to one side, and instantly the .45 was in his hand. He pushed the panel open all the way.

They looked down on a dark stair. It ended at a door.

"Have you a flashlight?" whispered Timuroff.

"All good boy scouts do," Pete whispered back, gun ready. "But I'm going down ahead of you—that's my job."

"No, Pete," Timuroff smiled at him. "This is *my* canary. I'll find the keyhole; it's probably not hidden. Then douse the light and follow me. I'll open up and duck inside, to the left. If nothing happens, follow me but go right. And save the light till we find out if there's a switch inside."

"I don't like it one little bit," Pete said.

Timuroff moved softly down the stairs. He tried the door before he tried the key. It was unlocked. He signaled up to Pete. The light went out. He waited until Pete was only a foot or two behind him. He threw the door open.

It opened on dead darkness, on cold air confined, on the smell of stone.

There was not a sound.

Timuroff darted through and to the left. He heard Pete follow, to the right. With his free hand, he explored the wall, and found a light switch where it ought to be, an old-fashioned metal and porcelain affair screwed to the doorpost. "Switch," he whispered, to alert Pete, and twisted it.

A light glowed, a dusty naked bulb suspended from the ceiling, its ancient wire filaments casting their yellow glow as reliably as they had in Albright's day. The passage they were in was virtually a chamber, at least six feet wide and fifteen long. Its floor was stone. Hewn stones formed its walls. To his left, Timuroff saw another passage branching off. There was no one there . . .

He heard Pete gasp, and whirled. Seated cross-legged in the other corner, on what appeared to be a hassock or a stool, eying them coyly over a filmy veil, was a raven-haired, beautifully bare-breasted girl in scarlet silken pantaloons, with a brilliant blood-red jewel gleaming in her delightful navel.

Long before, Timuroff had learned that the instant of letdown is when one must especially stay on guard. He resisted the temptation to guffaw, remembered to keep a watchful eye on the passage to his left, and said politely, "Miss Muriel Fawzi, may I present Inspector Cominazzo of the San Francisco Police Department? He is investigating your outrageous kidnapping."

Tactfully, Miss Fawzi made no comment.

Inspector Cominazzo muttered something mildly obscene.

"Thank you," Timuroff said graciously. "Do you suppose the villain brought this unfortunate child in from there?" He pointed at a dimly lighted passage near Miss Fawzi. "It probably connects with one leading right up to her bedroom, where there's not supposed to be any. That could explain the laughter we heard up there."

"Do you have to be so goddamn right *all* the time?" Pete growled.

The antique bulb shone cobwebs down on them; and now, for the first time, they really saw the chamber they were in. The long stone wall before them was broken by a door, a door of iron held to the solid stone by a steel hasp almost as heavy as a railroad rail. It, in turn, was secured by a brass padlock weighing several pounds, which Timuroff recognized as one of those unpickable ten-lever locks used in the Far East to protect godowns full of precious goods.

"Now what the hell's in there?" Pete asked.

"Possibly something very valuable," answered Timuroff. "Or horribly illegal. At any rate, something tremendously intriguing. But I'm afraid we won't find out tonight. We couldn't even if we had the key." He lifted the great padlock an inch or two. "Look at the keyhole. They've poured the whole thing full of melted lead."

The years had turned the lock a deep, dark greenish brown, the lead so gray that it was almost black.

Timuroff dropped it. "Well, it'll keep. Where do we go from here?"

"We know which way he brought her down. Why don't we reconnoiter down there to the left and find out where that leads?"

"To the outside somewhere, I'd guess. The spot where it comes out is probably well screened."

"Let's take a look. This time, I'll go ahead."

Timuroff did not demur, and they set off. They turned a corner and found another set of narrow steps descending, another ancient light bulb.

"We're already on the basement level," said Timuroff, "but back inside the hill. Here we'll go underground, beneath the courtyard, probably. From the way that passage down there angles off, I'd guess it ends up somewhere round the stable."

Pete halted momentarily. "I'm sure glad that angle's there. Otherwise we'd have *no* kind of cover going down."

He approached the angle cautiously, hugging the wall, and Timuroff followed him around it. Nobody shot at them. Here again the passage was of stone, and there were two more dusty light bulbs. As they advanced, the interplay of their own shadows peopled the thirty yards ahead of them with spectres. They reached a final flight of steps, and climbed them. The narrow landing was in darkness, and Pete's small flashlight was required to reveal the door to their right. Here there had been no attempt to hide the keyhole or the iron handle under it.

"Where are we?" Pete asked.

"It's all wood here," said Timuroff. "Weren't there a lot of cupboards along the back wall of the garage, with stairs up to the Hansons' living quarters somewhere near?" He slid the key in, turned it, pulled the handle back. The door opened inward, letting the damp night air in with it. It was a massive slab of oak, with a now-visible false front of thin-cut stones, their edges alternating back and forth to match those against which they had been designed to fit. It moved slowly and very silently. It was not the sort of door that could be banged, even deliberately.

Pete held it open while Timuroff went out. Two yards off stood the stone wall separating Grimwood's courtyard from his neighbor's garden to the east. A few feet to the left, a chimney jutted out a foot or so. Beyond it, shrubs and bushes grew, hiding the area from the service alley running from Kemble Street to Baker—an alley where, under the No Parking At Any Time signs, everybody parked.

"Well, that's how he does it," Timuroff remarked. "Let's find out where his keyhole is."

Pete handed him the light. On the door, and to either side of it, there were a few rusty bolt heads, like untidy architectural afterthoughts. One of them, reluctantly, pulled out and turned, and there the keyhole was.

Timuroff came in again, and let the door close to. It did so solidly, without a sound.

"We'd best be getting back," he said, leading the way. "Traeger may be here by now, wondering what swallowed us."

"All right, we've got a phantom," Pete grumbled. "The loudest noise he makes is his electric watch. I still can't understand how come the Hansons haven't heard him creeping in and out."

"People hear what they think they ought to. Mrs. Hanson probably would tell us that she and Hanson are plagued by heavy-footed mice. As a matter of fact, Albright may have soundproofed that one little stretch, with chopped cork or something primitive like that. He seemed to think of everything."

"Okay, what do we do now? Seal up the works?"

"I don't think so, Pete. Of course, we'll have to talk to Heck, but what I'd like to do is install a doorbell."

"With a little sign saying Please Ring?"

"No, with a little gizmo that tells us when he's there. I'd really like to meet the gentleman. From what you say of Traeger, he should be able to cook up something of the sort quite readily."

"No sweat. He's a real wizard on the electronics end. He'll have the thing in and tweeting in half an hour. I think it's a hell of a good notion. If Grimwood isn't happy with it, we can pull it out tomorrow. In the meantime—" Pete sighed wistfully, "maybe we'll catch Kielty."

"That would be nice," said Timuroff, "but I'm afraid not. It would've taken three Kieltys to hang up van Zaam."

When they reached the iron door again, he greeted Muriel Fawzi ceremoniously, and promised her that Dr. Grimwood would make mechanical amends for her indignities. "How about going back the way we came?" he said to Pete. "Traeger'll have to be taken on a tour anyway, and we can check that other passage then."

"I'd just as soon come up for air right now," Pete agreed fervently. "Your creepy-crawly tunnels down here underneath the opera are plain unhealthy. Tim, I never knew so much could happen in one day. It's less than twenty-four hours since you found van Zaam."

They went back through the armoire, and found Traeger in the library, drinking coffee and listening to Mrs. Hanson's woes. He was tall and flat and pleasant, a few years older than Pete—just old enough, guessed Timuroff, to have fought for a couple of years in Korea, and solid enough not to be soured by it.

Pete introduced them; saw that they liked each other. "Bill," he said to Traeger, "how much do you know about this deal?"

Traeger grinned. "I read the papers, and there's been lots of talk. Also I called Jake Harrell after I heard from you, and he sketched in some more of it, mostly about Chiefy and that Kielty bastard. I told him if both of you are sure they're pulling something dirty, that's enough for me. He said you'd fill me in."

"I'll whisper it while we pussyfoot along the secret passageways," Pete told him. "Our first stop will be the sewers of Paris." He opened the entrance by the fireplace dramatically. "Follow me, *mes braves!*"

As they retraced their route, it became obvious that Traeger had already formed a surprisingly accurate picture of what had happened and what was going on. His questions were brief and to the point, and Pete had very little filling in to do except where the comings and goings of the phantom were concerned.

"Who do we tell about this phantom bit?" asked Traeger. "Nobody?"

"*No*body," Pete answered. "If Kielty learns about the other passages, it'll just give him another rope to hang the doctor with. Right now, how could we prove there is a phantom, even if they'd give us half a chance? Tim thinks we ought to bug the alley door to let us know when he comes in or out."

"And if he does?"

"For the time being, just make a note of it," said Timuroff. "He doesn't seem to be out to do any real damage—he seems to have something else in mind."

They stopped in front of the armoire.

"So that's where they hung up van Zaam?" Traeger remarked. "He really must've been right out from under the flat rock. Every time anyone talks about him, the smell comes through."

"Have you run into him before?" asked Timuroff, opening the heavy doors.

"No, I'd have remembered him." Traeger frowned. "It was the name that rang a bell. Wasn't he mixed up with Hanno a couple years back?"

"You just don't like Hanno," Pete said. "Can't say I blame you."

"I pulled the whistle on them once when they were engineering one of their nasty half-threat, half-blackmail jobs. That was when Kielty and his pal—he hadn't yet made chief—went all out to get my license. They never did forgive me when the state suspended Hanno's for six months instead."

Pete slid aside the rear panel, they went through, and no more was said until the light went on to reveal Miss Fawzi and the padlocked door.

"All the comforts of home," Traeger said approvingly. "Well, there's no point in giving me the rest of the grand tour; I'll go exploring after my boys get here. I'll get my junk out of the car, and set the bug up then. I'd like a closed-circuit spy-eye, or maybe a surveillance camera, but they'd take too much carpentry. Maybe we can work one in a little later."

"Let's go back up the way she was brought down." Pete pointed to the passage on the right. "It's the only one we haven't had a chance to check."

"Okay." Affectionately, Traeger patted Miss Fawzi's pretty cheek. "I'm just a dog of an infidel, sweetheart, but I love you. Don't worry, I'll hurry back."

"No funny stuff, chum. Remember what happened to our mayor when he tried it."

"Don't tell me Lover Boy was really making passes at Lucrece?"

"It's not for publication," Pete said, "but he had his

pants off. Bill, I'm not kidding—you ought to see the pictures."

"*Tsk-tsk*," murmured Traeger, "the poor, besotted man —and him going to confession every Sunday, without a doubt."

The passage upward ended, predictably, in Miss Fawzi's closet, and they went back to the library, where Mrs. Hanson met them and told Timuroff his lady friend had called.

"Oh, she's that sweet and dainty you could almost eat her!" She giggled. "And maybe, sir, you'll have to. She called to tell you you could take your time, because your omelette's been et up."

Timuroff thanked her, and told her not to worry about Mr. Hanson and to get a good night's sleep; and, as Traeger walked them to the door, he realized that for the first time since the phantom had made his presence known, he felt at ease about the doctor's house. He told Traeger so, and they shook hands warmly.

"By the way, Bill," he asked, handing him the keys, "you said something down below about having had a dust-up with that Hanno crowd when they were doing someone's dirty work. Whose was it, do you recall?"

Traeger's expression hardened suddenly. "It was some rich-bitch female moneylender, trying to grab a shady title company. She wasn't in it personally—just a business name she was using as a front—so all I got was rumors. The outfit called itself Russian Hill Estates, and later on they changed their name or folded up—I don't remember which. You want me to check into it?"

Pete and Timuroff exchanged glances. "Maybe later," said Timuroff. "What about van Zaam? Was that when you heard he'd been mixed up with Hanno?"

"No, that was later, after Hanno got his license back. I can ask around and try to pick the lead up again, but I wouldn't guarantee anything."

They left. The door closed, and its bolt clicked solidly behind them. They said nothing more until Timuroff had pulled out from the curb into the street.

"Interesting, very interesting," he remarked thoughtfully. "First Traeger thinks he's heard about van Zaam working with this Hanno crew. Then he tells of Hanno being employed by someone who can't be anybody but Miranda Gardner. A strange connection."

"Dammit, I can read your mind," Pete said. "And suppose it *is* all connected somehow, and Hemmet and Medusa are behind it all—where does that put us? With the setup they have now, we wouldn't have a chance of even saving Hanson and Doc Grimwood! No, Tim, it's got to be coincidence—you know, dirty birds run together. Haven't we enough other strange connections to look into?"

"Yes," said Timuroff, "and before long we'd better spend an hour or two talking over all of them, trying to sift the gold out of the garbage. Lise's going to have a lot planned for tomorrow to take our guests' minds off their troubles. She'll probably drive them down to visit an old friend of hers, a composer and director from La Scala, who's living in Los Gatos. She won't need me along. Why don't we get together around noon?"

"All right." Pete sighed. "With Bill here holding down the fort, we ought to be able to accomplish something—at least if that damn phantom doesn't pull something really wild on us."

"I'm glad that you're an optimist," said Timuroff.

X

There Was a Young Man from Kaprust

It was not quite one thirty when Timuroff got home, and he found Liselotte and their guests relaxing, full of good cheer. "Well, Heck," he said, "you can tuck into bed tonight without worrying about your house. Traeger is an even better man than I expected, and everything's secure."

"That *is* good news, Tim. Penny's been waiting up, just hoping you'd tell us that."

"It's been wonderful," Penny Anne declared. "This apartment, and Liselotte's omelette—I ate your share of it all by myself—and her lovely voice, and everything you've done for us. And tomorrow she's going to drive us to Los Gatos to meet Maestro Umberto Mancinelli. He's asked us all to dinner, and that nice inspector's wife is coming with us." She kissed the doctor on the forehead. "Good night, dear. I know I'm going to sleep beautifully."

Timuroff said good-night to her, and she went out with Liselotte.

Hector Grimwood turned to him eagerly. "Tim, did you find out anything about that laugh and where it came from?"

"Yes, that's what took so long. We don't know anything about the phantom, but we know how he gets in and out, and how he kidnapped Muriel Fawzi—"

He told the story as briefly as he could, trying to play

down the drama of it and the mystery of the iron door and
newfound passages; but Dr. Grimwood listened impatiently,
crying out that it was tremendous! the most exciting news
he'd heard in years!

"I wish we were back there right now!" he exclaimed.
"So I could see it all and bring poor Muriel back upstairs.
But I suppose we'll have to wait at least till Monday—I
wouldn't miss tomorrow for the world, and Penny Anne
would leave me if I suggested such a thing! Is Mr. Traeger
going to try to catch the phantom?"

Timuroff outlined the measures they had taken. "I hope
they meet with your approval, Heck," he urged. "Both
Pete and I believe the phantom isn't out to do you any
serious harm, and Traeger will be right on top of things.
But we ought to find out who he is and what he's really
up to before we try to grab him."

They talked for a few minutes, Hector Grimwood weaving fantasies about the iron door. "It's very odd," he said,
"that no one told me. The whole affair was handled by
Mrs. Albright's own attorney, old Jefferson, who should've
known—but of course Albright was frightfully secretive.
I suppose it's anybody's guess."

Finally he announced that he was going to take one of
Penny Anne's sleeping pills and go to bed. "If I don't, I'll
roll and toss all night, wondering about it—and worrying
about poor Hanson in that jail. I forgot to tell you young
Coulter phoned. There's nothing he can do, at least till
Monday. He was quite upset. He said that Hemmet wasn't
any help at all."

"Somehow," said Timuroff, "I'm not surprised."

He sneaked into the bedroom, where he undressed as
quietly as he could, trying not to awaken Liselotte.

She waited until he was beside her before she stopped
pretending. *"Beast!"* she whispered in his ear. "Do not tell
me! I know you will not come with us tomorrow to see
Umberto. He will be hurt, and I will have to make up foolish stories to explain."

"Tell him that Pete and I are hunting down the Phantom
of the Opera. He, of all people, should understand."

"You mean that you have found out something?"

"We found some secret passages Heck didn't even know
about, with Muriel Fawzi sitting very primly in one of
them. I told him all about them." He yawned. "Why don't

you let him tell you the whole story while you're driving down?"

Liselotte pinched him in an especially vulnerable spot. *"You* will tell me the whole story, and you will hold me very nicely while you do it!"

Timuroff sighed, and held her very nicely, and told her the whole story. Finally, kissing her good-night, he made her promise not to wake him up for breakfast.

When he awakened, it was eleven o'clock and everyone had gone. Liselotte's maid, Emilia—who looked like a late-Renaissance female poisoner, and who adored him—was grumbling around, preparing a mixed grill, which she knew he loved and which she swore no true Christian would have eaten before sundown. While he consumed it, she sat across from him by invitation and, with many a pungent comment, read him the morning headlines.

There was no shortage of exciting front-page news. A dramatic account of Hanson's arrest was followed by an announcement from the board of supervisors: meeting in extraordinary session, they had unanimously elected Mario Baltesar mayor pro tem. Munrooney's party had also chosen him to run for the office at the forthcoming election. Finally, a Mrs. Dorene Enzwilger of Daly City had proclaimed, through her attorneys, that Errol Vasquez Munrooney had been, not only her off-again, on-again common-law husband, but the father of at least two of her several children. There were pictures of Munrooney and of Baltesar, and a sentimental shot of the plump Mrs. Enzwilger and her brood, posed in front of her modest residence.

Emilia, rapping the paper ominously, declared that it was all a plot aimed at that fine Inspector Cominazzo, at Dr. Grimwood and his pretty friend, and—saints preserve us!—at Mr. Timuroff himself. "Look!" Angrily she pointed at the Enzwilgers. "What do you think of that?"

"I think," said Timuroff, "that it is probably a mayor's nest."

"How can you joke? Do you understand? They are not married!"

Timuroff smiled. "You mean like Madame Cantelou and me?"

"That is different. You love each other. Besides, *la signora* gets much money from the one who was her husband, he who owns the ships. Also, you are very careful and do not make babies. It is the innocents one must be sorry for!"

Timuroff sighed with her over the immoralities of a wicked world, complimented her on a delightful breakfast, and phoned Pete. Twenty minutes later, he was in the Cominazzo kitchen, drinking coffee and listening to a run-down on what was new, while Pete finished his ham and eggs.

There wasn't much. Traeger had bugged the alley entrance, and installed two more telltales, one near the iron door, the other in the chamber to which Miss Fawzi had been abducted.

"You'll never guess where he put the second bug!" Pete chuckled. "Under Miss Muriel's pantaloons, where no high-minded phantom would dream of looking for it! Would you believe that she's as complete as anyone could want?— just like Lucrece and Evangeline. Only those rods that she had goosing her, the ones that made her work. Bill says it was almost more than he could bear just to look at 'em."

"Maybe Heck can work out some less painful way of doing it. What else has happened?"

"Well, Jake called and so did Stevens. Both of 'em say that Kielty's on to something he thinks can be worked into a real headliner, only he's not telling anybody what it is. Also, he's got half the bureau digging into Grimwood's history, with emphasis on right-wing politics—Goldwater, for God's sake! There's all sorts of pressure being applied. Looks like they want it wrapped up for election day."

"That makes sense," commented Timuroff. "A rightist plot could win them the election hands down, especially if they drag a racial angle in—and probably they will."

"Speaking of that," Pete said, "it's being dragged in already, only in reverse."

"How's that?"

"Denny Wallton. It's like I told you—ever since the killing, the militants and left-wing noisy boys have been giving him a stinking time, hinting he took a payoff to stay downstairs while Munrooney was being killed. Today he wandered in, Jake said, and he was all shook up. One of his kids got put into the hospital by some sort of rat pack on the way home from basketball. Denny's all ready to resign. He never did like that Munrooney detail—he felt

Munrooney only wanted him to show off because he was black, and he resented it."

"He's a good man?" asked Timuroff.

"The best."

"Could they have any other reason for attacking him? Right now, with Munrooney as a martyr and Chiefy knuckling down to them, they've not been riding the Department. Why pick on him?"

Pete shrugged. "Maybe to discredit anything he says. Perhaps they're scared being that close to Munrooney he maybe heard too much."

Timuroff sat back and looked at him. "Well, it's one more question. Let's choose a few, make sure they're the right ones, and try to find some answers."

"Which ones would you suggest?"

"For a starter, *What happened to old Jefferson, who was handling Albright's legal business when he died?* Our phantom, and probably Munrooney's murderers, had to find out about those passages; they had to get the keys from someone. Even if Albright never told his wife, he may have left instructions with his lawyer. Next, *How did the khanjar get away from Socrates?* But both of those will keep. The final one's the best, *What does the poet know that's so important?* It could be direct, scene-of-the-crime evidence. He has already talked to Kielty—perhaps enough to worry Kielty and his friends. I think we ought to go up there right away."

"You mean today?"

"Why not? Heck and the ladies are going to be at the maestro's until late tonight. We can run up to Stitchgrove's ashram, question him, stop at three or four better wineries, sample their wares, eat a decent dinner, and still get back in time."

"Timuroff," Pete said, "you're a hypocrite. You want to get out there in the grape country, and sip free wine, and drop in on a few antique stores where probably you'll find a rare old sabre or spontoon. But I'm a simple, dedicated policeman, and I can't agree without a formal protest." He put his dishes in the washer. "Let's go. Maybe I'd better call ahead and see if we'll be welcome."

He dialed, told the phone who he was, reminded it of his conversation with the poet, and said that, yes indeed, he and his friend were sort of seeking for enlightenment.

"Okay," he told Timuroff disgustedly, "we're approved

of." He slipped a miniature tape recorder in his pocket. "If we pick up something really hot on Kaula orgies, I'll mail it to Chiefy with *'Wish you were here. Love from Disneyland.'* It ought to make his day."

Timuroff's Mazda was waiting demurely at the curb, and its rotary engine responded instantly. "Hey," Pete exclaimed, "you know that character Rop Millweed, on the *Chronicle?* He called up half an hour before you came, trying to pump me about friction in the police department, and was anybody plotting against me personally, and that kind of crap. I told him Kielty was my only friend, and Chiefy had been like a father to me, and then he took another tack. It seems there's a new craze being started up, mostly by the press—making up dirty limericks about Doc Grimwood and his girls. Your car reminded me."

"My *car?*"

"Uh-huh." Pete read from his notebook:

> " 'The gears from her ass to her ankle
>   May occasionally grind or go clankle,
>   But believe me she can
>   Help a weary old man—
>   Her vagina works just like a Wankel.' "

"The Hindoos," remarked Timuroff, "achieved much the same effect without modern technology. The lady, bottom down, was in what amounted to a large net shopping bag suspended from the ceiling by a rope, the rope was twisted, and the rajah—he must have been at least a rajah—well, I'm sure you follow me."

"I'm way ahead of you," Pete said. "Which is probably what the girl told the rajah. Millweed read me one more. He said he got it from an editor of *Ramparts:*

> 'Dr. Grimwood, ancient and lewd,
>   Displayed his Lucrece in the nude.
>   He announced, "My invention
>   Will relieve sexual tension—
>   A girl who comes easily unscrewed!" ' "

Timuroff considered it solemnly. "It clearly reflects the tortuous psychological writhings of the New Left: dark undertones of frustration, penis envy, and possibly impotence. A limerick should be simple, forthright, tightly plotted. Any nuances should simply contribute unobtrusively to its dramatic gestalt effect."

"I'll keep that in mind for next time he phones. May I quote you? And have you heard about 'The Young Man from Kaprust'?"

"I don't believe I know that one."

"As we're paying him a visit, maybe you should. It's not one of Mr. Millweed's. It's traditional:

> 'There was a young man from Kaprust—
> Obsessed by abominable lust,
>   He ravished a hen,
>   A turkey, and then
> A little green lizard, which bust.' "

Timuroff laughed. "Perhaps the young man we're calling on has written poems about his own disappointments, which he'll recite for us. And what did Rop Millweed say after he had presumably softened you up with pornographic verse?"

"He hinted that his public was just panting to find out what went on between our expert, Mr. Timuroff, and Madame Cantelou, and whether Doctor Grimwood's little ladies were *really* capable of sexual intercourse, and he intimated that a red-hot newshawk like himself, with Influential Friends in City Hall, could do big things for a struggling homicide inspector."

"And what did you tell him?"

"I told him to perform a flying Kaula ritual on a galloping goose. Only I put it in terms he could understand."

"An excellent rejoinder," said Timuroff.

The day was bright and blue and wonderful, with a wind ruffling the blue-green Bay and filling the sails of swarms of Indian summer yachtsmen between the Marina and Marin. They crossed the bridge in silence, Timuroff trying to remember which of his Drummond-Mowbrey relatives, retired after a lifetime in the Central Provinces Police, had told him about the Kaula sect.

The traffic was light, and the Mazda disposed of the miles expeditiously, following far enough behind a white-striped scarlet Stingray so that its less blatant speed would escape the notice of the highway patrol. They circled round the Bay, headed for Napa and Highway 29.

"It's a strange world, isn't it?" Timuroff said finally.

"Ghastly stuff that used to be safely embalmed in dirty limericks being taken seriously as the cultural harbinger of a Great New Age. My Uncle Cedric used to talk about these far-out Sakti worshipers—never, of course, when there were ladies present. The Kaulas were the most extreme of all. I don't recall whether they went in for decapitating their blood sacrifices or not, but they were very nasty generally. I wonder how Mr. Stitchgrove happened on them, and what his academic sponsors—I understand he's lectured at U.C.—would think if they could witness the real thing."

"Hey! You don't think he could've been mixed up in either of our murders, do you?"

"I doubt it. Even though Sakti also appears as Kali the Destroyer, I'm sure she'd have preferred a nice fat goat or water buffalo to either Munrooney or van Zaam. Let's hope he's a better witness than he is a suspect."

"Well, we'll soon find out." Pete slapped his notebook. "Look at *that*—all we've picked up so far is Dun and Bradstreet stuff, pretty much common knowledge—and damn near all the gossip's about Munrooney's friends. Miranda Gardner has fun with gigolos. Socrates Voukos likes fat women—*not* boys—or so they say. Also the word is out that ever since Hemmet and his wife split up, his sex life's been getting kinkier and kinkier—no homo stuff, but girls who're real kooks. About Munrooney's enemies, there's nothing, though everybody knows he was a sort of Johnny Appleseed where murder motives were concerned. All right, whether or not his friends, or some of them, did become his enemies, how does our phantom fit into all this?"

"He fits in very nicely," said Timuroff. "Remember what I said about the khanjar being all wrong? Now we quite safely can assume that our phantom stole it, or had it stolen, for the express purpose of substituting it for another weapon, and thereby spoiling a very tidy plot to pin the mayor's murder on Heck and Hanson. As we know, he didn't spoil it completely, but he certainly made things tougher for whoever planned it."

"What does that tell us?"

"First, that he was no friend of Munrooney's; he made no effort to prevent the killing. Next, that he either was a party to the plot betraying his co-plotters, or that he found out all about it some other way. Thirdly, he may have been somebody's hired hand."

"If he was working from outside, how would he even have caught on?"

"Perhaps he wasn't completely an outsider. He may have known what motivated whom. A shrewd guess could have put him on to it, or simply accident. He may have been prying into something for profit or revenge or political advantage. Munrooney's murderers must be his enemies—otherwise why bother? Why take the risk?"

"You mean he could be almost anybody who's been connected with Munrooney—whether we've heard of him or not?"

"No, it's much more likely that he's tied in directly with Munrooney's close associates, especially with the people at the party. That makes him one of half a dozen, at the most eight or ten. And by this time, the killers know that he's after them, which means the pressure on them has increased. They may do something ill-considered and betray themselves. But best of all"—he smiled grimly—"*he* knows who they are, and eventually we'll have him. Then, if we play our cards right, we'll get the answer."

"*If* he comes back," Pete said.

"If he doesn't, perhaps we can induce him to."

"It's a damn shame we can't just call Jake and the boys in—but if we do, we've had it. Kielty'd tell the press, and then our phantom would be spooked for sure. The next step would be to say Grimwood was the phantom, playing tricks to get the law off his tail."

"Exactly. And we're going to have to be completely sure it's in the bag before we tell the world about it. When the news breaks, it's going to have to clobber Kielty and his friends—not strengthen whatever case they're building against Heck."

Presently, Timuroff found a horrifyingly purple Porsche to tag behind; the Mazda moved even more swiftly than before; the miles rolled out behind them and disappeared. Then suddenly, just south of St. Helena, they were at their turning.

"Hey, watch it!" Pete exclaimed. "Malvoisie Lane—that's ours!"

Timuroff braked, backed on the shoulder, and made the left. Malvoisie Lane was a road of vineyards being turned willy-nilly into suburbs. Where there had once been acres of well-tended grapes there were rows of unkempt vines which, though they furnished a thin excuse for the "California ranch-type" houses erected in their midst, could neither have paid for nor supported them. Among these, a few serious vineyards, large and small, bravely held their temporary own.

Malvoisie Lane thinned a little as it approached the foothills. Its houses became poorer, scruffier, and their viticultural justification even less plausible. Broken-down fences, tangles of barbed wire, weeds, strewn rubbish, and the corpses of dead automobiles hinted at shiftless and unsuccessful subsistence farming.

"It seems we have arrived," Pete remarked, as they slowed down beside a psychedelically daubed mailbox with a peace symbol, a large four-letter word, and STITCHGROVE scrawled on it, and a crude arrow saying ASHRAM pointing to the right. "Sort of looks like Dogpatch, doesn't it?"

Timuroff turned off, following a pitted washboard track to an untidy congeries of buildings clustered among dry, dead, and dying vines. The main house was a scabrous bungalow of pink stucco, in what Los Angeles had once believed was Mission style; it was stained and flaking, and was surrounded by a half-ruined barn, by tumble-down lean-tos, sheds, shanties, hog troughs, henhouses. A variety of domestic animals and fowl wandered at their ease, much like sacred cows on the streets of Mother India.

"It smells like Dogpatch, too," Pete said. "I wouldn't be surprised if Hairless Joe and Lonesome Polecat showed up and offered to take us through the Skunk Factory."

Timuroff killed his engine, and they got out.

"Could that be Moonbeam McSwine?" he asked, pointing at a young woman garbed in ragged jeans, huaraches, dirty long brown hair, and nothing else, who on the front porch was happily pretending to fight off the advances of a large dog who appeared to be part Boxer, part Airedale, and part happenstance. Next to her sat a long thin young man similarly attired but wearing also a double necklace of small plastic skulls, from which a long and gaily painted lingam was suspended. Clearly a person of some sanctity, he wore his hair and beard loosely braided, and smeared with a substance that Timuroff suspected was a mixture of ghee and cow dung. He was reading aloud from an open book, apparently to the farmyard creatures in his vicinity: a few ducks and geese and chickens, a moulting turkey, two bleary-eyed young pigs, and an aged spaniel bitch wearily suckling three mongrel puppies. The girl appeared to be sixteen or seventeen, the young man about twenty.

At Pete and Timuroff's approach, they stopped what they were doing and looked up, stiff with suspicion and hostility. The young man put the book face downward on the broken boards, revealing that its author had been Herbert Marcuse. The girl stared at them strangely out of vast dilated pupils, caressed the dog, and giggled softly to herself. Simultaneously, half a dozen of their co-religionists appeared abruptly from behind buildings and out of nooks and crannies. Male and female, they were very much of a type and of an age, upper-middle-class children somehow deprived of a real world and trying to contrive their own out of an ancient culture's dregs. All but one. Six or eight years older and several inches taller than the rest, he was magnificently muscled, hairy chested, with an almost Afro head of yellow hair. Except for his broad-brimmed floppy hat, he was naked, his body smeared vertically with clay, the Brahmin thread about his neck, his genitals in a foul cotton bag tied with a piece of string around his waist. In one hand, he carried a curved, broad-bladed sword, of the type manufactured by the thousands for the tourist trade and of wretched steel, but sharpened now to razor keenness. He said no word. He glared, and his mouth worked silently as he regarded them.

Timuroff and Pete, each sensing the sudden tension in the other, pretended to ignore him. No matter how accustomed one became to the counterculture's wild displays of kinkiness, it always came up with surprises—which sometimes could be dangerous.

"Like, you mothers lose your way?" the thin young man demanded with a sneer; and his companions snickered and growled appreciatively. A huge gray wolfish dog came up and circled, bristling, as though he too was troubled by clean clothing and the smell of soap.

"On the contrary," Timuroff answered cheerfully. "We've found our way. Mr. Cominazzo here phoned not long ago, and we were invited to come up this afternoon. So here we are."

There was a hint of general relaxation. The girl with the dilated pupils and the amorous hound said *Shit!* very rapidly several times, but obviously she was not addressing the remark to anyone.

The thin young man made a guesture of dismissal. "They're a couple pi— uh, cops up to see Guru-ji," he declared, "the ones he said knew about his poetry and talked all right, not like that prick we had up here this morning."

"Somebody been bothering you?" Pete asked solicitously.

"He tried to bug us with a mess of questions—a squinty, red-faced little guy with a great big one sort of guarding him."

Pete glanced at Timuroff.

"We said the Master'd gone off to a sensitivity get-together down at S.F. State, and after maybe half an hour he gave up. I had him figured for an SPCA bigot, but he was big-city fuzz."

Mr. Stitchgrove's followers began to wander off. The naked sadhu spat into the dirt and strode away, waving his blade and scratching at his cotton bag. Somebody else obligingly picked up a broken rake and belabored the gray dog until it fled, yelping and limping slightly.

"Now I shall take you to the Master," the young man announced formally. "He is meditating in the henhouse, where he has been for several hours, but he has ordered that you be brought to him immediately. Believe me, it's not something he'd do for just anybody."

"Thank you," said Timuroff, bowing slightly. He was fascinated by the lingam suspended around the young man's neck. Not only was it extremely lifelike—it was enclosed in what was without doubt a condom. Very politely, he inquired why.

At once, a look of profound awe and reverence passed over his guide's ascetic countenance. "You won't understand, but I'll tell you anyhow," he answered. "I'm the Master's lingam-bearer. This is the lingam of the Lord Siva, sacred to our Goddess Sakti. It must be kept for her alone. It is infinitely potent, infinitely fertile. Guru-ji says if we don't keep it in this gizmo here, there's no telling what'd happen. Hell, we can't give the Pill to every sheep and turkey on the place, can we?"

Timuroff agreed that it would be impractical; and they set off. The henhouse was a long, low, badly sagging shed between an old three-holer and the barn. It had been patched with broken plyboard and rusty tin. At its door, the young man stepped aside. "Go on in," he said. "He awaits you. You may address him either as Master or as Guru-ji."

Very few smells are less refreshing than those of a neglected henhouse, on a balmy day especially; and Timuroff, entering through the hinge-sprung door, wondered for a moment if the poet had not staged the interview as an exercise in one-upmanship, for it is difficult to decide whether to breathe and perish or hold one's breath and perish anyhow. On one side were arranged the perches, some cracked and broken, one or two supporting ailing fowl. The other side was given over to shelves for laying, and on one of these, on matted, musty feathers and other souvenirs of long habitation, sat Elia Stitchgrove. Surprisingly, he did look like a Hindu holy man, one of those who cluster wherever poor and frightened pilgrims flock in their multitudes. His attitude was a traditional one, feet resting on his thighs, hands folded at his loinclothed crotch, eyes lowered to perceive his navel. His biceps and pectoral muscles were almost nonexistent; his flaccid flesh fell in pale moist folds; his round, soft face wore a mysterious smile; and his tranquillity was in no way disturbed by the brown hen who, having established herself on his right shoulder, which she had adorned copiously with droppings, was seeking something edible in his tangled hair. He had painted his forehead with vermilion, and from his necklace of Benares bells hung an Egyptian ankh.

"We are here, Guru-ji," announced Timuroff respectfully. "This is Inspector Cominazzo, and I am Timuroff, his friend."

The poet's eyes remained on his navel. He raised a hand. "Peace!" he replied a little shrilly. *"Om mani padme hum!* You need information, and I shall give it to you. But first we've got to, uh, *communicate."*

"Yeah, sure," Pete agreed. "We'll jibe vibes."

"Some people might put it in those terms"—the poet nodded graciously—"but I prefer to say that we must reach an understanding. I have achieved a cultural and religious breakthrough. It's like the first man landing on the moon, only a lot more so. No one before has penetrated the true meaning of the *Kaulopanishad—"*

Timuroff and Pete had lowered themselves gingerly to the thin edge of a feed bin, and now they sat there quietly, tried to sort out the smells—which included those not only of chickens, rats, and decaying vegetables but of mystic incense and mind-blowing pot—and let him speak his piece. Some people, he informed them, claimed the *Kaulopanishad* was false. That was because they didn't understand its message regarding man and what the materialistic West called the lower animals. It all went back to a Brahminical misunderstanding. When the Lord Krishna, as a boy, had disported himself among the cowherds, it had been neither their wives nor the milkmaids to whom he had been sexually attracted, but the cows themselves. That was the real reason cows were sacred. This revelation had come to him during an especially lovely trip, and the sequence of poems resulting from it—privately printed under the title *Cowla*—had received such a splendid accolade in the underground and academic press that Professor Marrow, the famous intuitional psychologist, had given him the vineyard and all its appurtenances for his ashram.

Timuroff recalled that there'd been something of a scandal while Dr. Marrow was at Berkeley. He had bought the vineyard in the vain hope that wine of his own making might, at imaginative bacchanals, not only stiffen his own flagging libido but overcome the apathy of certain of his lusher students. Before he'd chucked the whole thing as a bad job, he had blundered by inviting up a singularly vulgar columnist, who had made the most of the occasion, on the spot and in print afterwards. Subsequently, after the Academic Senate had formally denounced the governor and the Board of Regents, he had been promoted and transferred to the new, multimillion-dollar Barstow campus.

For some minutes, while the hen watched his listeners with a suspicious eye, Elia Stitchgrove spoke of his progress and his problems; of the gratifying interest shown by the general public (even an aged sheepherder in Montana had asked to be converted); of an inquiry recently received from *Penthouse* regarding a possible feature article with color shots of Kaula rituals; and of what he called the Kali hang-up—the failure of so many Westerners to appreciate the dual nature of the goddess and the deeply spiritual nature of sacrifices. Finally he sighed. "I know you'll never really understand," he said, "but I do hope we're *communicating.*"

"Master, *I* understand!" Leaning forward, Pete stared at him intently. "I was an Indian in my last incarnation. I was a sergeant in the Central Provinces Police, used by my British masters to oppress my brothers."

Guru-ji looked up so abruptly that the hen, with an excited squawk, abandoned him. "And you *remember* it?"

"Every bit of it," Pete assured him. "That is, the important parts."

"What caste did you belong to?"

Pete hesitated, and Timuroff, who had kept a straight face, saw that he'd have to get him off the hook. "He was a Rajput and a Kshatriya," he put in smoothly. "He was beaten to death by his officers for refusing to arrest a great sanyasi—a saint who preached against Queen Victoria's tyranny."

"I sensed it!" Mr. Stitchgrove cried. "Instantly, when I heard your voice over the phone, I knew that we had formed an astral bridge! Look, man, tonight we're having a real chakrapûja. Why don't you stay? Maybe in that life you were pretty orthodox and never got asked in on one, but you've advanced by now!"

"I'm sorry, Guru," Pete answered dismally, "but it's my karma. Because of what I did back then, I've got to be a pig in this life too, at least till we get this murder of Munrooney solved."

"Munrooney was an ancient soul. He befriended the poor and humble and oppressed. He listened to me with great interest when I told him all about my doctrine at the party."

"Okay, so what was it you saw at Grimwood's, Guru-ji?"

Surprisingly, the poet giggled. For a moment, he lost his sacerdotal dignity. "At Grimwood's? I didn't see a thing at Grimwood's, man! That was just something I cooked up for fun!"

"Just something you cooked up *for fun?*" Pete almost shouted. "For Chrissake *why?*"

"To put your pig lieutenant off the track. He spoke to me as if I was some sort of criminal or, well, charlatan. His kind of fuzz are always trying to freak you; they're the shitty-gritty kind. What I really saw was the geek who got killed afterwards—van Zaam, the papers said his name was. I knew him right away, even though it'd been more than a year."

"You mean you'd seen him previously?" said Timuroff.

"It was just after I beheld the True Inwardness of

everything, before I got this ashram going here. We had this pad in Berkeley, in a big old dump on Grove Street. Its door was on a kind of alley out in back—you know, two little porches right together. The other one was Leda Minden's. I used to tell her with a name like that she'd be a natural for us Kaula cats, but she just wouldn't groove—she was too jacked up with her horse."

"Her *horse?*" Pete couldn't keep the disbelief out of his voice. "You mean right there in town?"

Again the poet giggled. "Yeay! Right there. Four blocks from the big pigpen back of city hall." He made a graphic hypodermic gesture. "*That* kind of horse. The big H. Heroin. Anyway, that night we'd held a service—chants and rock vibes and a sitar, all pretty traditional—and about three A.M. I drifted back to take myself a leak out of the door because there was a couple busy in the john. I opened up and there he was, just leaving Leda's pad."

"You're absolutely sure?" Timuroff asked, very quietly.

"Sure I'm sure. My light was on, with a real turned-up moon, and there his face was right in front of me. Man, but *no*body could forget those fisheyes. Besides, even if, that was the night she died—when she got horse-kicked dead, dead, dead. Next day the narcs and pigs were there all over us, pushing us around. We had to squawk to the ACLU before they let loose."

The cold and airless wind that van Zaam's death had not dispelled touched them once again.

"Any idea what he was doing there?" Pete asked.

The guru slowly shook his head. He shrugged. "He wasn't peddling Girl Scout calendars. We talked about him later on. None of us figured Leda was all that far gone, but hell! you can't ever tell once they get on that stuff."

"You told nobody about seeing him? No cops, that is?"

"Uh-*uh*. I tripped on acid, and had a talk with Sakti, and she came to me, and she was in her other, darker self, with her four arms and her hungry red tongue hanging out, and she was beautiful, and I could see that she was pleased with me because we'd kept it to ourselves, and we were at the burning ghat, among the bones, and then she straddled me like I'd become Lord Siva—" Guru-ji's eyes had closed; his smile hung open; he started swaying slowly back and forth, and the front of his grubby loincloth betrayed what seemed to be a rather undersized erection.

The hen, clucking excitedly, flapped back upon his shoulder and glared at them antagonistically.

"Looks like the interview is over," Pete said. "He's on a kickback to his trip." He rose. "Thank you very much, Master," he intoned. "Perhaps you have helped to solve the murder of your friend, Mayor Munrooney. The world is grateful to you."

The poet showed no sign of having heard, and they backed out into the air. The thin young man, hunkered against the wall, was waiting for them. "Hey, you sure made out, didn't you?" he said, rising to his feet.

"We were deeply impressed," Timuroff replied.

"It's his charisma. Man, he's lousy with it!" The young man stared at Pete, and plainly he too was impressed. "He must've known you were an Indian last time around. That's why he's a Master, feeling these things. Nobody else'd have the balls to ask a couple of lousy cops to stay over for a chakrapûja."

He led them back toward the car, steering them apprehensively away from a newly built, ramshackle shed where multitudes of flies were buzzing, explained that it was *Her* shrine, and waved good-bye to them politely but with obvious relief.

"Well," remarked Timuroff, as they pulled away, "what do you think of Guru-ji?"

"My considered judgment," Pete replied, "is that he's sort of chickenshit. Say, what is a chakrapûja, anyway?"

"Some sort of Lucky-Pierre-ring-around-the-rosy, I believe. Under the circumstances, I'd rather not speculate."

"My God, somebody ought to give that place a firehose enema! And there's one of his disciples who ought to be checked out real quick—that great big bastard with his tool in a tobacco sack. He's something nasty looking for a place to happen—maybe not the first time. I'd better put the sheriff's people on to him."

They reached the road, and found their way blocked by a mail truck, a little right-hand-drive affair drawn up by the box. The driver looked them over, grinned, and walked up with a letter in his hand. "You two don't look like you belong in Creepsville," he remarked, pointing with a navy-tattooed hand.

"We've been bill-collecting," Pete told him.

"Well, don't let 'em give you any garbage about being broke. Take a look at this—Special Delivery." He held the

envelope against the sun. Its return address said J. Ellis
Stitchgrove, D.D.S., somewhere in the Midwest, and it was
addressed to J. Ellis Stitchgrove, Jr. The check inside was
clearly visible. "More than I make in two months, and
they come all the time, some from his old man, some from
a female with a different name who I guess may be mama.
That's what keeps this mess alive."

He tossed the letter in the box, wished Pete and Timuroff good hunting, and drove away.

"He's right," Pete said morosely. "Daddy and mom buying junior off to stay the hell away. Except for that, we'd
only have an under-the-counter culture, the way it used
to be. Okay, we drive sixty miles and waste an hour
brown-nosing a dirty little parasite any sane society would
lock up in a booby hatch. And what for? To learn he
saw van Zaam a year ago, for God's sake! Suppose it was
the night some poor twirp dealt herself out—so what?
I'll tell you what *I* need. I need to crawl off to some quiet
cellar somewhere and get a nice cold bottle of Gewürz
Traminer to wash the taste away."

"I know the very place, not five miles away; and while
we're waiting for them to serve the wine, you can use
their phone."

"What for?" demanded Pete suspiciously.

"To call that friend of yours in Berkeley—isn't it
Burgoyne? Remember what you told me—that half the
women in the world are in disguise? False names, false
hair, and unreal faces. We'd best find out who Leda Minden
really was. If she was tied in with van Zaam, there may
be something we can't afford to miss. Besides, you do
owe me a favor."

"Come again?"

"You never told *me* about your last incarnation, and I
came nobly to your rescue over that business of your
caste. My Uncle Cedric's rolling over in his grave at the
idea of your officers beating you to death—that was strictly
against regulations."

Pete smiled, grinned, and laughed aloud. "You win," he
said, "but I warn you—it's a waste of time."

They reached their destination, and Pete called Burgoyne. "I got him at his home," he informed Timuroff.
"He's going to look into it and let us know."

Then the Traminer, cool and exquisite, was served to
them over a dark old barrelhead. Half an hour later, feeling

better, they sallied out to raid antique stores, and Timuroff presently unearthed and purchased five Japanese blades: a tachi, three katana, and a wakizashi. Probably liberated during the Occupation, fortunately none of them had been abused. The dealer referred to them as "samurai harikari swords," and Timuroff saw no reason to hurt his feelings by correcting him, especially as his price was a small fraction of their actual value.

"I think I hear someone purring," Pete remarked as they drove off again.

"Quite loudly," Timuroff admitted. "That tachi is a joy and a delight, late Kamakura Period—it could be Kagemitsu or somebody like that—and its Higo mountings are extraordinary. As for the others—well, I've hardly had a chance to look at them, but there's not a bad one in the lot."

"I'm glad somebody's happy," grumbled Pete. "Here we go out into the boondocks to solve a sordid killing, and instead you make a killing in swords."

"Well, let's hope it's the only kind of killing we run into from now on," said Timuroff. "We'll celebrate. I'll buy the dinner."

XI

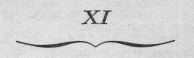

A Killing in Swords

At midnight, when Liselotte and her party returned from the maestro's, Timuroff and Pete were waiting for them. They had spent nearly three hours over an epoch-making dinner at La Bourgogne, in an atmosphere more conducive to optimism than that of Mr. Stitchgrove's ashram. Then, at Timuroff's apartment, Pete had phoned Traeger and Jake Harrell. All was well on Kemble Street, and Harrell reported only that an anonymous informant had tipped the media off to the mayor's nakedness, and that much was going to be made of it. After that, they had settled down happily to examining Timuroff's acquisitions.

The five swords had been placed, with ceremony, on a lacquered sword stand, and Timuroff had gone over them carefully, checking signatures against illustrations of fully authenticated specimens, and estimating their worth. He had decided immediately that the Higo tachi would have to join the carefully culled half dozen comprising his almost-never-shown personal collection. "Tomorrow," he told Pete, "I'll call Amos. He can see the others after lunch. He's sure to take at least two. I'll give him a very decent price and still get all my money back, which will be nice. But I won't tell him anything about the tachi—it'd spoil his day."

"That's *true* humility," said Pete.

For a few more minutes, they talked swords. Then Liselotte swirled in, her party following in her wake. *What were they doing?* she cried out. How could two grown men sit there and play with swords when there was so much splendid news? Heck had told the maestro all about Lucrece and Muriel Fawzi and Evangeline, and he had responded with wild enthusiasm—as indeed who would not? He was going to compose an opera about the house on Kemble Street, an opera in which she—Liselotte Cantelou—would sing the leading role!

Timuroff at once thought of a roly-poly tenor, minus pants and drawers, singing Munrooney's dramatic dying aria in Italian. Wisely, he did not mention it.

"Now all of us must go to bed!" she ordered. "Heck cannot wait to see his new secret passages. Also he wants to finish his Evangeline so that Umberto can be properly introduced. Penny Anne will stay with me, and we will spend the morning lazily before we get Olivia to take her out to lunch."

Timuroff, who had already planned the doctor's subterranean tour, smiled obligingly, and the party broke up in a round of kisses and good-nights, Timuroff allowing Liselotte to shepherd him to bed, where he told her just enough about his day to keep her happy.

He fell asleep immediately, and slept—he told Pete later—like a man who has just made a killing in swords, which was very satisfying. After wolfing breakfast with the doctor, he drove him back to Kemble Street, introduced him to Traeger, and—while one of Traeger's men mounted guard behind the alley door—showed him the mysteries which for so many years had lain unknown beneath his feet. Hector Grimwood was ecstatic. He groaned with disappointment when they urged the necessity of leaving Miss Fawzi at least temporarily *in situ* and deferring the opening of the iron door.

"I suppose you're right," he said, knocking on it impatiently. "But it's going to be terribly difficult to wait. I don't know what I'd do if I didn't have Evangeline to keep me busy."

Timuroff walked with him to the workshop, and watched while he prepared his instruments and turned the sheet back to reveal the young Evangeline, waiting immodestly on the surgery table.

"Heck," he said, "would you tell me a bit more about how your parties are arranged? I know that some of your friends are free to bring almost anyone they please."

"Yes, as long as their guests are interesting. Usually, my poker players are told first—Baltesar and Voukos and Amos Ledenthal and the rest."

"Who are the rest?"

"Well, Hemmet has been coming fairly regularly, and Arnold Tesserault the architect, and in the last few months we've seen a good deal of Reese Guthrie, Amos's partner, though I've tried not to have him come when Hemmet's there, and vice versa. Guthrie dislikes him—I think there's been bad blood between them—and icy politeness doesn't help a poker game along."

"What kind of players are they, Heck?"

"Baltesar is flamboyant—every hand is a front-page case in court. Socrates is shrewd and hard, but rather unimaginative. Amos—well, he's himself; he terrorizes new players until they see that he's all bark and very little bite. Tesserault is wonderful—he always loses so obligingly. Hemmet is cold and tough and calculating, but he doesn't win as often as he might, and he's not much fun to play against, perhaps because there's so little humor in him. Guthrie's a good sportsman, and his card sense is infallible. He's pleasant to play with, and impossible to read. Then, of course, we have a few who come only once or twice a year, like Penny's cousin Jeremy, and Admiral Melmoth. Wade Kalloch's been here too, but I don't encourage him—he always wants to play no limit poker."

"Do they have the run of the house when they're here?"

"Pretty much so, the regulars at least."

"Do you ever lend them your passage keys? During parties or anything like that?"

"Oh, yes. I'm not sure about Melmoth, but all the rest have taken their friends through at one time or another."

"I . . . see," Timuroff said. "Just out of curiosity, which of them helped most in organizing that last party?"

"I'm not really sure. Penny thinks she phoned two or three who were tied up, and then that lovely wife of Amos's, who did a lot to help."

By this time, what Dr. Grimwood was doing to Evangeline had become so very intimate that Timuroff, though he recognized its scientific spirit and anatomical necessity, began to feel like a voyeur. Promising to pick the doctor up in time for dinner, he took his leave. Downtown, he parked in the garage opening on Magruder Alley, took his four blades from the trunk compartment, and—trying to purge his mind of the limerick about the girl who came easily unscrewed—ascended to his place of business.

Olivia, of course, was already there, and his carefully stacked and sorted mail was awaiting him. So, to his surprise, was Ledenthal, seemingly very pleased with himself.

"Amos," he exclaimed, "it's good to see you."

Ledenthal's eyes fastened on the swords. "Goddamn it, Tim! Why don't you tell your friends about these goodies? What're you doing—hogging 'em all yourself? If I hadn't dropped by on my way back from the Hall of Justice, and if this sweet lady"—he bowed chivalrously—"hadn't told me, I'd likely never heard about them!"

"I'd intended to call you up before I left the house, but I had to run out to Grimwood's, and a lot of things came up—"

"Timuroff, you damn fool, are you still mixing into that miserable Munrooney business? After what I told you?"

Smiling, Timuroff put the swords down one by one on the table in front of Ledenthal. "And what were *you* doing at the Hall of Justice, Amos?"

"I got myself arrested!" roared Ledenthal triumphantly. "I'm out on bail, but I had to go down there again this morning. Jessie and I were having a quiet drink out on the deck late yesterday, just before dinner, when up came that goddamn pipsqueak Lieutenant Kielty. He had a big cop with him, a nice, quiet sort of guy. Anyhow, he wanted to ask questions, so I said, 'Okay, you pest, I'd as soon answer them here as anywhere.' He started right in, too—the same old stuff. Did I know Mayor Munrooney, and how well? What did I think of him? Where was I exactly when His Honor was up there getting himself killed? Was I a close friend of Dr. Grimwood's? Then he started getting all smirky, and dropping dirty hints about Lucrece and the other girls, so I asked Jessie to go bring some coffee out, and the big cop said could he help her? Kielty must've figured I was harmless, because as soon as they were in the house he sort of leaned toward me, and smirked some more, and asked me if Mrs. Ledenthal had ever known Munrooney, and had she known him *well,* and had our marriage ever had its little difficulties? And did I know what he meant?"

Ledenthal's brows drew down, and Timuroff began to expect at least a minor thunderbolt.

"And what did you say then?"

"Timuroff, I didn't say a goddamn thing. I reached out and grabbed the little bastard by the drawers—he was in one of our folding canvas chairs—and by the scruff of the neck, and I pitched the whole shebang into the swimming pool to see if it'd sink—just like I did that stupid MP captain back in Tokyo during the Occupation, only *he* went into the Imperial Palace moat."

Olivia burst out laughing. Timuroff joined her. "Just wait till Pete hears about this, Amos! Could Mr. Kielty swim?"

"Not so you could notice it. He splashed around, and snorted, and blew a lot of water, and said a lot of dirty words when he came up for air. Finally, Jessie and the big cop came running and asked what was the matter, and I told them, and the cop sort of apologized and fished him out. That was when I got arrested. I told him, 'Listen, you s.o.b., I'll ride in front with your friend here, who's civilized, but I'll be damned if I come anywhere near you, wet *or* dry. Anyhow, that's how they took me in, and—would you believe it?—the boys down at the Hall of Justice weren't hostile at all. You'd have thought I was an old pal coming home. My lawyer met me—Jessie'd phoned him right away—and I was out and home again before they'd even started the late show."

"Kielty's not exactly popular in the Department," Timuroff said, "but even so, Amos, was it wise?"

"Wise? Damned if I know. But it was a lot of fun and it was worth it." Ledenthal turned his attention to the swords. "Now, how exorbitant a price are you demanding for these hunks of Nagoya iron?"

"Flattery will get you nowhere," said Timuroff. "Examine them with care. Consider their beauty and their rarity. You'll be astonished at my pitifully small prices."

Ledenthal snorted, Olivia snickered, and Timuroff tried hard to look offended. For the next twenty minutes, they wrangled happily, and Ledenthal ended up buying two swords exactly as Timuroff had predicted. "And now," he growled, when the deal had been completed, "on top of being royally diddled, I guess I've got to buy your lunch?"

"That would be pleasant," Timuroff said politely.

They walked to Tadich's, and there, over his rex sole, he brought up the subjects they had discussed two days before.

"By God, Tim, you're just determined to rub your nose in that unholy mess, aren't you? What the hell for?"

"Because I like Hector Grimwood and I'm sure someone's trying to railroad him. That's one reason. Another is that Pete is getting pushed around because of it. Besides that, Amos, how deeply are *you* involved? Has it struck you that that little act of Kielty's could've been staged to set you up for something?"

"Set *me* up?" Ledenthal looked at him in astonishment. "Why should they? I'm clear out of it. Since I pulled out of Caldwell, Jolly I haven't been involved with them at all!"

"Well, you *have* been saying before God and everybody that Hemmet and Miranda were behind Munrooney's murder, and I've not forgotten the look she gave you at the shop. Amos, you do fly off the handle pretty readily, and a conviction for assaulting a police officer could really prejudice a jury in the future—whether you're the defendant *or* the victim. They may have dirty work in mind."

Ledenthal slammed his glass down on the tabletop. "Let 'em try!" he growled. Then he cocked an eyebrow and peered at Timuroff. "What is this, Tim? You're making noises as if you think maybe I was right about them after all."

"The idea's growing on me," admitted Timuroff. "The fact that Hemmet and Miranda have no motive we *know* about doesn't automatically shut them out as suspects. Neither does their apparent dependence on Munrooney. And the way the chief and Kielty have been operating makes me wonder whether there may be more at stake than the election, or even the Parks Master Plan—a quick cover-up, for instance. Besides, it's strange that nothing really seems to point anywhere else, except when Kielty and the chief are pointing it."

"I'm glad you've seen the light," Ledenthal grunted.

"Don't misunderstand me, Amos. I'm not convinced, not yet. But it's a new perspective. Mind if I ask a question?"

"Poop ahead."

"Do you have any *solid* information—even if it's something you aren't free to talk about—linking Hemmet and Miranda to the killing?"

"I told you, Tim. I don't know a damn thing the whole world doesn't know—but I know *them*. Okay, maybe it's like Reese keeps telling me and I was a goddamned fool shooting off my mouth the way I did, but I know I'm right. You can smell 'em everywhere."

"For instance?"

"For instance that crazy dagger he was stabbed with. I was at Socrates' party, and God knows there was enough confusion. Every collector and his brother came—Baltesar, Melmoth, Kalloch, even Tom Coulter. Then there were a lot of friends of Socrates', and all the arms dealers except you, because you were away, and some weird professor who wrote a book about the Coptic scriptures. Jessie and I brought Reese along. Even Heck and Penny Anne showed up."

"Did all of them stay late?" asked Timuroff.

"Socrates doesn't often dish out hospitality, but when he does he's pretty good at it. Even after the dagger had been locked up again—or anyhow its case—the party kept on going for an hour."

"Did you see him lock it up?"

"Not exactly. After he'd passed it round in that morocco box he keeps it in, and everybody'd *oohed!* and *aahed!* enough, I sort of remember somebody putting it away, and Socrates, all smiles, twisting the combination dial. We'd had a lot to drink by then, and he'd already started hauling out all sorts of other junk to show us."

"Pete says no one agrees on who last handled it. Any ideas?"

Ledenthal drained his wine glass, and held it out to be refilled. "Hell, I just got through telling you. The whole thing spells Miranda Gardner."

Timuroff, recalling his own ideas about the khanjar, looked dubious.

"Think it over. Here's a far-out weapon, covered with gold and jewels and worth a mint—sure to add more confusion and publicity. Then you come in—an expert hostile to the deceased. Besides, it's a cruel-looking sticker—just the sort that'd appeal to her. Let's say the two of them decided they had to kill off Munrooney. The time to do it would be before election—before he could get in again solidly. There'd be a hell of a lot more pressure then than afterwards, and they'd have a lot better chance to pin it on their scapegoat, Heck. He's made to order for them. Real wild, and the khanjar fits right in. I tell you, Tim, Miranda must've brought the bowie in her handbag, with Hemmet covering for her while she made the swap."

"And what about van Zaam?"

"A hired killer, like the papers say."

"Then why was *he* killed?"

"How do *I* know?" Ledenthal's voice began to boom again. "To keep him quiet, I guess. Maybe Hemmet did the job himself, or one of Kielty's cops. Dammit, Tim, can't you understand? Those two aren't human. Miranda's worse because she's smarter, but Hemmet's like van Zaam, only more complex and sneakier. He gets his kicks from hurting people—his poor damn wife, for instance. Remember what he did to Reese awhile back?"

"I was going to ask. What did he do to Reese?"

"Damn! Reese wanted me to keep my stupid mouth shut, but I guess you're going to hear it anyhow. It was just after Reese finished his second tour in Vietnam—when they were winding the whole business up—and he'd come back here to take his father's place with me. There was a girl named Marianne Denham, whom he'd met somewhere way back when, and he'd been seeing her each time he was on leave. Reese is the kind who takes that part of living seriously. She was for keeps, and all his plans were based on her. Then Hemmet ruined it."

"Hemmet?" Timuroff was genuinely shocked. "For God's sake, *how?"*

"I don't know. The son of a bitch has something, at least where certain women are concerned. Jessica always has detested him, but we were on friendly enough terms in those days. Anyhow, he met Marianne, and the next thing Reese knew she was halfway shacked up with him, and his wife had moved out across the Bay. Reese didn't try to interfere; he's too much of a gentleman to raise that kind of stink. Then, a few months later, we heard Hemmet had dumped her for something a lot younger, and she just disappeared. That was when Reese told me all he wanted was to get away, out of the country, and I let him talk me into a planned liquidation for the company."

"This I hadn't heard," said Timuroff.

"No, we've kept it quiet, and I'll ask you to do likewise. We've already shifted almost the whole business overseas. We're going to operate mostly in South America and Africa to start, and maybe later on in Asia too, developing more modern river transportation." Suddenly, Ledenthal's voice rang with a new enthusiasm. "Brazil alone has half a world you can hardly reach except by river. With shallow-draft vessels and new techniques, plus helicopters, we can explore it, develop it, and do what people did right here years ago! Reese has already made half a dozen trips, bringing small outfits down there in on it. When we get rolling, he'll stay down there and I'll be doing the flying back and forth—"

For the moment, Munrooney's murder and its train of troubles were forgotten, and Timuroff listened to plans common enough in Albright's day, but now too often red-taped out of existence before they started. Then he very gently brought the conversation back to the here and now, asking whether Ledenthal wanted to return with him to get the swords.

"Hell, you don't think I'm going to *leave* them with you?" Ledenthal roared so loudly that the waiter almost dropped his tray. "No, sir! I'll be too busy to come down again, and there's that sale of Kalloch's Wednesday afternoon—you've heard about it, haven't you?"

"Not yet," said Timuroff.

"The greedy bastard bought Gottschalk's whole collection, and he's giving all his dearest friends first crack at it. I won't dare miss it because Gottschalk did have a couple of good blades."

Timuroff laughed. "So Kalloch's doing it again! He'll peddle off the cream, then try to unload the rest on me. He never learns. They're always treasures from some great estate. They just don't happen to fit into his collection, but *I* can make a fortune out of them. I always tell him no, I knew the man who owned them. Then he gets irritated and goes away. Well, you can count on getting potent drinks before the bargaining starts, so be careful."

After Ledenthal had picked up his purchases and gone his way, Timuroff tried to settle down to his correspondence. But now the albatross around his neck refused to be denied. "Albatross," he said aloud, "let us take counsel with ourselves."

Let us assume, he thought, *that Amos is right about Hemmet and Miranda. Where do we stand? Obviously, they've been aware of the phantom ever since the murders, but they don't know who he is, or at least aren't sure, and they can't know about his new activities. Next, whether or not they know that Heck and Penny Anne are staying with us, they know that Pete and I are on his side, and that we'll do everything we can to keep him and Hanson from being railroaded. For the moment, because of their power position, they seem invulnerable, but they're under pressure— the upcoming election, the possible activities of people like myself, the phantom. No matter how desperate their urgency may seem, they can't afford unnecessary risks. But they can't afford not to act if the necessity arises. Or to slow down. And where does that leave us?* He paused. *We're much more vulnerable. Heck and Hanson are already being attacked. Pete's job leaves him wide open, but while they'd probably neutralize him legally, they'd have a harder time defusing me. So my own vulnerability may actually be greater. Liselotte, Olivia, Penny Anne? No, that's the kind of stuff they can't afford. The phantom—he's something else again.*

It seemed to hang together nicely. The question of who the phantom was he put aside. There were too many possibilities. Even Judson Hemmet might be a candidate—who knew what his relations with Miranda really were?

All right, where do we go from here? he asked himself; and the immediate answer was a simple one. He, Timuroff, would have to keep on sticking his nose into other people's business—but Pete would have to stay as far out of the case as possible, at least until some sort of break made it worthwhile for him to take the risk. *I wonder if I can persuade him to,* he thought. *It's all speculation up to this point, but the point does seem to be pointing somewhere. Might as well follow it.*

The phone rang. He answered it. Would Mr. Timuroff speak to Mrs. Miranda Gardner's secretary? . . . Mr. Timuroff said that he would, and the secretary's voice came on, fluting delicately. Mrs. Gardner wanted to come down, but she was very, *very* busy—could she come immediately? It was about the pieces Mr. Timuroff had set aside for her the other day. Would fifteen minutes be too soon?

Timuroff said he'd be in, and hung up, wondering at the coincidence. Could someone have been tailing Amos Ledenthal? Even after the Kielty episode, that seemed unlikely. More probably, he was the one being watched, either officially or unofficially. He shrugged, and started Glinka's *A Life for the Czar* going on the record player.

By the time Miranda Gardner arrived, he was solemnly reading a Swiss auction catalogue. He put it face down on his desk, conspicuously, and bowed her in, marveling again at the contrast between her lovely legs and youthful figure, the taste and flair of her coiffure and everything she wore, her sculptured, carefully decorated face, and her hard, watchful, unrevealing eyes. This time her secretary was with her, a tall and willowy young man, full of sighs and posturings, and with a brand-new permanent of which he seemed extremely proud.

In Timuroff's office, she sat down, glancing at the bar; and he obligingly poured her Canadian on the rocks. "You've met Jeffie, haven't you?" she said. "Find yourself a seat, Jeffie, and tell Mr. Timuroff what you want to drink."

Jeffie obediently sat down, and asked if he could have a crème de menthe. Timuroff poured it, made himself a highball, smiled at them both, and proposed a toast. "To my customers," he said.

Miranda Gardner's thin, scarlet lips drew back very slightly from her teeth. She drank. "Mr. Timuroff," she said, "could you find Jeffie a book to look at while we're doing business? He's terrified of weapons." She patted Jeffie's thigh. "He says they make him feel all creepy-crawly." She laughed, a high and strangely hollow sound. "I can't imagine why."

Jeffie shuddered obligingly, and Timuroff found him a copiously illustrated volume on the religious art of southern Russia. Then, for almost half an hour, he showed Miranda Gardner knives and daggers. She bought the two he'd put away for her, and asked for more. As he brought them to her one by one, and as together they surveyed his cases, she became, if not friendly, at least so avid, so obviously excited, that he could detect in her none of the frozen antagonism of her previous visit. Very much to his surprise, where he had expected at least some attempt to influence or intimidate him, she made no reference whatsoever to the murders, or to his own role in the case. Instead, she discussed technicalities, of origin, of workmanship, and of the weapons' actual use.

Finally, standing beside him with a scissors-katar in one long, blood-rubied hand and her glass in the other, she said, "Your shop is wonderful, Mr. Timuroff. You choose your things so well. I'd really miss you if you went out of business."

Timuroff smiled at her again. "I've no intention of it, I assure you. I've prospered here, and built up a good stock."

Her fingers closed and opened, working the three blades of the scissors-katar so that the two outer ones opened with a dry, harsh, shearing sound to reveal the third. "The Indians were so imaginative," she said. "I'll have to buy this too." She looked around the room again. "Your inventory must be quite valuable," she commented. "Isn't there a high risk involved? I mean, burglary?"

"Well, actually the rarer and older your weapons are, the less chance you take. It's a lot harder for the average thief to get rid of a several-thousand-dollar sword or snaphaunce than a hundred-dollar shooting iron. But of course I have insurance, and good alarms, and my locks are the best ones I could buy—though that's just to delay anyone breaking in. You can't stop a real expert from picking them."

The scissors-katar fascinated her. Its blades opened, and closed again hungrily. "Unless you fill your locks with melted lead," she replied abstractedly. "But then you'd have a hard time getting in and out." And the katar's blades opened and closed again.

"So would my customers," laughed Timuroff, "and that would never do."

His expression did not change, but he thanked the powers that be that she was watching the katar and not, like an astute Hong Kong jade dealer, the pupils of his eyes. Amos's conjecture no longer was an albatross around his neck. Now he was certain it was right.

When she was through, Miranda Gardner had bought seven more items from him. Most were from India and the Near East, needle-pointed, curiously curved and blood-guttered, but there was also an enormously expensive seventeenth-century main gauche and an ancient Japanese kwaiken, or woman's dagger. She accepted a final drink, wrote him a check for all of them, ordered Jeffie to his feet, and, still smiling her artificial smile, bade him a brisk good-bye.

Locking his door again, he walked back slowly to his chair. The realization that she knew about the lead-filled lock had shocked him, but there was more than that. She had not threatened him. She had not probed for information. And had her mention of the melted lead *really* been accidental—or was she testing him? He decided that, under the circumstances, the chances were heavily against its being deliberate—but the doubt remained.

Then he sat down—and the idea hit him suddenly. Whatever else she was, Miranda Morphy Gardner was completely and coldly practical. Perhaps, for reasons best known to herself, she seriously expected that he'd go out of business. Perhaps she simply had decided to buy up what she wanted while he was still around.

The notion was, to say the least, disquieting. Timuroff thought about it, and about what could be done about it, and came to the conclusion that there was nothing he could do but wait—at least nothing overt. The next move must be theirs. But there were other things that he could do. If he could get Pete out of town, that would help—it would look as though he and Pete were giving up. And there were the lines of inquiry he had already opened.

He phoned Hector Grimwood at Kemble Street, learned that Evangeline was practically complete, and said, "Heck, while I think of it, there's something I've been going to ask you. You mentioned a lawyer called Jefferson, who represented Mrs. Albright. What happened to him?"

"He died quite a long time ago, right after Mrs. Albright did. In fact, the other members of his firm had to finish winding up her estate. The firm was Braidstone, James, and Jefferson, and—"

"Braidstone?" interrupted Timuroff.

"Yes, John H. Braidstone. He was the last of them to go, and of course that was after Baltesar and Hemmet and Munrooney had been taken in. Why? Is it important?"

"I don't know, Heck," Timuroff said, "but it's interesting. It'll take some looking into, and we can talk about it later on."

They exchanged pleasantries, and he hung up, feeling that a window had been opened, that light was being let in—into the problem, and into the dark chamber where Muriel Fawzi watched the iron door and its leaded lock.

Then he called Norman Edstrom, the Treasury agent, who immediately turned the conversation on to guns, suggested that they meet for lunch at noon next day, and asked Timuroff to pick him up near the new Federal Building.

There seemed to be nothing more for him to do, so he settled back to scan the morning paper, trying to divert his mind from its insistent speculations. The press, he found, was too preoccupied with Mayor Munrooney's nether nakedness to have any further interest in the mechanics of his demise. The headlines trumpeted Chief Otterson's flat denial of the report; the news stories quoted "reliable police department sources" affirming it; and a boxed editorial cried aloud that the mayor's reactionary enemies would stop at nothing to defame him, even in death. The columnists, of course, were best of all. One of them, after delivering a solemn threnody on the city's sad bereavement, suggested that Dr. Grimwood, while he was about it, could have ensured Lucrece's chastity simply by installing an adequately large cigar cutter in the proper place —thus preserving at least a large part of Errol Vasquez Munrooney for his constituents.

Timuroff found himself bemused. Absurdly, he had the sudden feeling that the modern world had passed him by, leaving him in a dead backwater where nothing happened or could be accomplished. After Miranda Gardner's revelation about the lock, and after a link had been established between the lawyer who had been in Albright's confidence and Judson Hemmet, he knew logically that it was an absurd way to feel—but he cherished it anyhow, telling himself that it would be a good line to take with Pete in order to get him out of town.

At three thirty, when Olivia rather shamefacedly returned from lunch, he tried it on her, but she was not impressed.

"Henhouse nostalgia!" she answered cruelly. "Some people expect life to be one uninterrupted succession of excitements."

"So Pete told you about that, did he?" Timuroff laughed.

"He did, and made me promise not to tell a soul. But I think you boys have very nasty playmates."

Quietly, she went to work; and presently Pete himself showed up, looking like the end of a dismal day. He had picked up one useful item of intelligence: part of Kielty's evidence consisted of the khanjar's missing sheath, allegedly discovered when he searched the Hansons' quarters; the rest of it consisted of a key.

"He says he found the key downstairs," Pete declared, "and that it had no tag or chain attached to it. He claims that it was missing from among those in Hanson's key holder."

"That's not how Pambid told it," said Timuroff.

"You're damn right it isn't. Hanson's own key was palmed when they were booking him—it must've been. Kielty's bollixing the evidence—as if we didn't know."

"How about gossip?"

"There's plenty, but my God! again it's all about Munrooney's *friends*. The federal boys are being awfully cagy, telling all they can without really saying anything. I didn't get to see your friend Norm Edstrom, but the rest of 'em kept changing the subject back to Hemmet and Miranda. It isn't what they say; it's how they *sound*—the narcotics guys especially. After listening to a few of them, I talked to our own people and to Burgoyne. The way I'd piece it all together as of now is that too many really big drug busts happen on her property—not property she owns personally, but places owned by her dummy companies. As for Hemmet—and most of this is from our own boys or from state—his involvement, like Munrooney's, has always been as some dirty-bird's attorney, but the word is he's sold his soul in Vegas, and that it's only dear Miranda who's kept the axe from falling. They're all wondering did Munrooney know about it. And does Baltesar?"

"Surely a little thing like that wouldn't spoil their beautiful relationship?" remarked Timuroff, saying nothing about what he himself had learned.

"Who knows? Anyhow, Hemmet's credit is still good, and he hasn't misappropriated any funds or anything like that, so it's no one's business but his own—*yet*. The same is true about his sex life, so we keep getting gossip instead of solid information. But there's plenty of it, and from some weird sources. They say he's taken to playing funny games."

"With whom?"

"Women, I guess is all, but the kind who're tabbed oddball even in the Tenderloin. He's quiet about it, but it's been leaking out. Maybe it's female wrestlers rubbed with olive oil."

"At this point," Olivia said disgustedly, "I'd believe anything, even a windup sheep."

"Dr. Grimwood is too much of a gentleman," Pete informed her, "even to consider making one."

"That business of the scabbard and the key is interesting," commented Timuroff. "What else turned up?"

"Well, Burgoyne remembered that Leda Minden thing, though he wasn't in on it himself. They traced her through fingerprints—no previous record, but she'd held some sort of federal job a year or two. She was from Pennsylvania someplace, and her real name was Schelfield—all very respectable and well-to-do, he said; they sent the money to cremate her, but without a message. He thought maybe it was Maxine Schelfield, but he wasn't sure. He'll look it up and let me know. After that—" Pete accepted the drink Timuroff offered him. "After that, something happened that really shook me up. I'd called Burgoyne on Jake Harrell's phone—which I guess was stupid—and then I went on to the lab to chew the fat. I'm not there five minutes before there's a call from Chiefy's office, and Inspector Cominazzo's wanted there right away. So I trot up, and cool my heels outside for half an hour before they let me in. Chiefy has on his God-the-Father-punishes-be-cause-he-loves-you look, and he lays the situation on the line. I keep my nose out of the Munrooney case or get suspended and sent up before the board for insubordination."

"What did you say to him?" asked Timuroff.

"Not what I wanted to. I almost did, but I figured just in time that that way I'd give him exactly what he wanted. So I 'yes, sirred' him from hell to breakfast, until he gave me another sales pitch on Disneyland and his permission to get lost."

"Well, at least we keep on eating for a while," Olivia said.

"We would anyway, sweetheart—my wife works. But this way at least we keep on snooping."

Timuroff shook his head. "You can't afford to, Pete—at least not unless things change. Anyway, after this, some of your sources are going to dry up immediately. Even close friends of yours and enemies of Kielty's are going to have to move with care. Chiefy and his friends can cut your throat from ear to ear, and theirs too."

They looked at each other somberly. "Let's have a drink," suggested Timuroff. "You need another one. I had a feeling earlier that somehow events were going to pass us by, for a time at least. Olivia described it as 'henhouse nostalgia' and hinted that I was missing the excitements of the Stitchgrove barnyard and the Great New Age, but somehow I don't think so. I think we really may have reached one of those points where it's just no use pushing things. I'm going to make what I think's a pretty good suggestion—you know, rash youth being wisely counseled by prudent age. If I were you, I'd do exactly what Chiefy told you to—take off for Southern California. You won't have to stay more than a few days—just long enough to send Wifey her pretty little postcards and lull him into perhaps thinking you've given up. You two can fly down and rent a car. I'll take your messages and keep in touch by phone. If things break, you can always get back here in an hour or two."

"What you mean," Pete grumbled, "is that you want to catch that phantom all by yourself—in case he's carrying a rare gun."

"Now, don't be cynical," said Timuroff. "Think it over—the last place you ought to turn up for a while is Grimwood's."

"Tim, can you spare me?" put in Olivia eagerly. "Pete and I haven't been away together for a year."

Timuroff smiled at her. "I'll arrange with Heck to lend me Muriel Fawzi. Even if she can't learn to type, she can at least do a belly dance for customers."

Olivia giggled. "Just wait till I tell Mr. Karazoglu and Mr. Asterisk. The three of you are going to have a ball."

Suddenly the air had cleared. Though Pete was looking at Timuroff suspiciously, even he was more cheerful. "Tim, you wouldn't be trying to get me out of here so you can pull something too illegal for a homicide inspector to get in on?"

"Whatever gave you that idea?"

"Long association," said Pete.

There was a silence, and he could see that Pete was more than tempted—for there are times to get out from under, even if only for a day or two, and this was clearly one of them. "Look, Pete, if you two are really taking off," he said, "why not have dinner with us? Emilia's serving something quite enormous, so that'll be no problem, and I believe Maestro Mancinelli's coming up to talk to Heck about his wild opera notion. We can forget our fleas and have fun, and you'll be off to a good start."

Pete gave in. He also gave Timuroff the home phone numbers of Jake Harrell and Inspector Stevens, and promised to call them up before he left, so that they could pass any really important news along. "I'll let 'em know in Sacramento too," he added, "and maybe I'd better call Burgoyne right away."

Olivia dialed the number for him, and he got Burgoyne immediately. Burgoyne was sorry; he'd been overloaded; he wouldn't have a chance to dig into the files until to-

morrow. Pete told him what his plans were, and to call
Timuroff when he had anything.

"There's one thing we might try before you leave," said
Timuroff. "Your Sergeant Wallton was around Munrooney all the time, and Munrooney probably didn't see
him any more than he saw the furniture. I gather, too, that
there's no love lost between him and Chiefy's crowd. He
easily could have overheard something important. Perhaps
he knows how matters really stood in that Munrooney-
Hemmet-Baltesar-Miranda combine. Why don't you try
asking him?"

Pete thought it over for a moment. "Probably he doesn't
know a thing, but it'll be worth the try. Let's see if he's in."

He found the number in his address book, and dialed it.
"Hello? . . . Hi, there, Natalie. This is Pete Cominazzo. Is
the big guy home? . . . Yeah, I sure do. Can you put him
on the horn? . . . Thank you, ma'am."

A few seconds, and Dennis Wallton was on the phone.
They exchanged greetings and inquiries, talked bitterly
and briefly about what was happening, and then Pete said,
"Denny, officially I'm out of this. Chiefy slapped me with
three weeks' leave and told me to get lost. Olivia and I are
taking off for Disneyland. . . . You heard about it? Okay,
then there's no need to explain. I think Kielty's way off
the beam, but Chiefy won't even let me tell him why. You
were around Munrooney and his friends a lot—you know,
Hemmet and Baltesar and all that crowd. I thought maybe
you'd heard some juicy gossip that'd throw a different light
on some of this. . . . No? Well, I just thought I'd have one
try before I ran out on the deal. . . . *How's* that?" Timuroff
could tell that Pete was trying hard not to sound surprised.
"Denny, thanks for reminding me. I haven't even been out
to the range for two, three months, and with what's been
going on chances are I would've clean forgot it. . . . Sure,
you can leave it for me with Mr. Timuroff, where Olivia
works. Sure, when you can, in a day or two."

They spoke for another minute about wives and families;
then Pete hung up.

"Denny didn't know a thing," he said. "He's never heard
them say a word, except maybe on the weather. But he
wants to give me back my target Smith & Wesson. He'll
leave it for me here."

"Sensational!" remarked Timuroff sarcastically.

"It could be paydirt!" Pete grinned. "I've never owned

a target Smith & Wesson, and I've never lent Denny a gun of any kind. He must have something really hot for us."

From that point on, and throughout the evening, everything was euphoric. It was, thought Timuroff, like those sweet, cool oases of hours and days in time of war, when the reality seems mercifully unreal and the brief escape becomes the only true reality. After the party, when he and Liselotte were once again in bed, he was able to persuade her and himself that, for the moment anyhow, nothing more could happen. But he awoke at three, puzzling over what motivated people like Hemmet and Miranda Gardner, and who the phantom was, and what course of action he should follow. He was awake for half an hour, and before he went to sleep again, he had decided to talk the whole thing over with Bill Traeger in the morning.

After breakfast, he drove Hector Grimwood out to Evangeline, and, over a cup of Mrs. Hanson's coffee, briefed Traeger on what had taken place, omitting none of it. "I've told neither Heck nor Pete about Miranda and the lock," he said. "It might upset Heck to the point where he'd upset the applecart, and Pete's much too vulnerable to stay involved at this stage of the game."

"Don't worry," Traeger assured him, "I won't say a word. You know, the whole thing makes a crazy sort of sense, their being the kind of characters they are. Getting Pete out of town was sharp. It looks like maybe they're running scared, which could account for Chiefy's pushing him around. People have been awfully busy-busy here around the house—old panel truck parked where it hadn't ought to be, and stuff like that. But Hemmet and Miranda being behind it all—well, it makes you wonder just who the phantom is, and why."

"There's been no sign of him?"

"None at all. He could be anyone—even Lawyer Hemmet."

"I thought of that," Timuroff said, "but it's unlikely. I only hope he won't turn out to be a friend."

"Well, I guess it'll be up to us to catch the guy."

Timuroff smiled wryly. "It may be mostly up to you. Anyhow, I hope we get him before the jaws close down on Heck and Hanson."

"We'll try," Traeger promised him.

Timuroff said good-bye to him, and drove down to his shop. There he checked the answering service and found a message from Burgoyne, who had been wrong about the dead girl's name. Instead of Maxine Schelfield, it had been Marion Schofield. They hadn't gone too deeply into it because she was a known addict—maybe the federal people had—but call him anytime if he could help.

Timuroff made a note of it, and settled down to his ordinary routine. He missed Olivia. His mail was neither stacked nor sorted; the envelopes weren't neatly opened; he had to rummage in the files himself; and he was reminded more than once that his typing was by no means as neat as hers. It was with considerable relief that he kept his noon appointment with Norman Edstrom.

It was a friendly meeting, but unproductive from the outset. There was some discussion of the Munrooney case; and Hemmet and Miranda Gardner kept entering the picture, by way of guarded references and questions asked which had to be more than just coincidental. But he learned nothing new. While Edstrom ate his hearty lunch, he nibbled a crab sandwich and listened, saying very little. The conversation turned again to guns; they drove back to the shop; half-heartedly he made a half-cash, half-trade deal for a flintlock pistol Edstrom wanted; they drove once more to the Federal Building. Finally, at the curb, he remembered the question he had intended to ask from the beginning. "Did you ever hear of a Marion Schofield?" he asked.

"That Berkeley case? Heroin. Dead of an overdose, and self-administered. Isn't that sort of a long way from Lover Boy Munrooney and Lucrece?"

"Perhaps," said Timuroff. "Perhaps not. Do you know anything about the girl?"

Edstrom looked at him a little strangely. "No. Do you think I should?"

"It might be an idea."

Edstrom opened the car door. "I'll look into it," he said. "If anything turns up, and if I can, I'll let you know." He stepped out onto the sidewalk. "By the way, her name wasn't Marion. Berkeley had that wrong. It was Marianne —you know, as in *Vive la France!*"

For a few seconds, until he remembered that he was in a red zone, Timuroff sat there. He was disturbed. Marianne Denham had left Reese Guthrie for some sort of fling with Judson Hemmet, and Hemmet had abandoned her in turn. Marianne Schofield had died miserably in Berkeley of an overdose of heroin. The wild idea came to him that perhaps a curse had fallen on girls named Marianne—and that was followed by the thought that possibly the two Mariannes were one. He drove back to the shop again and called Amos Ledenthal.

Jessica answered, and told him that Amos was busy at his lawyer's. They liked each other, and for a few minutes there was only pleasant general conversation, Jessica pretending to be angry at her husband for Kielty's involuntary swimming lesson, but still obviously pleased with him for it. Then Timuroff asked her his questions. Did she remember if that girl friend of Reese Guthrie's had been married previously? One of his customers thought he'd known her. Jessica wasn't sure; Marianne hadn't often talked about herself. She came from somewhere back east, but she'd graduated from a Southern California college—was it USC?

Could Jessica recall anything at all?

"Well, just what she looked like," said Jessica, "because she really was a lovely little thing. Oh, yes—she had a silver cigarette case she was very proud of. It was really beautiful, with a cabochon sapphire catch, and her monogram all over it in gold, MSD all intertwined."

Timuroff thanked her and rang off. He phoned Burgoyne and asked him if he knew the name of Marianne Schofield's hometown. Burgoyne did—it was Wallis Heights, Pennsylvania. Timuroff dialed the area code plus 555-1212 for information. The town had two Schofields listed and one Denham, Wilbur F., Sr. He wrote the data down, and called the Denham number, but no one answered, and he decided not to try again until the rates went down at five o'clock.

He was perturbed; he didn't like the way things were pointing, and there seemed to be nothing useful he could do, so he went out again to Kemble Street.

Though Hector Grimwood had gone back to working on Evangeline, he too was thoroughly disturbed. Coulter had been unable to get Hanson out on bail, partly because the crime was murder, and partly because Hanson had jumped bail once before. Then Eisenstein and Primrose, his senior partners, had come in to help, and finally bail had been set—but at five hundred thousand dollars. Hem-

met had urged the doctor to underwrite it, but his own
lawyers said he shouldn't. If Hanson disappeared, for whatever reason, it would be financially disastrous. Hanson had
said, "Hell, no! I been in brigs before, and I can stay in
this one a few days." But the doctor was still torn between
his sense of duty and good sense.

Besides, several friends had called to tell him that
Kielty, with a detective and a police stenographer, had
come to visit them. He had arrived without warning, and
had bombarded them with questions, all aimed at one
point: whether Dr. Grimwood, privately or publicly, had
ever threatened the late Errol Vasquez Munrooney's life
or person. And had they, at Dr. Grimwood's house, ever
encountered a Mrs. Twinkle Mossmaker, described as a
teaching assistant in sociobionomics at Pinole State College?

"I don't believe it," said Timuroff. "No human being
could be named Twinkle Mossmaker."

"She is," Hector Grimwood assured him. "I remember
her—a long blonde girl with a long nose, long hair, an
almost nonexistent skirt, and a great many scarlet toenails,
drinking too much and arguing with people. Her friends
call her Twinkie. She must be saying dreadful things about
me."

Timuroff, who guessed that she was one of Kielty's
prime witnesses, agreed but did not say so. He asked what
else had happened, and learned that Mario Baltesar had
phoned. Baltesar was embarrassed—he knew that Heck
was not involved in Errol's murder, in spite of what was
being said, but there was his position, now that he was
mayor. And his wife was Errol's sister, after all. And he
was sure there'd be no misunderstanding, would there?
Dr. Grimwood, a little cynically, had promised him that
there would not.

The picture was definitely unpromising, and Timuroff
was relieved, when he got home, to learn that Liselotte had
again invited operatic dinner guests, friends of the maestro's more concerned with the dramatic possibilities of
Lucrece and Muriel Fawzi and Evangeline than with the
slaying of any mere politician. He made his mind up that,
come what might, he would enjoy the evening.

Pete phoned shortly before supper to say that Olivia had
prepared several postcards which an aunt of his would
mail from Disneyland, while they themselves went on to
San Diego, mostly to see the zoo. He sounded cheerful

and relaxed, and Timuroff did not trouble him with new developments. Then, from the phone in his study, he called the Pennsylvania number once again. It rang and rang, and finally an old man answered.

"Is this the Marianne Denham residence?"

There was a long silence before the answer came, its words spaced far apart, as though produced only with great effort.

"Who . . . is . . . speaking?"

"I knew her when she was working for the government," said Timuroff.

He waited. Then the voice said, "Did you know my boy?"

"No, sir," answered Timuroff.

"She married him." The old man seemed almost to be talking in his sleep. "It only lasted a few months. She is dead now. Something happened to her, and she died. Her mother lives here. Do you want her number?"

Timuroff said that he did not, and thank you, and he was sorry to have troubled him.

"It was a terrible thing," the old voice said. "Good-bye."

Momentarily, a Muscovite depression threatened Timuroff, and he used all his Scots resilience to defy it. If the signs were not pointing where they should, one couldn't force them to. He went back to the party grimly determined not to worry.

Next morning, having enjoyed the evening after all, he ran Hector Grimwood out as usual, and came back to the shop in a fine seventeenth-century mood, looking forward to his luncheon with Clayton Faraday. The only call had been from Mr. Millweed, and he ignored it. Then, at about eleven, Faraday phoned apologetically to take a raincheck until next day—he was being consulted in some urgent matter.

Timuroff was disappointed, and said so. "I'd really hoped we'd have a chance to talk, Clayton. This Munrooney business has taken some strange turns—some of them almost unbelievable."

"Tim," the judge sighed, "—*nothing* is unbelievable, not anymore. Ten years ago, who'd have believed Watergate? Or Chappaquiddick? That's why I'm genuinely concerned about your being involved in this. But we can talk about it all tomorrow."

Timuroff, again depressed, made the best of it by surprising Liselotte and Penny Anne, and taking them to lunch at the Jade Pavilion. Afterward, he forced himself to concentrate on his neglected correspondence.

He was interrupted only twice.

At around three o'clock, the answering service told him a Mr. Wallton wanted to talk to him, a Mr. Dennis Wallton. Timuroff placed him just in time, and had her put him on.

"Mr. Timuroff?" a deep voice said.

"You're Sergeant Wallton, aren't you? Pete's friend?"

"I'm a friend of Pete's all right, but I'm not sergeant anymore. I turned my badge in yesterday, and I'm going to be working out of town for the state, a sort of temporary deal starting right away. I've got this target gun Pete lent me, a Smith & Wesson. I guess he told you all about it. I figure it'd be safer left with you while I'm gone, if that's okay. Any chance we can get together sometime tomorrow afternoon?"

"Of course," said Timuroff. "About when?"

"Four or four thirty would be best for me. I'll bring it by."

"Fine," Timuroff told him. "I'll put it in my safe."

He hung up slowly, wondering what Wallton really had.

The second interruption came at half-past four, when he was tidying up before taking off to pick up Hector Grimwood. This time, the answering service put the call through directly, as they had been instructed to.

"Jake Harrell here, Tim. Listen closely. I'm calling from a booth and I've got to make it fast so Kielty won't catch on. I'm on my way back to the station from Kalloch's place—"

"You mean *Wade* Kalloch?" Timuroff broke in.

"Yeah, Wade Kalloch. You heard about his selling all those guns and swords and stuff?"

"What happened?" rapped Timuroff.

There was an instant's pause.

"Tim, Judson Hemmet killed Amos Ledenthal."

"What?"

"I'll give it to you as quickly as I can. It looks like self-defense. Ledenthal went out into the patio with one of these two-handed Jap swords, to get a better look at it, he said. Hemmet went out a minute later, with Miranda Gardner. He had been looking at a rapier, and he took it with him. He said something as a joke to Ledenthal, and Ledenthal turned on him without warning, called him a dirty bastard, and aimed a cut right for his skull. Hemmet says he parried it, and lunged out automatically to protect himself. Anyhow, he got Ledenthal right through the heart."

"He *parried* it?"

"That's what they say, both Hemmet and the Gardner woman. He 'parried it in six' was what he said, whatever that means. I've got it written down, and it's all on tape."

"Damn him." Rage welled in Timuroff. *"May his soul burn in hell!"* Then, before Jake could speak, he asked, "Were there any witnesses?"

"Well, yes and no. Only Mrs. Gardner saw it, really. The rest either weren't looking or couldn't see enough. Kalloch's place is all glass onto the patio, but he's got great big plants around the doors, and about all anybody saw was Ledenthal's head and the flash of that big sword. They heard him yell, '*You dirty bastard!*' and saw the flash, and then Miranda started screaming her fool head off. And that was that. Look, I'll call you later, when I get a chance. I've got to go."

For several minutes, Timuroff simply sat there, eyes narrowed, nostrils slightly flared, fingering the tight white scar across his cheek.

In his mind, the scattered pieces came together, each in its place, each fitting neatly and inevitably. He had already been quite certain about Hemmet and Miranda Gardner. Now he *knew*.

He knew that they had had Munrooney murdered. He knew that Hemmet had murdered Amos Ledenthal. He knew who had been the Phantom of the Opera, and who had killed van Zaam.

But there were still two things he did not know—why Munrooney had been murdered, and how to prove his case against the murderers.

XII

The Weight of the Evidence

The death of Ledenthal was the keystone. From it, all else derived; on it, all else now depended. Where there were pieces missing, Timuroff's mind interpolated them, bridging the gaps logically. Carefully, he planned what he would have to do. Then, taking a sheet of Olivia's best notepaper, he wrote on it in his bold, clear hand:

> If the abductor of Miss Muriel Fawzi will meet the writer of this message at nine this evening in the apartment where he left her, he will be given information about the murder of Amos Ledenthal, and will find it otherwise to his advantage.
>
> The meeting, and anything which may transpire during the course of it, will of course remain completely confidential.
>
> Sincerely,
A. A. Timuroff

It pleased him, reminding him of notices in the Agony Column of the *Times* in Sherlock Holmes's day. He folded it, sealed the envelope, addressed it, and put it in the inside pocket of his coat. Then he phoned the Ledenthals' residence.

Jessica's sister answered. A married daughter was driving up from Redwood City; Reese Guthrie had been over, very much upset, and had gone off again after the doctor came; Jessica was pretty much in shock, but there was a nurse there now.

Timuroff asked her to tell Jessica that he had called, and, trying to control his voice, said all the futile words required on such occasions.

After that, he took off for Kemble Street. He had expected days or weeks of apprehensive waiting, of inaction, of trying to fit inadequate data into a coherent pattern. Now the rapier that killed Amos had cut that Gordian knot, and—because he is primarily a man of action—his doubts, frustrations, and annoyances had vanished. Cold anger drove him—cold anger and hot anticipation.

He found Hector Grimwood still busy with Evangeline —now fully clothed and seated in an antique high-backed chair appropriate to her time and place in history. He murmured his appreciation, and sat down on a corner of the workbench.

"Heck," he said gently, "there's bad news about Amos Ledenthal. You'd better sit down while I tell you."

The doctor saw the expression on his face; he put down the fine jeweler's pliers he was holding; he fumbled for a chair.

Timuroff told him what had happened. He answered his shocked questions. "I'm absolutely certain, Heck," he said, "that Hemmet didn't lunge in self-defense. Amos was murdered just as surely as Munrooney was—by one of Munrooney's murderers. He was notorious for his violent temper, and he was under indictment for assault—the timing of the incident and Kielty's provocation show it was rigged deliberately to pave the way, if not for what occurred, then for something like it."

"But, Tim! My God, why would Hemmet want to kill Munrooney? They were partners—they were in everything together!"

"That's what I don't know. But a third murder has just been committed—and I can prove it. Take my word for that. And a calculated attempt is being made to falsify evidence and pin the first two killings on you and Hanson. We can't waste any time. We're going to have to break the case wide open—in self-defense."

"H-how do you propose—?"

"I intend to have a talk with our Phantom of the Opera. I have the invitation in my pocket. If you approve, I'll meet him here tonight at nine o'clock, down in the room where Muriel Fawzi is."

"Who is he?" Hector Grimwood asked.

"Someone we both know. I'd rather keep his name to myself until I've talked to him. I just *might* be wrong."

"Can you be sure he'll come?"

"My invitation's worded so that I don't think he can refuse. Heck, I'm asking you to buy a pig in a poke, I know, but if anything goes wrong we'll be no worse off than we are already."

"We may not be, Tim, but what about *you?* If he really is the phantom, he killed van Zaam. You've done enough for me already. I don't want you running that kind of risk in my behalf."

"It won't be just in your behalf. I was fond of Amos, and Jessica is still my friend. Besides, I really doubt if I'll be in danger; I think I know my man."

Hector Grimwood closed his eyes; and Timuroff saw that now his years hung heavily upon him. Then abruptly the eyes flashed again with their accustomed fire. "I'll buy your pig, Tim," he declared, rising to his feet. "Amos was my friend too. How can I help?"

"You can call Liselotte," said Timuroff, "and tell her you're having dinner with me. We can take Traeger with us, and I can tell him all he needs to know. Then we'll come back here and he can disconnect the mikes downstairs; I've promised that our talk will be completely confidential." His expression hardened. "But the bugs at the alley entrance and in the passage must not be disconnected, and we ought to have an extra man or two around. If anything goes badly wrong, I don't want our phantom to get away with it."

"We don't have to go out to dinner unless you want to. Mrs. Hanson tells me a roast is in the oven—she enjoys feeding Traeger and his men—so there'll be plenty for the lot of us."

"Then everything's arranged," said Timuroff. "Now all I have to do is phone a messenger and send the invitation to our guest."

"There's one thing more." Dr. Grimwood smiled. "When this is over, you can explain it all to Penny and get me off the hook."

They went upstairs. The messenger was called, and came, and was instructed to report success or failure instantly. Forty-five minutes later, while they were at table, he phoned to say the invitation was delivered.

At twenty minutes to nine, they went downstairs, and Traeger, telling Timuroff politely that he was out of his cotton-picking mind, set about disconnecting microphones. Two chairs were brought down from the poker parlor through the armoire and placed, one three feet to Muriel Fawzi's left, the other to her right.

At ten minutes to the hour, Hector Grimwood asked hesitantly, "What shall we do now?"

Timuroff sat down on the chair to Miss Fawzi's left. Out of his pocket he took the latest Christie's catalogue. "Just make sure all the doors are closed," he said, "and wait for me upstairs."

They left, and silence fell—that subterranean silence, broken only by dry crepitations and slow creaks, which live peculiarly under large old houses.

In the yellow light, he forced himself to concentrate on an exquisite fowling piece by Lebeda of Prague, presented to a princeling by his emperor, and by the princeling to a terribly rich American whose sister he had hoped to marry for her money.

When he heard the footsteps, he did not look up.

They were not cautious footsteps. They did not tiptoe. They did not hesitate. They approached firmly, steadily.

Timuroff did nothing until they broke their cadence a dozen feet away and stopped.

Then he closed the catalogue, and laid it in his lap, and looked around. "Good evening, Reese," he said.

Reese Guthrie stood looking down at him, jaw muscles knotted, his eyes deep bowls of shadow in his bloodless face.

"You knew?" he said.

"I wasn't sure," replied Timuroff, "not until today—until Judson Hemmet murdered Amos." He pointed at the empty chair, and suddenly command rang in his voice. "Sit down," he said, almost contemptuously. "And you won't need that pistol in your pocket. We're going to have to trust each other, you and I."

Slowly, Guthrie took the chair. "If I'd not trusted you, I'd not have come." His voice betrayed his turmoil, and as he spoke the accent of his native South became more marked. "I—I figured if Amos trusted you, well, I could too."

"You were fond of him?"

"He was the closest to an uncle I ever had. He—he used to take me fishing as a kid, and it was he taught me how to ride, and after Dad's death—" He broke off. "You know the rest of it. Tell me, Mr. Timuroff, what's all this about Hemmet *murdering* him? The police are pretty sure it was self-defense."

Timuroff's fingers strayed across his scar. "Hemmet murdered him. I know what weapons were involved. Gottschalk had only two Japanese katana, but both were excellent. One was by Yasutsugu, who was renowned for his blades' cutting qualities, and that was probably the one that Amos took outside. Hemmet told the police that Amos cut at him two-handed, at his head, and that he parried it in six —a standard parry for that sort of cut in sabre fencing. But I assure you, on the basis not only of expert knowledge"—he smiled thinly—"but of direct experience, that if Hemmet had parried such a cut made with such a sword, he'd have been lucky to have survived at all. The Yasutsugu would have sheared through the blade of any rapier ever made, and through the guard, and through the hand that held it—and it might not have stopped even then. Therefore it was deliberate murder. The flash of steel the witnesses describe came as the blade fell *after* Amos was run through."

"But *why?* Wh-why did he kill him?"

"Because he thought *Amos* had taken the Munrooney murder weapon and put the khanjar in its place. Because he thought *Amos* was ruining his and Miranda's well-laid plans. He may have thought so because Amos was so overtly hostile to him. He blamed it all on Amos—not on you."

For a moment, Reese Guthrie raised his eyes and looked at him. Then he bent his head, covered his face with his two hands, and wept. He wept without a sound, betrayed only by the shaking of his shoulders. Timuroff watched him silently, and Muriel Fawzi, on her cushion, smiled her small, pretty smile.

Presently, he took his hands away and raised his head. "If I could just have—have *guessed,*" he said.

"That it would end this way, with Amos dead?"

Guthrie closed his eyes and did not answer him.

"What did you expect?" demanded Timuroff. "What were you trying to accomplish?"

"It was after Marianne dropped out of sight. You know about her? About Marianne?"

"I know."

"She disappeared. Somehow I knew she'd gone down the drain. After that, because I knew that Hemmet was responsible—in a minute, I'll tell you about that—I tried to figure out some way of wrecking him." He looked down at his lean powerful hands. "I could've killed him anytime, but then my life would've been finished too. I—I'd hoped that maybe I still could have a life to lead."

"Amos told me about your river plans."

"Yes, we got started on that almost right away. Meanwhile, I hired a detective agency to tail Hemmet. It wasn't long before they started running into things, mostly about the kind of life he leads, the cash he drops in Vegas, and his women. You knew he was a sadist, didn't you? Nothing as crude as torture, no whips or anything like that. He just likes to destroy his girls, that's all, and sleep with them while they're being destroyed. Or—or maybe he just picks the ones he feels are certain to destroy themselves." Guthrie shuddered. "Marianne started on the softer drugs, then turned to acid. Finally, it was heroin. And—and then he had her killed."

"Van Zaam," said Timuroff.

"How did you know?"

"He was seen leaving her apartment. And how did *you* find out? By bugging Hemmet's office?"

"Not his office, no. We learned that once a week at least he'd drive out to an old three-floor office building way out on Balboa, park out of sight, and meet Miranda Gardner. She has a first-floor storefront business there. It calls itself a kind of letter shop, Xeroxing, multigraphing, all that sort of stuff, and with a sour old battle-axe running it—but it's a fake. In back, she had a little office, with a few filing cases and a wall safe, and that's where she kept her really private records and did her private dirty work. At that point, I told the agency I didn't need them anymore, and brought a friend of mine in. He was with me in Vietnam, and now he's a deputy and criminalist in Santa Clara County, and a real genius when it comes to electronics. There was a vacant office on the second floor, not right above, but just one notch over and in back, close enough so he could get his bugs installed without a hitch. I rented it, had a false name painted on the door, and he set up a sound-actuated rig inside an old TV set, and we just left it running. It picked up everything they said downstairs. Believe me, it was interesting. Finally, we got the two of them planning to kill Munrooney."

"Motive?" Timuroff asked sharply.

"Because he ratted out on them, they said. I never did find out exactly how, but it was all tied in with Caldwell, Jolly and that Master Plan. Also, it sounded like he told them he was going to clamp down on their personal rackets. Both she and Hemmet are knee-deep in narcotics. Not directly—that can't be pinned on them. But she owns people—people who manufacture them, importers, wholesale pushers—or she owns the companies that own the buildings where they operate. And Hemmet represents all of them. She owns that police lieutenant, Kielty, and she's got mortgages on several other cops, the chief included. Most of it's through her loan sharks or her own contacts in the underworld."

"How much of all this did Munrooney know?"

"Most of it, but he pretended not to. Baltesar—they used to laugh at him—never once guessed. Maybe he didn't dare."

To the dusty porcelain socket of the light bulb, a small brown spider had attached her geometric web. Now, quickened by the unaccustomed warmth, she was traversing it as though on an inspection tour. Timuroff regarded her admiringly, was reminded that the black widow spins the most mysteriously untidy webs of all, and realized that he had never heard what had become of Mr. Gardner.

"Women's Lib is wonderful," he commented. "Miranda sounds like a one-woman Mafia."

"She *is*. The plan to kill Munrooney was all hers—the plan, the place, all but the weapon and the date. At first, Hemmet was scared, but she pointed out that Grimwood and his man were perfect pigeons—and that they'd have a damn good chance to get this house and find whatever lies beyond that door."

"She knew about this?"

"Hemmet told her. I guess you know how he found out."

"Braidstone?" said Timuroff.

"Right. After Braidstone died, Hemmet found secret instructions left by old man Albright 'to be opened only so many years after my death.' "

"And he kept them secret?"

"Yes—except from Miranda. Anyhow, they took awhile to decide about Munrooney, maybe hoping he'd change his mind. But finally it was set—all except who'd do the actual job. Hemmet put it up to her, and she came back at him immediately. I can remember every word—I've listened to the tape too many times. 'Don't be a fool, Jud,' she told him. 'That man Hanno found to dust the girl off for you— that Denham girl—he's the man we want.'"

Guthrie's mouth twisted; for a moment, his hands fought each other on his lap. "Th-that was the first I really *knew* that she had died," he said. "The rest I found out later on. About the time she'd built up to a two-hundred-dollar habit—two hundred every day, that is—she started threatening Hemmet. And she'd picked up enough so that they had to silence her. I don't know how van Zaam got to her, but it was he who gave the overdose." He paused. "That was when I knew I'd have to take a hand."

"I see your point," said Timuroff.

"At first I thought of tipping off Munrooney, then I decided what the hell! He was the kind who makes it possible for people like Hemmet and Miranda—yes, and van Zaam—to survive and prosper. And suppose anybody had believed me? I'd have been trapped into investigations, trials, suits, and countersuits. I knew I could catch the next flight to Rio anytime I wanted to. I was already spending almost every other week in South America, getting the groundwork laid, but between trips I always made Grimwood's poker games. When I found out he had a master key and didn't even know it, I borrowed it one night to give some friends the guided tour, took an impression, and had a copy made. Then a few times I came in the alley door to learn my way around.

"They'd planned, when Grimwood gave the party, to have almost no one there who'd distract attention from Hanson and the doctor—and Hemmet was supposed to engineer it through Baltesar. But when Penny Anne told Jessica about it, I stepped quietly in. I made damn sure that almost everyone tied up with Caldwell, Jolly would be there, and all the arms collectors I could think of. And then there was the weapon. Hemmet had planned to use a boning knife from Grimwood's kitchen. He was going to hide it in the passage for van Zaam. I wanted something a lot more conspicuous, so I got hold of that fancy dagger Voukos had."

"At his ceremonial viewing, I suppose?"

"Naturally. Amos invited me along, after I'd hinted I'd like to come. I didn't think I'd get away with it, but I brought a bowie knife—not one of those enormous ones, but heavy enough to be taken for the dagger in the case. If Voukos hadn't served so many drinks, I'd never had the chance, but toward the end he crossed the room to show off a silver chalice or something of the sort, and they all drifted over with him—all but me. It didn't take a second. Voukos still had to put the case away, and I got ready to slip the dagger down between the cushions of the couch in case he opened it. But he came back, higher than a kite and talking a Greek streak and picked the case up, and kissed it, and locked it in his safe."

Timuroff nodded.

"I guess you've figured out the rest of it," Guthrie went on, a thin thread of despair still in his voice. "Hemmet's getting Munrooney up to Lucrece's room was simple. He kidded him with the spread-her-legs-apart bit, started upstairs with him, then happened to remember something he had to do—he'd follow in a minute. Munrooney went on ahead, and by that time van Zaam was ready in the passage. Hemmet and Miranda had it all worked out. As for me, I'd come in through the back door, taken the boning knife, and left the dagger in its place. I waited for van Zaam to use it, which he did, and when he came back down I killed him in the passageway—I've been well trained —and hung him up in the armoire. I took a business card out of his billfold, rumpled it up, and put it where you found it, and I took the key Hemmet had given him—he wasn't told about the iron door and all that. It had a chain with a St. Christopher medallion, the kind they peddle everyplace. I took a chance of being seen and chucked it out where somebody'd be sure to find it."

"Kielty found it. He took the chain and medal off, probably because he was afraid it might be traced to Hemmet or just to make it easier to pin on Hanson. And after that you went upstairs again and peeled the mayor's pants off?"

"Right. I wanted to stir up all the fuss I could, in the news especially. That's why I chose the weapon—that and so they'd bring you in. Amos always told me that once you get your teeth into a problem you don't give up until you have it solved."

"I try not to," said Timuroff, acknowledging the compliment. "I suppose that's also why you used the Turkish bowstring?"

Guthrie nodded. "I set out with two aims—to foul their plans up so they'd hang themselves, and to make sure Grimwood and Hanson weren't railroaded." Again his mouth twisted. "I've failed. Hemmet and Miranda are still riding high. Things look bad for Hanson and the doctor. My tapes are worthless because an officer obtained them for me; they're inadmissible as evidence. All I've accomplished is to get my best friend murdered."

Timuroff examined him. By now, he understood him well. He had known many men like Reese Guthrie. Some he had met only in the books they'd written. Some, like his Uncle Cedric, had been relatives. Others he had encountered in armies here and there—on horses, in tank turrets, flying aircraft. Others still had shown up in unexpected roles and places. Timuroff thought about them, and realized that, given the opportunity, every one of them—himself included—would have killed van Zaam.

"No, Reese," he said softly, "that's not all you have accomplished. Your tapes aren't any good *as evidence in court*—but they're not worthless. Their value's in their *information*—and information can be used to get hard evidence. You have them, don't you?"

"Yes."

"Can we assume that Hemmet and Miranda found out about them? At least about your bugs?"

"The day after they killed Munrooney, Hanno's boys turned the place upside down. I don't know what they found, but there was some equipment which might have been identified as Santa Clara County property; we aren't quite sure. Upstairs, we had to sneak the stuff out of the office in a hurry."

Timuroff thought about it. He said, "Reese, did Hemmet and Miranda say anything at all about what they'd do if they were really pushed?"

"Miranda talked about a rigged jail suicide, with a hearsay confession witnessed by a couple of Hanson's fellow prisoners. Hemmet argued that they couldn't sustain it in court, and then she pointed out that with it the media would convict Grimwood before he ever came to trial. They wanted Heck and Hanson indicted and arrested before election day, for the publicity. Of course, that was when they still expected to get Hanson for Munrooney's murder, not for the killing of van Zaam."

"They've done some clever jumping, considering the surprises you've arranged for them," commented Timuroff. "Perhaps we can arrange some more." He leaned forward. "From what you know of me, would you trust my judgment, Reese?"

"I . . . would," Guthrie answered slowly.

"Enough to gamble your whole future on it? Your freedom?"

"Yes."

"How many hours do your tapes run, all told?"

"Those between Hemmet and Miranda, or between her and people like that Hanno bunch? Twenty at least, maybe more. Also, we caught a lot of unimportant stuff, her talking to the old bat who runs the shop, or about more or less straight business deals. Why?"

"I'd like you to copy *all* of them without delay—even the unimportant ones. Do you have equipment?"

"I can rent it."

"Then I'd like you to take the copies out to Ledenthal's, and put them in a filing cabinet—I'm sure Amos had at least two or three. You can tell Jessica they're business records. When is he going to be buried, by the way?"

"Not buried, cremated. The service is on Saturday, at eleven in the morning."

"All right. Can you make sure that *no* one will be in the house? That there won't be anybody guarding it?"

"You sound as if you're setting up a burglary."

"Merely the opportunity for one. Hemmet'll have to carry through and try to find those tapes. Even if they can't be used in evidence, they're still deadly dangerous. Probably he'll have Hanno's boys do the job, and I want to make absolutely sure they succeed. Then he'll feel safe again, and that's just what we want."

"That makes sense," Guthrie said. "And then?"

"Think very carefully—did any of those tapes contain information which, if it could be used legally, would result in airtight federal charges against either or both of them? Or, more to the point, were there explicit references to concrete evidence which, seized with a legal warrant, would accomplish that?"

"I'm no lawyer, but I'm sure of it. On the narcotics end

alone there ought to be enough to send them up forever
and a day."

"And do the tapes tell where this evidence is kept?"

"She had most of it in her wall safe."

Timuroff frowned. "Yes, I suppose the past tense is appropriate. She must've cleared it out immediately. Do you
suppose that she's destroyed it?"

"She can't," Reese Guthrie told him. "Most of it's blackmail material against her zombies. It's her weaponry—her
life insurance."

"Then it must be somewhere, and Hemmet certainly will
know. Somehow, we'll have to jar the information out of
him."

"Just how do you propose to go about it?"

Timuroff looked judiciously at Guthrie, seated there; at
Muriel Fawzi, still smiling imperturbably; at the huge lead-
filled padlock and the iron door. He listened to the whis-
pering timbers of the house, and his fencer's mind engaged
the several problems confronting him. "I have one idea,"
he said. "I'm going to try to work it out. But the federal
people are already interested. If we can get them to listen
to your tapes, if we can show them that a search warrant
will *really* bring convicting evidence, if we can outweigh
Miranda's money and all their power and hidden influence,
then perhaps we'll get results. I can't imagine what else can
save Hanson, and perhaps Heck too, at this point."

"I can." Guthrie looked him squarely in the eye. "I can
confess."

"That," said Timuroff, "is what I'm trying to avoid. Your
confession would get Hanson off the hook, but it would
ruin our chances of clobbering Hemmet and Miranda, and
I'm not sure it'd clear Heck. If, through you, the federal
agencies get *legal* evidence that will convict everyone from
Miranda down, I doubt that they'll pursue you very eagerly.
But I don't see any need, at this point, to tell them who
you are. Tomorrow I'm having lunch with Judge Clayton
Faraday—you've heard of him, I'm sure. He's an old friend
of mine and Liselotte's. I'm going to ask a Treasury narcotics man to join us, and Pete Cominazzo too—I'll phone
him in San Diego when we've finished here. Besides that,
I'll have to fill Heck in on most of it, keeping your name
out of it for now. Reese, you have two choices. You can
take off for Rio immediately, and leave Hemmet and Mi-

randa riding high, or you can take a chance and play along."

"I'll take the chance," Reese Guthrie told him. "After the tapes are copied and—and taken out to Amos's place, what do I do?"

"Phone me at the shop around four tomorrow. I'll tell you what the situation is."

Simultaneously, they stood. Timuroff held out his hand. Guthrie took it hesitantly, as though the responsibility for his partner's death had deprived him of any right to do so.

"Good night, Reese," Timuroff said quietly. "You aren't to blame for Hemmet murdering Amos. Amos wouldn't have blamed you. Nor will Jessica."

"I wish I could believe that, sir," Guthrie answered. "But —but thank you anyhow. I'll call tomorrow."

He said good-night and turned away, and started slowly through the passage, his head bent.

Timuroff watched him for a moment. Then he let himself back into the house through the armoire. Using the phone in the poker parlor, he rang the library. Bill Traeger answered.

"All clear," Timuroff told him. "You can call in your man at the alley door."

"I have," said Traeger.

Timuroff's brows drew down. After an instant's pause, he said, "I'll be right up."

He took the elevator, opened the library door, and found Traeger at a side table on which he had just put a set of headphones.

"You have been listening." He made the statement in a voice abruptly very low and hard. "I told you I'd given him my word that everything between us would be confidential."

Traeger looked up at him and grinned. "It *is*," he said, "and it'll stay that way. Sure, I listened. Mr. Timuroff, it's my job to protect Dr. Grimwood and this house. I'd no more break my word to him than you would to Reese Guthrie. Fair enough?"

The anger drained out of Timuroff. "Sorry, Bill. I was looking at it only from my angle. Which bug did you leave alive?"

"The one under her bloomers," Traeger told him.

They both laughed, and Hector Grimwood, eager and excited, came back into the room. "Thank you for ringing,

Mr. Traeger. Tim, I hope all went well? I couldn't stand just waiting quietly here, so I attended to Evangeline. She's moved into her room. One of Mr. Traeger's men very kindly helped me to carry her, and Mrs. Hanson brought all her little things. She's really comfortable. And now, before you tell me what went on—I hope you've not been sworn to secrecy?—can we go right down to that dreadful room and rescue poor Muriel Fawzi?"

"I don't see why not. Coming with us, Bill?"

"You bet. I can't wait to disconnect that mike from Fuzzy Muriel."

They followed Miss Fawzi's anxious maker back to the iron door. They lifted her up gently, and she rewarded them with her accustomed smile, not even resenting the liberties Bill Traeger was compelled to take. They carried her in triumph to the elevator.

As they ascended, the doctor patted her affectionately. "You know," he said, "my girls are really getting famous. People are making up dirty limericks about them. I heard one just today:

> "They're guaranteed not to be fadeable,
>   Wearoutable, even abradable.
>   They never feel ill
>   And they don't need the Pill—
> But I still like mine biodegradable."

He chuckled. "To be quite frank," he told them, "so do I."

XIII

Dear Mayor Munrooney

Timuroff picked Pete up at the airport at ten fifteen next morning. Pete was alone, Olivia having decided to stay over one more day to do the zoo again, and he regarded Timuroff reproachfully.

"I told you so," he said. "You ran me off to Disneyland so you could have the fun of chasing down our phantom all by yourself!"

Timuroff, the night before, had spent a good half hour at bedtime soothing Liselotte, who was beginning to worry for his safety. Now he apologized to Pete with an almost convincing sincerity; and, between the airport and the city, told him everything except Guthrie's name. That, he explained, was a point of honor, but promised that in due time all would be revealed.

"Reese Guthrie," Pete said disgustedly. "Ledenthal's partner, and Hemmet did him dirt about a girl. Don't get upset—I'm not telling anybody."

Timuroff looked a little hurt.

"I ought to quote Shakespeare at you," Pete added, "but I can't think of anything but 'Friends, Romans, countrymen . . .' Okay, what do we do now?"

"First I'll drive you home so you can drop your bag and make a phone call or two. I'm worried about that notion of Miranda's—Hanson being found dead in his cell, an apparent suicide, with a hearsay confession ready for the press. It wouldn't be too hard for Kielty to arrange;

177

he must have contacts in the jail. Can you find out who his cellmate is, and who is in the cells on either side of him?"

"No sweat. Jake can manage it."

"Fine. Then, if they're hopheads or militants or anything like that, let's try to get them changed."

"And after that?"

"After that, you and I are having lunch with Clayton Faraday. Norm Edstrom is going to join us later at the shop. And I'm going to tell them just about what I've told you. We'll see if we can interest them enough at least to listen to the tapes."

"For a humble little antique arms dealer, you're doing fine. All we'll be doing is asking a top federal judge, the guy who throws the book at people, and a Treasury agent, one of the guys who puts the bracelets on them, to listen to illegal tapes illegally obtained with the assistance of a police officer by a man who has committed murder, and then to act illegally on what they hear. Don't you know the federal courts exist to protect the rights of really useful citizens like Hemmet and Miranda and van Zaam?"

"Don't be bitter. Anyway, I'm not going to ask them to act illegally on anything. We'll get them information on which a legal warrant can be issued. Clayton's a rare bird —he's more concerned with protecting honest men and their society than with twisting legal technicalities. That's why they turned him down for the supreme court five years ago. He'll at least listen."

"Dreamer! He'll probably issue warrants for our arrest. And if he does listen, then what? You said yourself Miranda's got another hiding place. A search warrant's no good unless you find out where to search. How do we do *that?*"

"I'll get it out of Hemmet."

"That'll be the day!"

"I'll get it if I have to kill him."

Pete shook his head. "The things folks say to homicide inspectors! Did you know you're wearing your Ivan the Terrible face again?"

"Thank you," said Timuroff politely.

"I thought you'd like to know. It might prejudice a jury."

The Mazda pulled into the apartment house garage, and they went upstairs, where Pete made his calls. He told Jake Harrell only that he'd left Olivia in the south and flown back because a cousin had been taken ill—which meant that Jake would call him back from an outside phone. He did so ten minutes later, and he already had the answers where Hanson was concerned. His cellmate was a very nasty character named Ollie Upshed, known in the East Bay as a sort of criminal handyman, with everything from purse-snatching to dope-peddling on his record. He had replaced a forger the day before. Jake wasn't sure who was in the adjoining cells, but he'd find out. Anyhow, he'd arrange that Hanson was surrounded by nothing but honest burglars from now on—or at least enough of them to make sure nothing happened. As for Upshed, they'd best get word to Hanson to pick a fight with him, late on the swing shift preferably, so there'd be a real reason to put somebody else in. It'd mean another charge for Hanson, but what the hell.

Pete hung up. "That should take care of it," he said.

"Good," said Timuroff. "I'll phone Heck."

He called the doctor, who was busy getting Evangeline ready for her final programming, and was assured that Mrs. Hanson would take the message when she visited the jail later in the day.

"That," declared Dr. Grimwood, "is the kind of legal advice he'll appreciate. He detests his roommate."

Timuroff said he'd see him toward suppertime, and put back the phone. "We'd better hurry," he told Pete. "The judge is going to meet us at the Jade Pavilion. I don't want to keep him waiting."

Pete looked at him mournfully. "Behold the whiskered Muscovite," he declaimed, "blown by the ill wind of his own madness to his doom!"

"That isn't *Shakespeare?*"

"No, it's Cominazzo—but it fits." Pete double-locked the door behind them. "Except your being whiskered. I put that in because Muscovites ought to be. Anyhow, think about it when the judge bears down on you."

On this foreboding note, they drove to the restaurant, where Clayton Faraday was waiting for them. At first glance, people always thought him frail—and were surprised to find that he was as tough as whalebone, both spiritually and physically. Any perceptive man, thought Timuroff, needed only to look into his eyes, gray and alert and absolutely steady under his level brows, to forget his size and age completely. He was full of a cold fire, a tempered strength.

They lunched, and at first talked very generally about the world and its affairs, moonflights and lunacies, rivalries and fashions, works of art and riots of destruction. Then, without noticing how the change was made, Pete realized that suddenly they were discussing the Munrooney case—or rather that Clayton Faraday was asking subtle, penetrating questions about its background, about Hector Grimwood and his house and girls, about Amos Ledenthal, Hemmet and Miranda Gardner and van Zaam, Hanson and Kielty and the chief, about old weapons and older ways of killing men—and that as he asked them they seemed much less like questions than innocent grace notes dropped casually into the stream of conversation.

Pete realized again then that, if you happened to be very far on the wrong side of the law, Judge Clayton Faraday was a man really to be feared.

"Tim, this has been delightful." The judge bowed his appreciation. "But I want to hear your real story. Let us go and meet our Mr. Edstrom."

There was only casual conversation on the drive over to the shop, and they found Norman Edstrom already there. He knew Pete, but he had never really met the judge, and he was obviously impressed, especially when Faraday remembered him and complimented him on his testimony in two separate cases. They entered. The judge took a seat. Instantly, a courtroom dignity mantled the room.

"Let's get to business," he said.

"Very well," said Timuroff. "I am going to ask you and Norman here to listen to more than twenty hours of tapes, or at least to their more important sections. They were surreptitiously recorded with the assistance of a police officer, and—as I understand the law—are not admissible as evidence. In short, the whole thing is and was illegal. However, these tapes reveal the truth regarding the murder of Munrooney—for which two innocent men are now being framed—a murder in which the man van Zaam was a mere instrument. They tell of the murder, by van Zaam, of a girl in Berkeley. They also point to concrete evidence which can be seized legally, and which will, I believe, break the back of a criminal deeply involved in the hard narcotics traffic in this area, and employing every weapon from blackmail and bribery to murder."

"A tall order," murmured Faraday. "Go on."

And Timuroff, episode by episode and point by point, told them the whole story as he knew it, holding back only what he—as a seventeenth-century gentleman—felt he could not honorably reveal. It took him a little more than an hour, and he was interrupted only by a few questions, all Edstrom's, and by Faraday's occasional quiet comments, which always seemed inconsequential until seemingly un-heralded facets of the story displayed the almost clairvoyant reasoning and perception on which they had been based.

Finally he finished, and for a moment there was quiet. Then Clayton Faraday leaned forward, pressing his finger-tips together. "I hope, Tim," he said, "that you didn't promise this man you call the Phantom of the Opera that I'd shut my eyes to crimes he has committed, or keep this matter secret, or protect him from the law?"

"I told him I had no authority to promise anything," Timuroff replied. "But I did tell him what I thought your reaction at this point might be."

"And that was?"

"That, in my opinion, your concern was as much with decency and justice as with the letter of the law—especially when the law itself was being tampered with to pervert justice. I told him I didn't think either you or Norman would act against him while a chance remained that the testimony of his tapes and the charges he himself has made were true."

Faraday's face was stern. "You were right—but you had no right to be. You've placed me in a very difficult posi-tion, and Mr. Edstrom in one scarcely less embarrassing. Naturally—" He smiled suddenly. "I myself wish more citizens were like you, but that's because I do not share my profession's present esteem for criminals. Subcon-sciously, you know, men forward their own interests, and we lawyers have been no exception to the rule. To many of us, criminals are not liabilities but assets. We are the only men who really need them. Only we can remain un-criticized when we become deeply involved with them—like Hemmet and Munrooney and how many more? They make our reputations. A few dramatic prosecutions can propel a sharp DA right into orbit—a governorship, a Supreme Court appointment, perhaps the Presidency itself. And because we lawyers govern you—we are an absolute majority in both houses of the legislature—we have contrived a legal system which makes both prosecution and defense too complicated, too sensational, and very profitable indeed. Consider the Sirhan trial, or Manson's. However, these are the laws with which, for the moment, we must live. The people you are challenging are people of great power and considerable prestige. They are people who live not just by breaking laws but by manipulating all their technicalities—so successfully that it has been impossible to root out either political corruption or the organized crime that thrives on it. Regardless of the content of your tapes, these people aren't going to be easy to attack." He smiled again. "And now you've seen how cynical I am, tell me—why did you come to me, Tim, instead of the law enforcement agencies, who I'm sure would have listened to your tapes without asking too many questions or making too much fuss?"

Timuroff looked at him. "Because," he said, "the people we're challenging *are* what you said they are. Time and red tape are always on their side. If you consent to enter into this, and if after listening to the tapes you are convinced, then when we strike we can strike instantly. That is the only way they can be caught off balance."

"Exactly," growled Edstrom, and Pete nodded his agreement.

"It seems I'm destined to play devil's advocate," said Clayton Faraday. "You have more than twenty hours of taped conversations. Electronics experts can cut and patch and make almost anything out of that much talk. Even if none of it is to be used as evidence, what if the fact of its existence becomes known? That alone could be highly damaging, regardless of your concrete evidence. Cases have been tossed out of court for less. Wait!" He raised a hand as Timuroff started to protest. "We must examine every facet of this. There's one especially with which I'm not satisfied—the motive for the alleged murder of Munrooney. From what you've said, the conversations do not make this clear—and yet you may be forced to make it clear in court, especially if no supporting evidence is found. Remember, your adversaries won't let you keep it simple."

"Sir," put in Edstrom, "we may not need to charge them with the mayor's murder. If what we've heard is true, there'll be enough other felony counts against them to really knock them in the head."

"And will that clear Mr. Hanson and prevent Dr. Grimwood's prosecution?"

Even Timuroff remained silent, and the judge answered his own question. "There is an excellent chance that it will not. Lieutenant Kielty's possible involvement in such things as bribery and the narcotics traffic will not necessarily invalidate his testimony in an apparently unrelated murder case; nor will the prosecuting attorney necessarily drop the charges simply because of a sensational exposure of civic rottenness and police corruption. No, I'm afraid that you're going to have to show a motive, and wrap up the Munrooney murder with the rest of it."

"But that may be impossible," said Timuroff. "Perhaps no evidence exists, and Hemmet and Miranda certainly aren't going to be very hel—"

The doorbell rang.

"Now who the hell is *that?*" Pete exclaimed. "Stitchgrove, with the SPCA hot on his trail?"

"My God! Pete, I'd forgotten. It must be Sergeant Wallton. He phoned while you were gone, saying he'd drop your target pistol off today. Will you let him in? I'll get our drinks started."

Pete opened the door carefully. "Denny!" he cried out. "It's good to see you. Come on in."

"Hey, Pete in person! I thought you'd be down south." Wallton entered, a powerful black man with a military moustache. "Look, I hope I'm not bulling in at the wrong time. I see you've got some high-powered company."

"God, no." Pete took him by an elbow. "We've had developments in the Munrooney business, and we're just about to have a drink to celebrate."

"Will you join us?" called Timuroff.

"Happy to."

Pete made the introductions. Like Edstrom, whom he already knew, Wallton had never met the judge personally, and he too was impressed.

Timuroff took their orders. They sat down with their drinks. "Cheers!" Wallton said to Pete. They drank.

He had put down the shoebox he was carrying, and Pete's glance fastened on it. "What's this you have for me?" he asked.

Wallton grinned. "That's window dressing, in case the wrong people saw me coming here. Throw it away. What I've got could be a lot more important." From the inner pocket of his jacket he took a long manila envelope. Then he looked a little hesitantly at Clayton Faraday.

"Go ahead," Pete told him. "It's all part of the same deal, and the judge knows just about as much as any of us."

"Okay." Out of the envelope, Wallton drew another, from which in turn he took a folded letter. "Pete, I had no use for Mayor Munrooney. To him, I was a nigger—a black who couldn't live without his kind of busybody to think for me. Those of us, like my old man and me and plenty more, who'd made it on our own were just Toms to him, like to the shiftless bums and Mau-Mau militants, because we didn't need him any more than we need them. He had me on the guard detail not because I was a good cop, but as a showpiece." He looked around. "Anyhow, while I was on it I caught on to a lot of high-level political conniving that probably he thought I couldn't even understand. One piece of it was in this letter." He unfolded it. "I found it on the car seat where he had dropped it, and I brought it back to him. He must've guessed I'd looked at it, because for a second he was all shaken up. Then he turned on the personality, and put his arm over my shoulders, and thanked me. 'I very much appreciate this, Sergeant Wallton,' he told me, 'and I want you to keep this letter for your boys. Someday it may be worth quite a piece of change. But, because it is important, I want you to promise me that you'll not say a word about it, not to *any*one.' Well, of course I promised, but recently I got to thinking how this case really stinks, with the chief and Kielty trying to job Pete the same way they did me, so when Pete phoned I had no trouble making up my mind. And here it is."

He handed it to Pete.

Pete glanced at it, drew his breath in sharply, read it through again.

"Would you mind reading it aloud?" said Faraday.

Pete did so, very slowly. It was from a gubernatorial mansion in one of the North Atlantic states.

Dear Mayor Munrooney:

As you have known since our conversations at the last Convention, I am deeply impressed by your progressive attitudes and policies, your political genius, and your great sincerity.

After much consideration, I have decided that there

is no man in the United States whom I would rather have as my running mate if I have the good fortune to be nominated for the Presidency.

Needless to say, this must be held in complete confidence for the time being—there's no point in giving advance information to our enemies. However, I would appreciate your giving it your immediate and serious consideration, and advising me of your decision as soon as possible.

With all good wishes for your continuing success.

Cordially yours . . .

The letter was signed by his party's front-running candidate.

"May I see it?" asked Faraday.

Pete gave it to him, and he examined it. "There's no doubt that this is genuine," he said. "Do you know what his decision was, Mr. Wallton?"

"Yes, sir. I guess they thought the limousine partition was closed all the way. What he said was, 'The bastard means I can get him lots of votes.' Then the character in the back seat with him asked, 'You're going to turn him down, aren't you?' And Munrooney came back with, 'Are you crazy? Turn down a chance to get within one jump of the White House? Hell no, I'm going to accept.' The other fellow sort of gasped. He said, 'Errol, what about the Master Plan?' And Munrooney said, 'It's down the drain —it and a lot of other stuff.' "

"And who was the man he said this to?"

"It was his partner, that lawyer Judson Hemmet."

"Mr. Wallton, would you be willing to testify to all of this in court? Perhaps in my court?"

"I would," said Dennis Wallton.

Now Faraday stood up, the letter in his hand. "Tim, this is your lucky day. Here is your motive for Munrooney's murder. It is concrete evidence which cannot be denied." His eyes flashed. "Very well, I'll listen to your tapes."

XIV

A Crash in Uruguay

The next three days were busy ones for Timuroff. The first order of business, of course, was listening to Reese Guthrie's tapes, or rather to those of them that Pete and Edstrom thought would be especially interesting to him. Guthrie had delivered the originals, and had assured him that a set of copies was now in one of Ledenthal's filing cabinets; and Pete, off duty, had undertaken to do the preliminary scanning, with Edstrom helping whenever possible. It was a fascinating but sordid business. Half the conversations were between Miranda Gardner and Hemmet. Most of the rest—and these were often the more interesting—were between her and a variety of other people, men and women, some of them trapped in debt, others whom she controlled by other means, and a few who, seemingly unafraid, simply appeared to be in league with her.

Pete listened carefully, keeping a log of every name, of each address, of each transaction. He worked at home, after he and Edstrom had gone over the apartment and found it clean, and every afternoon and evening the judge would join him, look the log over, and choose the tapes he wished to listen to. Timuroff stayed away, to avoid attracting any attention. He had asked Pete to note those tapes that contained references to the relationship between Hemmet and Mrs. Gardner, and especially any in which, behind his back, she hinted at friction or distrust or possible betrayal on either side.

187

His was a very special interest, and at first nothing turned up that satisfied him. By Friday evening, though Pete and Edstrom and Clayton Faraday were excited by what had been disclosed, he was impatient, and his impatience had communicated itself to Liselotte, to Olivia, who had come back to work, and to Dr. Grimwood, who was beginning to feel left out of things. He did his best to pacify them, but succeeded only with the doctor, who at least had some idea of what was in the wind. Liselotte, presciently apprehensive, had given him a bad time on Friday night, and he was sure that Olivia, who had been looking at him reproachfully all day, was doing the same for Pete.

On Saturday, he went with Dr. Grimwood, Penny Anne, and Liselotte to the services for Amos Ledenthal, and while everyone was gone the Ledenthal residence was quietly burgled. A TV repair truck pulled up in front of it, and two men forced the door latch with a plastic card after ringing the bell ostentatiously. They carried tool kits and a large carton. Presently they came out, once more carrying their gear. Several readily salable articles were stolen—a stereo set, a portable TV, some silver and some jewelry, a shotgun, and a pocket watch. So were the tapes, together with a few oddments from the study. A couple of Bill Traeger's men, observing from the house of a cooperative friend of Ledenthal's almost a block away, recorded the proceedings with a telephoto lens; and Timuroff, when he heard that everything had gone off as anticipated, temporarily forgot his own frustration—until Pete called him at eleven o'clock that night to tell him that the tapes still had not yielded what he wanted. When Mr. Rop Millweed phoned at a few minutes to midnight to say excitedly that a national syndicate might be interested in the Timuroff memoirs of the case "as told to Rop Millweed, internationally known correspondent," his answer was so picturesque that Liselotte refused to speak to him for half an hour.

Sunday began more favorably. By noon, the tapes had all been listened to, and Pete had phoned to tell him a couple of them might be what he was looking for. He drove out to the Cominazzos', first dropping Dr. Grimwood off at Kemble Street, and listened to them. After he had listened to them twice, he decided that they could scarcely be better for his purpose. He told Pete he wanted

copies made, and learned that Pete and Edstrom had anticipated him.

Shortly afterward, Judge Faraday arrived, was given a
quick summary of the final tapes, and listened to pertinent
sections of a number of them. Abruptly, then, court was
again in session.

"Gentlemen," the judge said, "can you sum the situation
up for me as it now looks from the police point of view?
Naturally, I've formed my own opinion, but I would like
to hear what you think."

"Pete and I are pretty much agreed," said Edstrom. "Go
ahead, Pete, you tell him."

"Sir, we've got enough to wreck the works," Pete stated.
"But almost none of it is stuff on which we can act instantly. I mean, we have a map telling us where to go and
how to get there—but we've still got to drive the distance,
and look for signs, and maybe ask our way. There's a
hell of a lot of police work to be done before we get the
thing wrapped up—unless we want to run the risk of blow-
ing it. We need Miranda's personal papers, but God knows
where they are, since Guthrie spooked her."

"That's my opinion too." Faraday nodded. "Still, somebody must know exactly where she keeps them. The problem's *who*. And how will you find out? Remember, there
must be no mistake. Any warrant issued on faulty information could ruin us."

"Judson Hemmet knows," Timuroff said quietly. "He
must know."

"He'll never talk," Pete protested. "No more than Miranda would."

Timuroff's jaw muscles tightened. "He'll talk to me.
Under the right circumstances, I think he'll tell me everything he knows."

"What are those circumstances?" asked Clayton Faraday.

Timuroff evaded the direct question. "I can arrange
them—with a little help," he said.

"I . . . see." The judge looked at him narrowly. "My
instinct as a man urges me to press the point until you
tell me what you have in mind. However, my intuition
as a judge instructs me to the contrary. There are some
things it is perhaps better for judges not to know, and I
suspect that this is one of them. I will ask you one favor,
though—for Liselotte's sake, not my own."

"Sir?" said Timuroff.

"Tim, I really know you very well." Faraday smiled, and his face shone suddenly with kindness and concern. "I quite agree with Lise that you belong in an earlier century than our own. I hope you won't do anything anachronistic that could get you into serious trouble in this one."

"I'll try not to," Timuroff promised him.

There was some further conversation about what could be done with the information the tapes contained. Then Faraday left, after accepting Timuroff's dinner invitation for the Tuesday following.

"Okay," said Pete, after the door had closed behind him. "What kind of crazy plan have you cooked up? How're you going to pry that information out of Hemmet—with a sword?"

"Possibly," Timuroff replied, not smiling. "Actually, my plan is pretty much complete, but I'm going to have to bring Heck in on it, and Bill Traeger too. Why don't we get together this evening out on Kemble Street, if it's all right with Heck? Then I can tell you what I have in mind, and we can go over it step by step."

Pete agreed grudgingly, and Edstrom said he could arrange to be there at about eight. Timuroff thanked them, and took his leave. He drove directly home, and called Wade Kalloch. Kalloch said, no, he wasn't busy, and for a few minutes they chatted inconsequentially about old weapons. Then Timuroff asked casually which of Gottschalk's rapiers Hemmet had used when he killed Amos Ledenthal, and learned it was a monstrously long German blade. "God damn the bastard!" Kalloch shouted. "I got it back after the cops said self-defense, but it's got a sort of scratch all along one side, I guess where it rubbed against that Jap sword Amos tried to cut him with, and even that's been damaged. The guard was bent all out of shape when Amos dropped it, and there are scratches on it too, only I'm not sure they weren't already there. By God, sometimes I think I'll start collecting clocks instead!"

"Hickory, dickory, dock," Timuroff said sympathetically, and wished him luck.

Next, he phoned Florencio Pambid, who was out working, and asked his wife whether one or both of them could be available later in the week, he wasn't sure just when. She told him that, even if he was engaged, Florencio would be glad to cancel for Mr. Timuroff; and he promised to call again that evening.

Finally, he played the tapes he had received from Pete and Edstrom, listened to them very carefully, marked them, and went out to Kemble Street, where he found Bill Traeger in the library.

"I know Heck's busy with Evangeline," he said. "I'll see him later. Right now, I want to talk to you." And he told Traeger how Judge Faraday and Pete and Edstrom had heard the tapes, and how they had agreed that only the seizure of Miranda's personal files could crack the case wide open. "I have a plan," he said. "I think I can make Hemmet talk, if Pete and Edstrom go along with it. Bill, it's going to be rough. I'm going to explain it this evening, and then you can decide. Meanwhile, I've brought you a few tapes. They contain the makings of what Hemmet has to hear Miranda saying. I'd like to know if you can cut out what we don't want and put the rest together so nobody'll know."

"That'll be simple," Traeger answered. "Ordinarily, I wouldn't touch it—it's more in Hanno's line. But this time —if we can make it work—the bastard has it coming."

Timuroff left him and joined Hector Grimwood and Evangeline, now comfortably settled in her room.

"Heck," he asked, "would it be too much of a job to re-program our pretty little friend?"

The doctor patted their pretty little friend with pride. "Not really. This time, I have her tape-controlled, like a computer. It takes a little planning and a little time, that's all. Her conversation can be coordinated with her actions —turning her head, smiling, using her hands and arms." He beamed. "I'm really very pleased with myself, Tim. Her mouth responds to the words she uses just as if she were really speaking them. I'd hardly hoped to succeed so well."

He activated an unseen remote control, and Evangeline turned toward Timuroff, lowered her lids demurely, raised her hands even more demurely to her décolletage, smiled, and said, in Penny Anne's soft voice, "I like you, Mr. Timuroff. Dr. Grimwood thinks you're very nice, and so do I."

Hector Grimwood chuckled delightedly, and switched her off.

Timuroff bowed to her, and congratulated her creator. "Heck, she's wonderful! I could've sworn her mouth formed those words, and I must admit I find them much more pleasing than if she'd quoted Longfellow as Eric does. Besides, I'm glad to hear that she's so adaptable. It happens to fit in with what I have in mind."

Grimwood sat down and pointed to a chair. "So something is developing? Tim, I hope at last we're going to put an end to this! Tell me about it."

Timuroff told him very much what he had already told Bill Traeger; and they agreed to meet in the doctor's library at eight o'clock to talk over his plan. Then he went downstairs again, and listened to Traeger's report on the four tapes.

"See if I'm wrong," said Traeger. "I'm to cut out all the names and crud where Miranda's talking about Hanno and that other guy—the one who runs the warehouse—and make it like she's talking about Hemmet?"

"That's right."

"Okay, I'll have it ready by tomorrow. I can't guarantee he'll fall for it, but nobody'll ever know that it's been touched. Let's run them through again, and you can show me exactly what to do and where."

They played the pertinent sections of the tapes, and Timuroff indicated the cuts, insertions, and change of sequences.

"That gal's real weird," Traeger commented when they had finished. "Did you listen to that boyfriend she was talking to? The guy sounds like a nance. Do you suppose she sleeps with him?"

"I'd imagine so, though I've not speculated on the details. She's had a lot of these young men, and they've all been alike. As soon as one disappears, another comes along. Maybe she eats him up after they've mated."

"Of her, I could believe anything." Traeger grimaced. "Anyhow, you're in business."

Timuroff thanked him, promised that he'd be back at eight, and drove downtown again to look in at the shop, check his mail, and brave Olivia's silent disapproval. Even after he had attended to the correspondence and glanced through the one sale catalogue that had come in, from Paris, there was still time to kill. Liselotte and Penny Anne had taken off for the maestro's. Hector Grimwood was having dinner at the Engineers Club with an old friend who was going to pick him up and bring him back again. And Olivia rather conspicuously said nothing about his dining with the Cominazzos. Finally, to quell his sudden doubts and apprehensions, he left her to close up, and went out to the Russian restaurant on Hayes Street. There he spent an hour or two trading nostalgic reminiscences with the proprietor and with the cook, who was from Vladivostok, and, while he ate his dinner and drank a bottle of good Gamay Beaujolais, reviewed his plan of action. It cheered him. When he returned to Kemble Street, he was once more optimistic.

Pete and Edstrom were already there, talking to Bill Traeger in the library, and Hector Grimwood joined them a minute or two later. Sensing their eagerness, he began almost without preamble.

"Gentlemen," he asked, "what is your opinion of Judson Hemmet? Does he impress you as fundamentally a brave man? Do you think that under great pressure he would refuse to break?"

"He's a murderer, not a hero," Pete answered. "But he'll never break without trying to bend every which way."

"From what I've heard," said Edstrom, "I think it'd depend on the degree of pressure. Hit him hard enough, and he might come apart."

"I intend to hit him hard enough," Timuroff told them; and he proceeded, step by step, to outline his plan. They listened to him spellbound, without question, without comment. His plan was simple. It only took him fifteen minutes to give them every detail. But before he was even halfway through, he realized that they would not support him.

He finished, and waited for their comments.

"My God, Tim!" Pete exploded. "Just how anachronistic can you get? Look, Norm here and I are cops—there's just so much we can get away with, anytime. Sure, it's a great plan—if everything you say is right, which maybe it won't be. But how many felony counts will there be against you and all of us if it just doesn't jell?"

"I'm sorry, Mr. Timuroff," said Edstrom. "I've got to go along with Pete. Anyhow, are we in all that hurry? Hemmet has his tapes. He probably feels safe again. Do we have to push it all that hard?"

"I think so," Timuroff told him.

"So do I," Bill Traeger said. "Maybe it won't work, but my hunch is to try it. What else can we do?"

"We can wait and start our police work," Edstrom answered, and Pete nodded his agreement.

For a few minutes, they argued back and forth, with Timuroff successfully concealing his annoyance, and no one challenging his position. Hector Grimwood, distressed, spoke of hiring some high-powered legal aid instead. "No, no, no!" he said. "Think of the personal risk that you'd be running, Tim. Suppose that everything went wrong? I never would forgive myself. And what would Liselotte say? No, no, we mustn't even think of it."

Finally, Timuroff gave in with reasonably good grace. "I see I am outvoted." He smiled at them. "I just hope you are right and I am wrong—and that someone comes up with something quick and positive that we can do."

Then he allowed the conversation to drift into less controversial channels—when they should consult Judge Faraday again; investigative avenues to be explored; agencies which might, in due course, be expected to cooperate. Dr. Grimwood summoned Mrs. Hanson, who twittered over them and served a round of drinks; and after not too long a while they dispersed. Timuroff was not happy. Instinct told him that prompt and drastic action was required; now action was denied him. He seethed inwardly, unable to be angry with the doctor, so genuinely concerned about the risk he himself might run, or with Pete, who was too old a friend, or Norman Edstrom, simply following his sense of law and duty. On the drive home, he conversed politely, mostly about Evangeline. Then, pleading weariness, he went to bed with his frustration, to doze and wake and dream, and toss uneasily for an hour or more, till Liselotte joined him and, by her presence, soothed him into a deeper and less troubled sleep.

It was not a sleep he was allowed to finish. At five fifteen, the phone burst into it, tearing it to shreds, bringing him wide awake immediately. He lifted it before it rang again.

"Tim? Is that you, Tim?" It was Pete's voice, and Pete was badly shaken.

Softly, trying not to rouse Liselotte, who had only stirred and mumbled in her sleep, Timuroff said, "Yes?"

"Tim. It's Hanson. He—he's dead."

Timuroff caught his breath. Then, "Hang up," he said. "I'll call you on the other phone."

Silently he rose, put on his bathrobe, went into his study. Pete answered instantly.

"What happened, Pete?"

"Jake's brother-in-law just called up. They found him in his cell during a bed check. It looks like he took poison."

"What kind?" snapped Timuroff.

"Cyanide, they think—the old reliable."

"Did Harrell's relative have any other information?"

"Nobody saw anything. Nobody heard anything. He was just dead, that's all."

"What about his cellmate?"

"That was kind of odd. They transferred the guy out on the swing shift, and didn't put anybody in his place. Hanson was alone."

Timuroff, trying to shift his mind into high gear, was silent.

"God, who'd have thought it?" Pete went on, his voice deeply troubled. "It looked like everything was safe for a few days anyway, with Hemmet and Miranda getting their tapes back and thinking all the pressure had come off."

Timuroff refrained from pointing out that everything had not looked safe to him. "Maybe that's the trouble," he replied. "Perhaps they started feeling too secure—secure enough so that they could have Hanson murdered and blame it on Heck. A poison murder's easy to pin on an M.D., and here they'd have the motive ready-made—so that Hanson couldn't break and confess that Heck hired van Zaam and then had van Zaam killed. All very plausible, especially with a hostile press and Hanson having no recent visitors except his employer and his wife. Listen, Pete, you'd better get in touch with Traeger right away. Kielty's going to be up there sniffing for cyanide as soon as he can get a warrant, and you can bet he'll find it. Traeger's going to have to watch him every minute, and Heck's attorneys had also better be there. It's a chemical with lots of other uses; for all I know, Heck even may have used it in making Muriel Fawzi or Evangeline. I'll ask him if there's any in the house when I break the news to him, and I'll call Bill immediately if the answer's yes. All right?"

"I'll call Bill now," Pete promised. Then he hesitated, and Timuroff could hear him swallow before continuing. "Tim," he said, "after I talk to Bill, I'll get hold of Ed-

strom. I was wrong. It looks to me as if we'd better set
your plan in action."

"As soon as possible," said Timuroff.

He wakened Hector Grimwood and broke the news to
him as gently as he could. He watched and waited until
the shock of comprehension had made itself apparent on
the doctor's face, answered his outraged cries and questions, and saw him pass through anguish and despair to a
revivifying anger. He had seen the phenomenon before.
For a few seconds only, at the first impact of bad news, his
friend displayed the symptoms of quavering old age; then,
as anger rose, they vanished suddenly; his huge frame came
erect, decisiveness replaced uncertainty.

"They *murdered* Hanson, Tim." His voice was under
tight control. "They murdered him, and probably they'll
try to blame me. Why is it, in spite of all that's happened
in my house, I can't believe the sort of people we're up
against? What can we do?"

"What I suggested. What else could possibly be quick
enough?"

Anger danced wildly in Dr. Grimwood's eyes. "It's
mad," he said, "but maybe where sanity has failed madness can succeed. All right, if Pete and Edstrom are persuaded, I'm willing too."

Timuroff called Pete, who had already been in touch
with Edstrom, and who reported that the Treasury agent
—after much convincing—had agreed.

"I'll have to wake up Penny Anne," the doctor said. "I
hate to tell her, but naturally she'll want to be with Mrs.
Hanson, and anyhow we'll have to have her here when
we reprogram Evangeline."

"Well, we can hold off for a day or two on that. How
much will she need to know? I'd rather it didn't get back
to Liselotte, at least not ahead of time. She's too intuitive."

"I'll simply tell her it's important, and swear her to
secrecy, and promise that I'll tell her the whole story later.
Don't worry. She'll take my word for it, and she's discreet."

"There are a lot of other things to think of, Heck. When
it'll be, for instance. We'll have to wait, of course. There'll
be formalities. And I suppose there's going to be a funeral
too?"

"I'm not sure. Mrs. Hanson may have his body shipped
to Lassen County, where her whole family still lives. It

seems to me she's mentioned their having a cemetery plot up there. I have a feeling, too, that she won't want to stay on here without him—which means I'll have to find somebody else. As if things weren't bad enough already!" He looked quizzically at Timuroff. "You know, Tim, I've never seen quite that expression on your face before. I can't quite put it into words, but you look twenty years younger, somehow. You're really looking forward to this confrontation, aren't you?"

"I wasn't as close to Hanson as you were, Heck," Timuroff replied apologetically, "and it is always good to get something finally settled."

Actually, he felt as if a spring too tightly coiled had been released, as though a beautifully precise mechanism perversely frozen had suddenly been set free to function and fulfill its purpose; and he realized that his expression and demeanor would have to be controlled so that they would not betray him. If his plan was to succeed, everything had to appear normal. For the time being at least, the seventeenth-century Timuroff would have to knuckle under to the humble twentieth-century antique arms dealer.

He managed it quite well. It was not difficult to discipline his countenance during the scenes of feminine distress he was compelled to witness, first when Hector Grimwood told Penny Anne the news, then when he himself had to tell Liselotte, finally—and much more poignantly—on Kemble Street, when the doctor picked Mrs. Hanson up to drive her on the round of sad necessities prescribed by law. He did not go with them. Traeger's men had already searched the house from top to bottom, finding no trace of cyanide. Young Tom Coulter had arrived, bringing another junior member of his firm, and everything was ready for Kielty's visit. Wisely, he decided that any such invasion would pass off much more smoothly in his absence, and went home to answer some of Liselotte's questions and parry others, and to learn that she and Penny Anne planned to bring Mrs. Hanson to stay with them until her relatives came down from Lassen. Finally, she went away to keep a luncheon date, and he was able to call Edstrom and Reese Guthrie. Edstrom still was not too happy; obviously he had agreed to go along only because he could think of nothing else to do. Guthrie's voice shook when he heard the news, and Timuroff realized that the ferocity of his eagerness—whipped up again by new guilt over Hanson's death—would endanger their success unless he was very carefully coached beforehand. He invited him down for lunch, and told Emilia, who wanted to go shopping, not to worry, that he would have the Jade Pavilion send something in. Then he phoned Florencio Pambid, and asked his wife to have him call as soon as possible as there was going to be an opening for a couple at Dr. Grimwood's.

From then on, he lived between impatience and the need for precise planning, preparation, and rehearsal. Kielty, accompanied by two detectives, appeared at Kemble Street on schedule. He had his warrant, and he quite openly was gloating. His manner changed abruptly when Traeger told him that each searcher would be accompanied and watched. He started to get nasty, but dropped the subject surlily when Coulter told him coldly that there'd be no attempt to interfere with him, but that he would either have to use force or obtain a court order to prevent surveillance. Traeger and Coulter accompanied him personally. He was tense and nervous now, and his search was perfunctory and impatient, as though it were only a routine he had to follow. He left empty-handed, and Traeger phoned Timuroff immediately. "It looks like we're in the clear for now," he said, "but give the bastard a few days. He'll be back."

"A few days is all we need," Timuroff answered.

Two days went by. Mrs. Hanson stayed the night with them, comforted as much as possible by Penny Anne and Liselotte. Next day, an uncle and a niece arrived, homely country folk set to do whatever family loyalty demanded, and moved her back to her apartment over the garage preparatory to taking her up north with them. It was announced officially that Hanson had committed suicide, but Jake Harrell had suggested cynically that it should have been called "suicide at the hands of a person or persons unknown." On the afternoon of the second day, Hanson's body was shipped north, and Mrs. Hanson and her kin left simultaneously, she with a check from Dr. Grimwood so generous that it started another freshet of her tears. On the morning of the third day, the Pambids were installed in their new jobs, keeping their edge-of-Chinatown apartment until Mrs. Hanson eventually returned for her possessions.

Florencio had called Timuroff back almost immediately, and Timuroff had taken him into his confidence. He had told him about van Zaam and the dead girl, about Guthrie and Amos Ledenthal, about Hemmet and Miranda Gardner and Hanson. "It is a very dangerous game we're playing, Florencio," he had said. "If it goes wrong, we'll be in serious trouble—though I don't think you'll run any great risk, even if you're there. But I want you to know exactly what the situation is."

"I have played dangerous games before, señor," Florencio had answered with a grin. "With the Japanese, and once with a man who came only to kill, like that van Zaam. Sometimes such games are necessary"—the grin vanished—"if we are to keep evil from the world. *Bastante*. You can rely on me."

After that, Florencio had been included in their discussions and rehearsals. Evangeline had been reprogrammed —though Penny Anne had balked a little when she heard her lines, and had required a good deal of coaxing to repeat them until they were as perfect as Timuroff demanded. Kielty had not yet returned. Hemmet had called personally to extend his sympathy, and twice again with legal advice and offers of his services should Hector Grimwood need them. To Timuroff's delight, for he had expected difficulties, Traeger had informed him that neither by his voice nor by his manner had the doctor given Hemmet any hint that anything was in the wind.

Meticulously, at Timuroff's insistence, they went over each detail again and yet again, until everyone was letter-perfect in his part. Allowing himself to entertain no doubts but one, he quieted theirs, reassuring them by his own inner certainty whenever they seemed momentarily disheartened. As a final triumph, he managed to persuade Liselotte and Penny Anne to accept another invitation from the maestro—an invitation for which he had to connive, wheedle, and almost bribe—and leave the city for a day or two immediately after seeing Mrs. Hanson off.

Only Olivia disquieted him. On his brief, infrequent visits to the shop she stared at him silently out of large, almost tearful blue eyes, asked him no questions whatsoever, and thereby let him know in no uncertain terms that she heartily disapproved of whatever he was up to. It was not until the morning of the third day, when he dropped in rather guiltily to scan his mail, that she broke her silence.

"You boys are brewing up something, Mr. T.," she told him. "I feel it in my bones, and I'm scared to death. I ought to call the cops, if we still had any cops to call. No"—

she waggled an old-maiden-auntish finger at him—"don't tell me anything. And don't worry—I'm not going to try and interfere. But I'm telling you right now, if this comes out all right, and you and Pete still have your skins on when it's over, I—" Her voice broke. "I'm damn well g-g-going to get that little station wagon out of one of you!"

Timuroff promised her she would, and kissed her on the forehead, and told her that he loved her, and went away feeling guiltier than ever—and still more certain of himself in spite of it.

He drove again out to Kemble Street, found the doctor and Florencio readying the poker parlor, and finally voiced his single doubt.

"Do you think he'll come?" he asked.

"He's been here every day," Hector Grimwood answered. "He'll come trying to pick up information, if for nothing else. If he can't come today, he'll come tomorrow. Shall I call right now? If he's in court, I'll ask him to call back."

"Let's get it over with," said Timuroff.

Hemmet was in his office. "Judson?" the doctor said. "I'm glad I caught you in. . . . No, there's been no more trouble—thank God! But really I've been under terrible pressure. I must do something to relax a little, so I'm going to have a poker game, just like I've always had—though I'm afraid there aren't too many of our people I can get. Socrates is too upset about his dagger, and Tesserault and Kalloch are both out of town, and naturally I can't even ask Mario under the circumstances. But can you come? . . . Oh, I hope you can! Mr. Traeger, who's been guarding me, is a good player, and we've scraped up a few more between us. . . . Good, good. Then we'll see you at the usual time? . . . Yes, eight o'clock. . . . Good-bye."

He turned to Timuroff. "Well, that's that. How did I sound, Tim?"

"Perfect!" Timuroff was enthusiastic. "You couldn't have done better. You made your voice sound just a little frantic without overdoing it."

"That reassures me. I've been a little worried I might spoil everything." Hector Grimwood paused diffidently. "By the way—well, I hate to mention it, but you do have that expression on your face again."

Judson Hemmet entered the poker parlor at three minutes after eight o'clock. The hanging Tiffany lamp was bright over the green baize center of the table. Otherwise, except for a faint light behind the burnished bar where Florencio was clinking glasses, the room was shadowed, and on the paneled walls a dark glow from the roaring fireplace danced its sunset colors.

Hemmet entered, and stood there for a moment, tall, almost unnaturally erect, his severe face all pale highlights and sharp shadows. And when he entered, Timuroff felt another shadow fall across the room, and, neck hairs prickling, recognized that here—though very, very differently—there was a certainty equal to his own.

Hemmet looked at the group seated at the table—Hector Grimwood banking, counting chips busily; Pete with shirt sleeves rolled up, helping him; Norman Edstrom sitting there relaxed, dealing mock blackjack hands to Timuroff; and, demure and beautiful between two vacant chairs, Evangeline.

"Hello, Judson," called Grimwood cheerfully. "Give your coat to Florencio and take a chair. You've met Pete Cominazzo?"

Hemmet smiled, a smile that seemed no smile at all. His glance touched Pete, and for an instant the smile flickered and went out. "Yes, we've met," he said. "How are you doing, Inspector?"

"Just fine, Mr. Hemmet." Pete waved a friendly hand. "You know Norm Edstrom here?"

Hemmet obviously did not. He smiled at Edstrom and at Timuroff, and asked if Edstrom was another policeman; and Bill Traeger answered, "Norm's a friend of mine. He's in pharmaceuticals."

"And who have we here?" Hemmet asked. He hung his jacket on a chair beside Evangeline, the one across from Timuroff—as if instinctively he knew his true antagonist. "Hector, you haven't introduced me to your girl friend. Don't tell me you've taught her to play poker?" He sat down. "The usual stakes?"

"Yes, a four-bit limit except for stud—then it's a dollar." The doctor pushed the chips toward him. "Here you are—twenty dollars' worth, and of course debtor chips."

"None for the little lady here? Maybe you ought to deal her in—there are only five of us."

"Do you want to treat her?" Grimwood chuckled. "Personally, I agree with Scarne that poker is an excellent

game for any number from two to seven." He broke open
a new deck, shuffled it, said, "High card deals."

Bill Traeger, to his left, received a noncommittal eight;
then Hemmet drew the ten of clubs; Timuroff, separated
by an empty chair from Evangeline, a five; Pete Cominazzo
a red queen, and Hector Grimwood nothing but a trey.
Pete took the cards, asked if the house rules allowed a
round of stud, was told they did. He shuffled while Florencio discreetly took orders for their drinks. They played.
Out of the round's five hands, Hemmet won two, folded
two others after his second or third card, lost one by
bluffing against two pair which Timuroff, to be at all plausible, had to bet. When the deal came to the doctor, he
chose seven-card stud, high-low, and again Hemmet took
half the pot.

Timuroff watched him carefully as he played. At first, he
had not been sure; now he decided that any suspicions Hemmet might have had had at least been lulled. Hemmet's face
showed he had been disarmed by the confirmed poker player's concentration on his game. It was a wax-museum face,
artificially contrived, held together—against what self-assas-
sinating hungry drives and hatreds, despairs and guilts?—
only by the hidden sinews of those Puritan restraints he
had inherited.

Timuroff quietly folded a heart flush, and allowed Hemmet to win once more with a hand which, at the very
best, could have been three of a kind only, and was probably two pair. Hemmet's pile of chips had grown to
thirty-five or forty dollars. He won again, at draw—a fat
pot called only after several raises.

Timuroff watched his face. He watched the faces of the
others there. They were just poker players' faces, cheerfully
rueful, slightly irked but hiding it, impatient for the next
deal around.

He nodded imperceptibly to Florencio Pambid.

Hemmet, having gathered in his chips, was stacking
them methodically; and now, slowly and gracefully, Evangeline turned her pretty head toward him, opened her eyes
wide, reached out her right hand and, barely, ever so ten-
derly, touched his forearm.

"My goodness, Mr. Hemmet," she said, in Penny Anne's
soft voice, her coral lips forming each word convincingly,
"you are *a clever man. Do you find poker very profitable?"*

Hemmet started; gathered himself together instantly. He

laughed. "You've really got her trained," he said to Hector Grimwood, and took her little hand in both of his. "Sweetheart," he told her, "sometimes I find it very profitable indeed."

She smiled up at him dazzlingly. *"More profitable than heroin?"* she said.

Silence struck the room. Her hand, abandoned suddenly, remained hovering there in front of her. A pile of chips in front of Judson Hemmet toppled over slowly.

And all the lights went on. The room flared with them. The lamp above the table paled into nothingness; the firelight perished. And Hemmet saw the faces of his fellow players. All but Evangeline's were set inflexibly, frozen in their cold hostility.

His voice cut like a knife. "Dr. Grimwood," he demanded, "is this a joke?" And he received no answer, and knew that it was not. And suddenly they felt the hatred flowing from him, inundating them.

Again he smiled his artificial smile. "Well," he said, "this all may be good theatre, but what's its purpose?" He placed his hands flat down on the table, as though about to stand. "You can't compel me to stay here and undergo all this."

"I think we can," Pete told him, flatly, with no inflection whatsoever.

Hemmet's face twisted. He half rose.

"Sit," growled Norman Edstrom.

"And who are *you?"*

"I am a Treasury agent. You've heard of us. As Bill said, I'm in pharmaceuticals—hard drugs, that is."

Hemmet did not sit down. "I'm afraid that I can't help you. I can't imagine what this is all about, but as a lawyer I can assure you that you're already in very serious trouble." He looked at them. Their faces were expressionless. "What do you want?"

"It's very simple, Jud," Timuroff said. "We want to know one thing. Where does Miranda Gardner keep her private papers?"

Outwardly at least, Hemmet remained unruffled. "Have you lost your minds? If Mrs. Gardner has private papers, it's not your business—and even if it were I wouldn't tell you. She's my client. Our relationship is privileged."

"An honest working girl trying to get along, you mean?" suggested Pete.

"Essentially that's true. Her business is legitimate."

"No heroin? No blackmail?" Timuroff was no longer making any effort to control the expression on his face. "Not even just a little bit of murder?"

"Don't be absurd."

"Where does Miranda keep her papers, Jud?"

Hemmet laughed at them. "This has gone far enough. It's time I left." He stood. "And I suspect that none of you will try to stop me. Gentlemen, good——"

A sharp hard knock, twice repeated, interrupted him. He stared. They turned around.

"Come in!" called Hector Grimwood.

The door of the armoire, where van Zaam had hung, opened slowly. Reese Guthrie stood there for a moment, framed in darkness, his face like granite, his eyes on Hemmet's eyes. He stepped into the room.

"Tell the man what he wants to know," he ordered. His Carolinian voice was deep and soft. He waited several seconds. "Did you really think it was poor old Amos who had you followed and then made all those tapes? No, Judson Hemmet. *I* did it. Because of Marianne. We've got them all, and quite a few we didn't leave you copies of. I ought to kill you here and now, like I did van Zaam, but these good people need your information. Give it to them."

Observing Hemmet, Timuroff noticed that whatever held that waxen face together seemed suddenly imperiled, as though the vicious, agile intellect that lived behind it at last felt shaken, but the impression lasted for an instant only.

"*Give* it to them," Reese Guthrie said.

"I don't have anything to give."

"That's your last word?"

"It is."

"Those tapes alone can hang you," Edstrom said. "Make it a little easier for us, and maybe you can make it easier for yourself."

"Mr. Edstrom, let us assume those tapes exist—that somebody has managed to contrive them. If any law enforcement agency had any part in getting them, they can't be introduced in evidence." Hemmet's smile formed again. "Suppose one piece of electronic gear, found on the premises, can be identified as police property—your tapes would never be allowed in any court. Even if that were not the case, the fact that Guthrie, having admitted van Zaam's murder, probably won't be here to testify would make it easier to discredit them. Such tapes may give you information, but the road from information to conviction isn't always an easy one."

Timuroff leaned forward. "It's not that simple, Judson. Let's be frank. We know that you're the kingpin here where heroin's concerned. Miranda is the money. You're the mastermind. *No*—" his voice hardened, "—don't argue. We know because Miranda told us so." He gestured to Florencio behind the bar. "Listen!"

Evangeline looked up. She looked at Timuroff and smiled. She looked at Hemmet. Abruptly her smile disappeared. Her whole expression changed.

She spoke, and it was in Miranda Gardner's voice. *"Darling,"* she said. *"Don't worry, Jeffie lamb. Jud thinks he's in the clear. If anything goes wrong, the hard-drug evidence all points to him. I just own property."*

"She's talking to her pansy boyfriend," Pete put in.

"That's how I've got it fixed," Miranda said, *"and, honey, Jud's expendable. I can't keep saving him from all those Vegas goons forever."* And Timuroff, watching her mouth work, could almost see Miranda Gardner sitting there.

Hemmet listened, still smiling his cruel smile.

"It'll work out nicely," Miranda's voice went on. *"He and the horse can go together when we're through with them. Now you just stop your fretting, Jeffie lamb—"* Grotesquely, the hard, harsh voice began to coo. *"Be a good boy, real goodie-good, and maybe next time—maybe this very night—mommy'll really let you get on top."*

Timuroff gestured. Florencio shut her off.

Hemmet swallowed. He snapped, "That's faked-up, and you know it!"

Pete Cominazzo threw his chair back. "For Christ's sake, how long do we have to bother with this creep? Let's get it over with and save the state a million bucks! Tim, tell him what the score is."

Timuroff's facial muscles had turned to steel. His scar stood out now, whiter than before. He stroked it carefully. He stood up, facing Hemmet. "The score is this," he said. "You are before a court of no appeal. We know exactly what you've done, to whom. We also know how hard it could be to destroy you legally. Therefore, as Pete said, we're going to save the state a million dollars. I'm going to do it personally, because Amos was a friend of mine, and you murdered him."

"I killed the man in self-defense."

"You lie. Amos was a good *kendo* fencer. He'd also been an expert *kata* man. Do you know what *kata* is? *Kata* means 'form.' It is a two-man exercise with the live sword. To do it without cutting up your partner, you must have absolute control. Amos had it, and his blade was splendid. If you had parried any cut of his in six with that long piece of European iron, he would have cut right through it into you."

Quietly, Florencio came from behind the bar, carrying a sword in either hand. The first he gave to Timuroff.

"Hand him the other one, Florencio."

His face as hard as all the rest, Florencio offered the long German rapier which Timuroff had brought. Hemmet shrank from it, then took it, backed two paces, held its point to the floor and to one side.

"It's almost the twin of the one you used on Amos," said Timuroff. "And this—" he drew his own blade from its plated scabbard, "this one is quite as good as his. Inouye Shinkai made it three hundred years ago, and my father captured it in Manchuria in 1904—something which didn't happen often in that war—and put his initials on the hilt in platinum. See? *A.T.*" He held the blade out. Its hilt was the gold-washed sabre hilt of the Meiji era, Western in style but lengthened to accommodate two hands. The blade itself was glorious. Its temper line was straight, a cloudy silver ribbon along its edge.

"Isn't it pretty, Hemmet?" said Timuroff. "And it cuts well. I'm going to tell you about a crash in Uruguay, and then you'll understand that, when I say you murdered Amos, I base my statement on practical experience."

"I refuse to stand here and listen to this kind of crap. There's no reason why I should!"

"I can think of several why you *will*. As you all know, when I was very young I was an officer in the army of the Argentine, the cavalry. They let me wear this sword. Because my father was a splendid swordsman and a fencing master, in my first year of service I became known as the best man with a sabre in the army, and that's why I got into the crash in Uruguay." As he spoke, Timuroff played the bright light along the blade, examining its workmanship. "In Paraguay, you see, they had a general named Arazabal.

His full name doesn't matter, but he was very arrogant and powerful and bad-tempered, and well on his way to pulling off a revolution and becoming dictator. This the Argentine army for some reason didn't want—so, never suspecting, I found myself appointed aide to one of our major-generals, and sent off with him on a diplomatic tour to Montevideo. I was proud as a peacock, naturally, and it seemed to me that all the Uruguayan ladies were not only beautiful but extraordinarily complaisant. So I was having a fine time when one day my general ordered me to run some errands for him in his car, and then to wait for him near the intersection of an avenue—I forget which one—named after 'the Heroes of the Twenty-third of August,' or something of the sort. We parked there in his open touring car, his chauffeur in the front seat, myself in back basking in the sunshine and in the knowledge that every passing woman was aware of me."

Timuroff sighed. "Of course, I had no notion that it was all a setup. I didn't even know that General Arazabal had come to town. I first became aware of it when, without a word of warning, the chauffeur started up the engine, gunned it in first gear, and plowed directly into a huge Mercedes in the intersection. Though nobody was hurt, the crash was horrible. Out of the front seat of the Mercedes leaped the Paraguayan soldier who'd been driving. Out of the back seat roared Arazabal, in his dress uniform and his worst temper. My chauffeur stayed exactly where he was, but I jumped out intending to apologize. General Arazabal, gold epaulettes and all, came at me like a berserker. Before I could as much as say a word, he'd drawn his sword—a Solingen sabre and a rather nice one, much better steel than that blade in your hand—and, when mine was only half out of its scabbard, he slashed my face. He really oughtn't to have done it, for I immediately forgot he was a general, or a Paraguayan, or anything but a damned unpleasant enemy. I attacked at once, using my sword with one hand, which was all I had been taught. I parried one or two tries he made to cut my head off, and waited for my chance—a good cut at his forehead. He parried it in six, just as you say you did." Timuroff's eyes flashed fire. "And of course the Shinkai sliced through his blade and guard and hand. By then, I really was excited, so I went on and finished up the job with one more cut. It was too bad, because when they pensioned me off after the affair had been hushed up by everyone concerned—even his own people didn't love Arazabal—I had to take my blade over to Tokyo to be repolished. So you see—" Very deliberately, he gripped the sword hilt with both hands, holding it out before him like a samurai. He fixed his eyes on Hemmet. He kicked off his shoes. His voice rang like a battle trumpet through the room. "You're going to have a chance to prove your story, murderer! *On guard!*"

And very slowly, poised, sharp edge cleaving the air ahead of him, he advanced on Judson Hemmet.

Hemmet raised his point a foot or so, backing uncertainly. His eyes moved jerkily from face to face. "Two of you are police officers," he cried. "You can't just sit there and watch murder done!"

"I won't," said Edstrom. "I'll watch an execution."

"I'm a homicide inspector," Pete declared, "and this is one homicide I'm yearning to inspect."

Bill Traeger simply gave him an obsidian stare, and from behind the bar Florencio Pambid watched him as he had once watched the invading Japanese.

"Hector!" Hemmet was still backing up as Timuroff came forward. "Hector, *stop* this lunatic!"

"I wouldn't think of it!" answered Dr. Grimwood cheerfully. "Tim's going to perform an operation on the brain. His technique probably won't be quite like mine, but I wouldn't miss seeing it for the world!" And his aged laughter, cracked and manic, echoed from the walls.

Hemmet was backing as slowly as he could, as though he dreaded the moment, fifteen feet away, when he would have his back against the wall and could retreat no farther. He had assumed the fencer's stance. His point was out, but not quite on guard.

"*Engage!*" said Timuroff, through his set teeth.

Hemmet drew his point back a little, continued his retreat.

"*Engage!*"

"No—" Hemmet whispered. "No—" He dropped his point.

"*Engage, I said!*"

They moved six feet in silence. In all the room, only their breathing now was audible.

"On guard," Timuroff whispered, and the Tartar in him glared out through his eyes.

Hemmet's lips had skinned back from his teeth. He gasped. Desperately, very swiftly, he brought his arm to full extension—and Timuroff exploded.

Everything seemed to happen simultaneously. His forte caught Hemmet's blade with one fast, powerful press. As fighting samurai and *kendo* fencers always have, he shouted out his great percussive *"Hai!"* Up only a few inches the Shinkai flashed, then like instant silver lightning it cut down—

"Holy Christ!" cried Pete.

Whatever animated Judson Hemmet fell apart. The rapier dropped from his suddenly nerveless fingers; his legs collapsed beneath him; the tight wax tissues of his face dissolved, showing the scars and furrows his life had graven there. He became only an ungainly bundle on the floor, sprawled on knees and elbows, eyes shut tight.

He was uninjured. Timuroff had done what only first-class *kata* men can do. He had stopped the flashing Shinkai in midair.

Hemmet's eyes opened—and he saw that cutting edge held motionless six inches from them. A shudder swept him visibly.

"Where are the papers, Jud?" asked Timuroff, in a low voice and very dangerously.

Hemmet covered his eyes with his left hand. "A-at Jeffie's place," he blurted almost incoherently. "She—she owns the apartment house he's in. A fireproof filing cabinet. It—it's built into the wall behind his bed."

"Where is the place?"

Hemmet moaned and gave them the address; and Norman Edstrom left the room to phone. They waited for him. His calls were brief, and he returned almost immediately. "They'll have the warrant right away. We should be hearing in an hour or so if he's been telling us the truth."

Timuroff pointed to a chair near the fireplace. "You sit there," he told Hemmet, "until this is checked out. Then—" His voice was utterly contemptuous. "Then you can go."

He sheathed his blade, picked up the rapier, handed the two of them to Florencio, and resumed his seat next to the doctor at the poker table. "We might as well play a few hands of stud while we're waiting," he suggested. "And I could use a drink."

They played again, and Florencio made them one more round. After forty minutes, the phone rang and Edstrom answered it.

"Well, it's all over but the shouting. She wasn't there, but we've picked up her boy. The papers are a gold mine. Now watch the bastards fall like dominoes! They want me over there tonight." He turned to Pete. "You want to come along?"

"Not at this stage," said Pete. "I'd better stay away until the PD picture clears up."

"It will," Edstrom promised him. He said good-night around, congratulated Timuroff, and left. Reese Guthrie stood up to follow him. Obviously finding it difficult to speak, he thanked them all. "I owe you a great deal, Mr. Timuroff—you and your sword." He stared at Hemmet, bowed over in his chair. "You can't know what this means to me. M-maybe someday I'll repay you properly. I guess I'd better rush along. You know where you can find me from now on."

He shook hands silently, and said good-bye, and the armoire door closed silently behind him.

Then, at a sign from Timuroff, Bill Traeger rose, and pulled Judson Hemmet roughly to his feet, and walked him out under their cold eyes, to set him free into an altered world.

"Don't worry," remarked Timuroff, after he had gone. "I have a feeling he won't run very far."

Then it was Pete and Hector Grimwood's turn to praise what Timuroff had done, and then Florencio's, who brought another drink, especially strong.

"Hell, Tim," Pete said, "it wasn't that damn sword that buckled him—it was your Ivan face again."

"I think we all did very well." Timuroff raised his glass. "Heck's wild laughter bit about the brain surgery sent shivers down my back. And now—" he bowed, "I shall propose a toast. Gentlemen, to Evangeline!"

And Evangeline looked up at him, and smiled, and dropped her eyelids modestly, and covered up her décolletage. *"Oh, Tim,"* she murmured, *"I do think you're simply wonderful!"* To everyone's surprise but Dr. Grimwood's, she blushed. "Veux-tu coucher avec moi quelque soir?"

"Heck, that's not in keeping for *Evangeline!*" protested Timuroff.

"No," Dr. Grimwood said, "I don't suppose it is. But I'm getting bored with Longfellow. I think I'll change her name."

XV

A Party for Evangeline

Next morning, Timuroff went down to the shop at what had always been his customary time before Monrooney's murder, and was relieved to find, awaiting him, a message from a pretentious Beverly Hills auction house insisting that he fly south immediately to appraise the hideously expensive, thoroughly nondescript collection of a millionaire recently deceased at Balboa Beach. Ordinarily, he would have turned it down, but Liselotte, on her return from the maestro's, had awakened him to assure herself that he was still intact and to extort an accounting of his actions in her absence. She was convinced that he'd been up to something desperate, and she refused to sleep until he gave her a highly censored version—all mention of sharp instruments deleted—of what had happened. Olivia was still another matter. Her look declared eloquently that *she knew all*, she disapproved, and she was keeping silent only out of her sense of duty as wife and as employee. The sole saving grace was an almost imperceptible undertone of the respect that heroes get, and Timuroff wasn't at all sure of that. He read the message, announced that he was taking off immediately, phoned Emilia and told her to inform Liselotte, called Kemble Street and left a message for the doctor, who today was driving himself out in his Rolls-Royce, and finally phoned Pete, who first accused him of chickening out on them, and then admitted that, as things were going, there was no need for him to hang around.

"When do I get my station wagon?" Olivia called out after him as he left the shop.

He drove south on Highway 101—he never flew unless he absolutely had to—and luxuriated in his new detachment from the murders and connivings and inevitable anxieties with which he had been living. He detoured in order to have lunch in Monterey, then drifted onward, reaching Santa Barbara in time to look in at a few antique stores before dining on the pier. By ten thirty, he was established at a motel in Pasadena, and had called Liselotte and Olivia to tell them where he could be reached. Very carefully, he neither turned the news on nor bought a paper, but read himself to sleep with a copy of *Blackwood's Magazine,* and dreamed vaguely but pleasantly of Liselotte and the Argentine.

He was not, of course, destined to escape so easily. The morning headlines screamed San Francisco's latest scandal at the world, and though he refrained from buying any paper, he could not avoid the millionaire's widow, a sinuous brunette whom the old man had purchased somewhere to spice up his declining years. She seemed much taken with him, perhaps because for the moment scandal made him a small celebrity. Occasionally she would rub up against him, purring rather loudly and hinting that he needn't rush his work—that really he'd be *much* more comfortable in one of her own guest rooms than in anything as impersonal as a motel. From her he learned that Mario Baltesar had resigned as mayor of San Francisco, announcing that he would not run in the election, that Chiefy too had quit, that there had been any number of arrests—she wasn't sure of whom—by federal officers, and that Miranda Gardner, mysteriously tipped off, had fled the country.

By the day's end, the widow's nose was somewhat out of joint, his work was done, and he was feeling properly self-righteous because of his fidelity to Liselotte. But he had given up any idea of walling himself off. He bought a paper, and read it while he dined. From it, he learned that both Hemmet and Lieutenant Kielty, for whom warrants had been issued, could not be found, and that Hanno and several of his men already were in custody. There also was a boxed front-page human-interest story, under the noted by-line of Rop Millweed, revealing (exclusively) how poor defenseless Twinkle Mossmaker had been brow-beaten and blackmailed by Lieutenant Kielty into mis-quoting Dr. Grimwood, who was a darling old man, really.

At the motel, there was a message for him to call Liselotte instantly. He did so.

"You ought to be ashamed!" she told him with asperity. "Think how you have hurt poor Hector's feelings, and also Penny Anne's!"

"I *beg* your pardon?"

"You have run away. You have been away two whole days, and you still will not be home until tomorrow. Hector and Penny have moved back into his house, and you have made him wait to open the big iron door!"

Suddenly, Timuroff realized that, in the tension of preparing for the confrontation in the poker parlor, and in the excitement of that confrontation—when, he now admitted to himself, he could quite easily have had a rapier through him—his mind had somehow diminished the importance of whatever lay behind the lead-filled lock. "You mean he's waiting till I get there?" he exclaimed, really touched. "Dearest, phone him immediately. Tell him I *am* sorry—that I'll get home as soon as possible, some-time tomorrow afternoon."

"*Besides,*" she continued, "Pete and Olivia have told me what you really did while I was gone. *They* think you were very brave. What *I* think—never mind, you will hear it soon enough! Now I shall phone Hector and apologize because you were so rude and inconsiderate."

"I love you, dear," said Timuroff, kissing her good-night over the phone.

He had promised to call at the auctioneers' offices before he left, and he couldn't very well get out of it. In the morning, he took off without breakfasting, got there just as they were opening up, spent nearly an hour dis-cussing what the millionaire's collection would bring in the New York galleries, and made himself eat brunch. Then he headed for Interstate 5 and home.

He drove fast, stopping only once for gas, and specu-lating on what might be behind the iron door—his curiosity now once more thoroughly aroused. A hundred miles from the Bay, he turned the radio on and learned that Hemmet had been found, dead in his car, in a broken-down garage in a squalid ghetto alley at Hunter's Point. The gun was there. It looked like suicide. But there were other factors, and the FBI had moved in to investigate.

Timuroff was worried. Was it possible that Guthrie, instead of sensibly catching the first plane for South America, had been unable to forego one final vengeance? The radio went on talking, reiterating what he had heard already, and he switched it off to wonder once again what that lead-filled lock had been protecting for so many years.

He arrived well before cocktail hour, and found that Liselotte had forgiven him—which, of course, was what usually happened. She told him that Reese Guthrie had phoned him from Belém, at the mouth of the Amazon, which took one worry off his mind. Then, at her insistence, he called up Hector Grimwood with explanations and apologies.

"Tim, didn't Liselotte tell you?" The doctor was once again his old enthusiastic self. "Both of you must come out here right away! I'm calling it a party for Evangeline, but it's in your honor really. I arranged it all as soon as I got the word that you were coming back this afternoon. We're going to have a drink or two, and then we're going to open up that iron door and find out what's behind it. When I told Florencio and his wife about it, they promised us a banquet 'just like those served at the Presidential Palace in Manila'—he said you'd understand."

"I do indeed," said Timuroff, again deeply touched.

"It's not going to be a big party—no more of those for me!—just your friend Judge Faraday, the Cominazzos, Edstrom and his wife, Penny and me, and you and Liselotte, and of course Traeger."

"Opening that lock is going to be a job," Timuroff said.

"It shouldn't be too bad. Mario Baltesar came to see me yesterday. He swore he simply had no idea what Hemmet and Miranda Gardner—and for that matter Munrooney—were up to. He was trying hard to make amends, and I believe him, Tim. He'd gone through Hemmet's office with the FBI, and he found the key hidden there, with Albright's original instructions to old Jefferson. He brought them here to me. Bill Traeger's sure he can manage it. He'll use a blowtorch to melt all that lead, and tongs and things to hold the lock itself and turn the key. Pete says he'll help him. Now please hurry. Penny and I want you and Liselotte to be the first ones here."

They were not quite the first. When they entered, Pete and Olivia had just arrived; and Timuroff could tell immediately that Olivia also had forgiven him—though perhaps a little grudgingly. Dr. Grimwood was in the poker parlor, Penny Anne told them, and they joined him there.

"Have you heard the news?" Pete asked.

"I had the radio on while I was driving up," Timuroff said. "What else has happened?"

Pete grinned. "They've made Jake Harrell acting chief, which means that my vacation's over as of now. But that's not all." Suddenly his voice became as hard as it had been across the poker table. "They've located Kielty. Less than an hour ago. He was as dead as Hemmet."

"Where was he?"

"In a public john way off in the park. He'd swallowed his own cyanide. I guess they'd sucked him deeper in than anyone."

Hector Grimwood looked at all of them. "I know I should be shocked," he said, "especially after all that's happened here. But I'm not. I am glad. Not long ago, I thought this house could never possibly feel clean again. Now it does. I'm sorry, but Mr. Kielty's death makes it feel even cleaner. It proves poor Hanson didn't kill himself, and that I didn't murder him."

"That was proved already," Pete declared. "We've been tipped off that Hanson had been having trouble sleeping, and how Kielty's man on swing shift gave him some kind of pill. The theory is they used a waker-upper—slipped it into his supper probably—to make damn sure he'd have to ask for something."

"Who tipped you off?" asked Timuroff.

"A trusty at the jail. He was afraid to talk before. And that's the way it's going—they're falling like dominoes, exactly as Norm Edstrom said. Either they're no longer scared to talk, or now they're scared not to. Besides, those papers told a lot about who had done what to whom, and some of it has been made public. Already there've been a couple of quick killings on the drug scene."

Hector Grimwood went behind the bar. "Florencio's much too busy to mix drinks." He draped a bar towel over his left arm, and beamed at them. "But I'm not. We won't wait for the others. They'll be along any minute now."

Expertly, he went to work, and Penny Anne ushered in the Edstroms and Judge Faraday while he was doing it.

Mrs. Edstrom, a petite dark girl whom Edstrom had married only months before in Baton Rouge, was introduced around. With Penny Anne's assistance, the drinks were made and served. "They're all doubles," explained the doctor. "I don't think I could stand it if we postponed the opening for two separate rounds."

Clayton Faraday regarded Timuroff severely. "Tim," he said, "I really shouldn't be conversing with you. I've heard of what went on here the other night, and after all I *am* a judge. I haven't tried to count the laws you broke deliberately. You are a malefactor and a reprobate. You have been saved only by the Nelsonian paradox."

"The *what,* sir?" asked Edstrom.

"The fact that sometimes it is necessary to lift the telescope to one's blind eye, as Admiral Nelson did when it became imperative for him *not* to see his commander's signal." He smiled at Timuroff. He raised his glass. "May your tribe increase!" he said.

They laughed and drank.

"Well," remarked Edstrom, "it's all turned out much better than I thought. Just one thing sticks in my craw— the fact that Gardner woman got away."

"Where did she get to?"

"Rio, Mr. Timuroff—where else?"

"In that case, she may have left the country, but I can promise you she's not escaped—at least, not for long. Brazil is where Reese Guthrie is. He phoned us this morning from Belém." Timuroff did not try to hide the grim amusement in his voice. "Miranda's going to wish she'd stayed at home."

"I'll drink to that!" growled Edstrom.

Finally Bill Traeger and Florencio came in. They were loaded down—a heavy toolbox and a blowtorch, two suits of coveralls, two pairs of work gloves, two welders' masks, a fire extinguisher.

"I've come prepared!" Traeger announced, setting the clutter down. "That lead in there may sputter."

He received his drink, and Florencio, explaining that he had to hurry back to help his wife, went out reluctantly.

"I wonder what we'll find in there?" Hector Grimwood said. "From what I've heard of Albright, it could be *anything.*"

"It is a dragon's treasure, like Fafner's in *Der Ring!*" Liselotte's eyes were bright; she was almost dancing in her eagerness. "How can you foolish men stand here drinking, when there are probably whole chests of rubies, sapphires, emeralds, golden necklaces?"

"We're working up our courage, Madame Cantelou," said Traeger, and he sang solemnly,

> "Sixteen men on a dead man's chest—
>   Yo-heave-ho and a bottle of rum!
> And drink and the devil may do for the rest—
>   Yo-heave-ho and a bottle of rum!"

"I'll tell you what I think we'll find," Pete offered. "We'll find a million dollars' worth of opium and the skeletons of four Chinese. Just our luck too—with Norm and the judge here watching us!"

"Hurry, hurry, *hurry!*" exclaimed Liselotte. *"Please!"*

In two gulps, Traeger killed his drink. He handed Pete a pair of coveralls. "These ought to fit you pretty well," he said. "Get into 'em, and we'll get going." He slipped out of his jacket and got into his own. "I don't think more than four of us ought to go down in there until the torch is out. How about you, Tim, with the extinguisher? And Dr. Grimwood too."

The doctor had opened up the doors of the armoire. He had opened the secret panel at its back, and the hidden door that Timuroff had found across the passageway. He had turned on the lights so that they could see the stairs leading down. "First we must show the ladies and Judge Faraday just what it looks like," he declared. "They can go in and look and come right out again."

The judge went first. The ladies followed him, shuddering at the hook from which van Zaam had hung, exclaiming at the chamber where Muriel Fawzi had endured her brief captivity, and at the massive door, the ponderous lock. They hurried back, and Pete and Traeger carried the tools in.

"You'd better stand well off to one side," Traeger told Timuroff and the doctor. He fired up the torch. He produced a huge pair of iron tongs.

"Looks like you robbed a blacksmith," Pete said.

"Just about. Now let's have the key."

Hector Grimwood gave it to him—iron, five inches long—and he passed it to Pete, with a stout pair of pliers. "When the lead melts, stick it in the keyhole and give it a quick turn. A lock works just as well in fluid as in air, and that's what lead is once it's melted. Okay, let's go."

With the tongs, he lifted the lock up almost at right angles. The blowtorch roared, and he played its flame as evenly as possible over the brass. "It'll take a little while," he told them. "There's a lot of metal here to absorb heat."

Now only the torch itself was heard. Behind them, the watchers on the stairs were tense and still.

Then the brass started to turn color with the heat. A thread of smoke rose into the air, a smell of ancient burning oil.

"It's melting!" Traeger said. "Wait till I give the word! . . . *Now!*"

Pete pushed the great key into the almost red-hot lock. With the pliers, he gave it a full counterclockwise turn. Bill Traeger pulled down swiftly with his tongs. Molten lead hissed and flowed and spattered down unnoticed—

And the vast lock hung there, open.

Bill Traeger turned the torch off. Carefully, with the tongs, he freed the padlock from the hasp. Then he took off his welder's mask. "Everybody can come in now!" he called.

They filed in, moving to one side or the other.

"Shall I open it?"

"Of course!" the doctor cried.

Traeger freed the hasp. He put the tongs down, seized the still-cold knob with his gloved hand, and pulled. Creaking its protest after sixty years, the iron door swung slowly open—onto darkness.

"Don't tell me we didn't bring a flashlight?" Pete said.

"There's probably a switch right by the door," suggested Timuroff. "There has been everywhere. May I?"

Traeger moved aside for him. He reached in to the right. The cobwebbed switch was there. He snapped it on. In front of them, hanging naked from the ceiling, another ancient light bulb glowed. And in its dusty yellow light they saw the room.

It was a large room with a stone floor, so large that— had it been empty—the solitary light would not have shown its corners clearly. Timuroff guessed it as twenty by twenty feet.

But it was by no means empty. Exactly in its center, under the hanging lamp, a plain deal table stood. Two kitchen chairs flanked it, carelessly, as though their occupants had only just arisen and departed. On the tabletop, there was a whiskey bottle, two glasses, and a book.

And all around the walls were wooden cases neatly stacked. Most of them were about four feet long and a foot deep, but eight or ten, toward the rear, were much larger. Dust lay on it all, but—considering the long intervening years—not too thick a layer. The air was stale but breatheable.

They entered, treading very carefully to avoid roiling up the dust. There was a chorus of exclamations and excited questions.

"What on earth is all this?" demanded Hector Grimwood. "What was Albright up to, anyway?"

"Heck, I can answer that right now!" Timuroff's voice betrayed his own excitement. "Look at those cases! Each of them say WRA—that's Winchester Repeating Arms Company, and they're exactly the right size. You probably have several hundred rifles here!"

"What big eyes you have, grandmother!" Pete whispered in his ear.

Timuroff did not answer him. He walked back to the larger cases, looked closely at them. "They're from Colt. I think—yes, they're Gatling guns! Heck, it's not what anyone expected, but you do really have a treasure!"

"Do you mean that Albright—?"

"I mean that Albright, among other things, was almost certainly a gun-runner. These must've been part of his stock in trade."

Liselotte stared at him wide-eyed. "Timmy!" she cried out, stamping her foot. "You cannot mean that all these cases have nothing in them except *guns?* How can you do a thing like this to me?"

Clayton Faraday saved him from answering. The judge had picked the book up from the table and opened it. Now it was he who was excited.

"You have more than just one treasure here, Dr. Grimwood! Look at this!" He held the open book before them, dust sifting down from it. *"Black Beetles in Amber,* by Ambrose Bierce, and I think it's a first edition! But that's not what's important. It provides one clue at least to the solution of another mystery. Bierce disappeared into Mexico in 1913, when he was seventy, and no one ever really knew why he crossed over. Now listen to what's written on the fly-leaf—

Albright, friend and enemy,

More friend than enemy, perhaps. I've never told you what I really think of you because then you might become more enemy than friend. And I won't tell you now. I'll leave a space for it instead. When I return, you and I will drain the bottle and I'll finish this.

He left a lot of space above his signature. He must have known Albright really well. And it is signed Ambrose Bierce."

"Why, that's wonderful!" Hector Grimwood was delighted. "Of course, I've heard about him and his disappearance. Old Mrs. Albright often talked of him. But I had no idea that they were thick as thieves!"

"Not thieves," laughed Judge Faraday. "Gun-runners. This at least tells us that, when he went into Chihuahua, he was adventuring and not just trying to end it all, as so many writers seem to think. He and Albright must really have been more friends than enemies. Otherwise Albright wouldn't have sealed this chamber up—guns, bottle, book, and all—when Bierce did not return."

"What kind of Winchesters do you think they are?" Pete asked.

"Let's have a look!" replied Dr. Grimwood eagerly. "I know that Tim can hardly wait. I'm so pleased with all this! For two weeks now, Albright's secret rooms and passages have brought me only fear and death and danger. It wasn't his fault and it isn't theirs. Now they're back to normal—carrying the spice of old romance, old mystery, adventure in the past. Bill, could you and Pete open one of these cases up?"

"Sure. I've got a pry bar with the tools. You want it opened here, or do we take it up?"

"Well—" The doctor hesitated.

"We'd better take it up," said Timuroff. "It's really pretty dusty here, and breathing's better in the poker parlor."

"There at least we can have another drink," declared Liselotte. "I shall drown my disappointment!"

They left the room, Faraday still carrying the book. Pete and Bill Traeger brushed the dust from one of the long wooden cases and, grunting and straining, brought it out and up the stairs. Timuroff spread two bar towels on the poker parlor floor to put it on. While Edstrom tended bar, they opened it. Timuroff carefully lifted out a rifle.

His face lit up. "Heck, look at *that!* They're Model 95's, and muskets, and brand new—no rust has touched them. And they're .30-40 calibre, and really hard to find in that condition—and with their bayonets!" He passed the lever-action rifle to the doctor. "They *are* a treasure—and those Gatling guns, regardless of their calibre, are much rarer."

Hector Grimwood examined the weapon in his hands. "What will I ever do with them?"

"Sell them, of course," said Timuroff.

"What are they worth?"

"I haven't counted them—let's say you have four hundred—well over a hundred thousand, without the Gatlings."

The doctor frowned. "Oh dear! That means I can't afford to sell them—it'd put me in an insufferable tax bracket. But I hope you'll each take at least one musket and one Gatling gun as souvenirs?"

"Me, I'd be happy to accept a musket," Norman Edstrom answered. "I'm a gun nut from way back, but a Gatling's just too valuable. It's too bad, too, because legally they aren't machine guns."

Pete and Traeger echoed him.

"Well, I can't just leave them there," Hector Grimwood said. He handed the musket back to Timuroff, and absent-mindedly accepted a drink from Edstrom. He sipped it. Suddenly his expression cleared. "I know exactly what I'll do!" he cried. "I can afford to sell the lot of them if I don't get too much. Twenty-five thousand dollars! Tim, would you like them for that price?"

Timuroff was embarrassed. He hesitated. He began stammering apologies.

"Nonsense!" the doctor told him. "You'll actually be doing me a favor. Here, let's shake hands on it. Is it a deal?"

Avoiding Liselotte's eyes, Timuroff shook hands.

"Talk about smelling like a rose!" murmured Pete admiringly.

Timuroff smiled at Olivia. "There's your little station wagon," he promised her.

"And also my new mink, and perhaps a big emerald," said Liselotte decisively.

Timuroff reached for the glass Edstrom was holding out to him. He raised it. "To our host and hostess!" He bowed to Hector Grimwood and to Penny Anne, and everybody drank. "And to successful gun-running!"

The phone rang. The doctor answered it. "Florencio," he announced, "tells me dinner's ready. After Pete and Bill take off their coveralls we'll go upstairs. What a shame it is that Evangeline couldn't be here, but she'll be sitting at the table with us, so you'll all have a chance to talk to her."

"Evangeline?" asked Timuroff. "I thought that after the way she's been behaving you were going to change her name?"

"I am. I just haven't been able to decide on one. I thought of *Juliet of the Spirits*—do you remember that Fellini movie years ago? What do you think of it?"

"I think she might prefer it to Evangeline."

"So do I," agreed Hector Grimwood. "It's not so—well, quite so *dated*. She seemed quite pleased about it when I told her."

They started out, Pete and Timuroff bringing up the rear. In the hall, Pete hung back a little, deliberately. "Tell me, Tim," he whispered, "did you really have that sword fight with the Paraguyan general?"

Timuroff smiled at his friend. He stroked his scar. "Pete," he said softly, "does it matter?"